P9-DNZ-642

ALSO BY ROBERT GRUDIN

The Grace of Great Things
Time and the Art of Living
Mighty Opposites

BOOK

A NOVEL

BOOK

A NOVEL

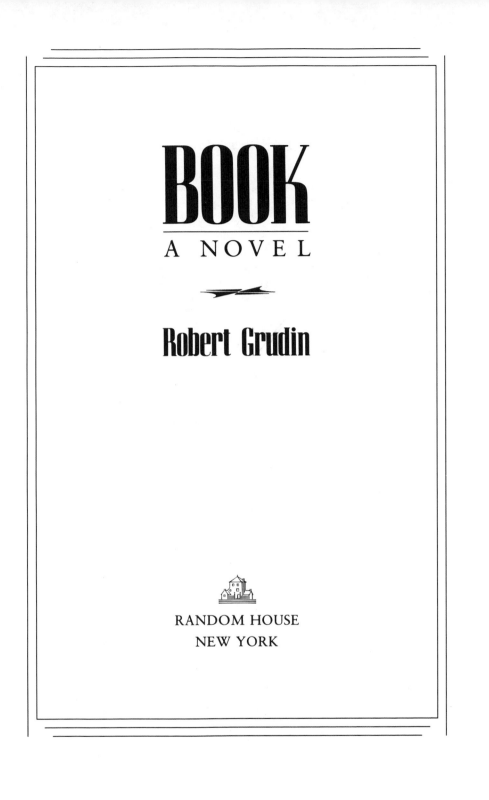

Robert Grudin

RANDOM HOUSE
NEW YORK

Copyright © 1992 by Robert Grudin

All rights reserved under
International and Pan-American Copyright Conventions.
Published in the United States by Random House, Inc.,
New York, and simultaneously in Canada by
Random House of Canada Limited, Toronto.

Grateful acknowledgment is made to
Encyclopædia Britannica, Inc., for permission
to reprint excerpts from two articles entitled
"Book" and "Bookselling" from the 11th edition
of the *Encyclopædia Britannica,* published in 1910–1911.
Reprinted by permission.

Library of Congress Cataloging-in-Publication Data
Grudin, Robert.
Book: a novel/Robert Grudin
p. cm.
ISBN 0-679-41185-2
I. Title.
PS3557.R787B66 1992
813'.54--dc20   91-50980

Manufactured in the United States of America

24689753
First Edition

Book design by Oksana Kushnir

To Michaela

Stretch'd on the downy fleece, no rest he knows,
And in his raptur'd soul the vision glows.

—Homer, *Odyssey,* Book 1,
trans. Alexander Pope

LIBER FONS LIBERTATIS

The characters and institutions in this novel are fictitious. Any resemblance to individuals living or dead is, at most, generic.

CONTENTS

POSTSCRIPTS

BOOK

A NOVEL

He sat on his haunches, his breath clouding the glass on the inside of the front door, his brown eyes intent on the far corner of the laurel hedge past the driveway, where he might first catch sight of his master returning. He sat completely still, postured like some Egyptian statue; yet no Egyptian artisan, ambitious to adorn Pharaoh's palace or tomb, would have condescended to depict the big black long-hair mongrel, with his rounded mastiff head, barrel chest and sashlike tail. He sat as though arrested in time, as though the hours that stiffened his muscles and wheeled his shadow clockwise on the rug were the single second before he saw his master, heard his step, felt his hand. Master of the loving hand, master of the endearing voice, master of the comforting smell, master of the heaped bowl.

His bowels ached and writhed. The need to be outside, to wander off at his master's side to the relief of some breezy alien forest or some field rich in odors of decay, oppressed him till his head pounded with the effort of restraint. His shadow slowly faded; the light grew dim. The little road outside was busy with returning cars. He rose and stretched forlornly and turned and with slow steps sought the remotest corner of the house, the broom closet behind the kitchen, to commit with infinite relief the unthinkable deed. Climbing the stairs to the darkened bathroom, he drank greedily from the toilet bowl. He came down the stairs and stood in the living room, listening. Now it was night again in the hungry house. Now neighbor dogs came by walking their people, dogs of easy familiar smells, masters who knew him and had petted him. He went to the big chair in front of the slightly opened front window and put his forepaws up on the chair's back and barked thunderously, cocking his ears as the echoes faded. He went to the front door and barked and barked, his great body shuddering with the agony of expression.

PART ONE

Book, the common name for any literary production of some bulk, now applied particularly to a printed composition forming a volume, or, if in more than one volume, a single organic literary work. The word is also used descriptively for the internal divisions or sections of a comprehensive work.

The word "book" is found with variations of form and gender in all the Teutonic languages, the original form postulated for it being a strong feminine *Bôks,* which must have been used in the sense of a writing-tablet. The most obvious connexion of this is with the old English *bóc,* a beech tree, and though this is not free from philological difficulties, no probable alternative has been suggested.

> —A. W. POLLARD, "Book," *Encyclopædia Britannica,*
> 11th edition

CHAPTER 1

THE VIEW FROM MAMMAL HALL

The meek shall inherit the entire earth, except
for a very thin layer at the surface.

—SOVRANA SOSTRATA,
Gesta

From the start of his academic career, J. Thoreau Marshall had shown professional qualities of an unmistakable character. Fresh out of college, with a Big Ten degree and a kaleidoscopic gamut of graduate options at his disposal, he had chosen as his heart's desire the field of business statistics. Set in this course, he then proceeded, from his dissertation years on through a brace of assistant professorships, to produce a succession of timid, short-sighted, derivative articles, couched in muddy meandering wearisome style. Marshall's comportment as a teacher was equally distinctive. Terrified of being at a loss for words, he wrote out his lectures which, sauced with redundancy, seasoned with non sequitur and served up at metronomic pace in a pained nasal monotone, induced narcosis in all who heard them. In committee meetings he was notably inarticulate, dead to nuance and phobic to original ideas. His other relationships were of a similar ilk. To his students he was autocratic and unfair, to his advisees distant and obtuse, to his colleagues earthbound and hollow.

It was eventually apparent that these characteristics, displayed consistently and noted by all, ideally qualified Marshall for academic administration, and before long he was welcomed into a confraternity whose members, by and large, shared his talents and propensities. Yet so far did he exceed his colleagues in these regards that he speedily rose to the summit of his profession, leaving the ranks of department heads and deans to become vice-president for academic affairs, or provost, at the University of Washagon, Dulce, WS. In this office he observed with unflinching purpose the timeworn obligations of his profession: bullying his subordinates and cringing before his superiors, stifling talent and rewarding mediocrity, promoting faddishness and punishing integrity, rejecting the most impassioned and justified individual plea yet acquiescing to every whim of political interest; avoiding confrontation, whenever possible, with the naked truth; shirking decisions and articulating such decisions as had to be made in memos so vague, oblique and circumnavigational as barely to deserve the name language. For these persistent efforts to maintain the standards and security of a great institution he was rewarded with the reverence of the faculty and the benevolent patronage of President Ralph Adorno who, "impotent and bed-rid," was awaiting imminent retirement.

Though the illness of the president (whom he had temporarily replaced and was rumored likely to succeed) gave Marshall additional power and responsibility, he nonetheless found time to relax now and then, leaning back in a great old leather swivel chair, alone in that spacious Mammal Hall office whose wide windows overlooked sunny lawns and the ivied Corinthian splendor of the College Pump, meditating wisely on things past, present, and to come. During these solitary seances, these necessary remissions of stress, his head would now and then tilt back, and a look that seemed to blend angelic patience with infant joy would cross his broad countenance. These were the moments when the noble man, now secure in public trust, could contemplate retribution against individuals who had abused him in the past. This year four colleagues were marked off for the working of justice.

There was Harvey Solomon, that feisty old historian, who, years before, had ridiculed one of Marshall's proposals in front of a titillated professorial assembly. Solomon was now postponing retirement in hopes of a pension-fixing salary increase; he would wither and wait in vain.

There was Jack O'Toole, the brash department chairman who had gone over Marshall's head to secure a new position. O'Toole aspired to a post in a prestigious national foundation; Marshall had on his desk a confidential letter of referral, compounded of gentle and pervasive slander, that would make O'Toole's name stink to high heaven—but stink so quietly and confidentially that O'Toole would never learn of the calumny done him.

There was Sarah Wilkins, that attractive young English professor with intense blue eyes and an evangelistic passion for the environment, who, instead of succumbing to Marshall's erotic overtures (hath rank no prerogatives?), had actually dared to contradict him at a planning-committee meeting. Her controversial tenure case was on his desk; it would go no further.

And there was Adam Snell, Wilkins' obscure colleague in English, who had written an objectionable novel, bizarre, anti-institutional, pernicious, meretricious, unscholarly and obscene, a book that brought negative attention to the university, a book that somehow offended colleagues from every ideological camp, a book that fortunately was a commercial flop. Now, oblivious to the effects of his own blunders and despite the fact that Dean MacCrae had told him to desist, Snell was writing another nonscholarly book, this one perhaps more odious than the first. Malfeasants like Snell shared a common fate at great universities, and Marshall was pleased in this case to be its executor. Glanda Gazza, Snell's department head, had come to Marshall with a scheme, touching the uncooperative novelist's post-tenure review, that would make Snell's life in Dulce the closest academic approximation of living hell.

But at two thirty-five on the afternoon of May 24, 1990, Marshall learned with some shock that his implementation of justice, at least with regard to Professor Snell, had encountered an unexpected obstacle. The intercom buzzer had shaken him out of a light doze, and he glanced out the window to notice that a great cumulus cloud, strange for that time of year, had come before the sun.

Clorene's voice over the intercom was strained. "Sorry to disturb you, Dr. Marshall. Professor Gazza's here. She says it's a crisis."

The acting president rose and straightened his tie. Crisis or no crisis, visits from Glanda Gazza, illustrious scholar, swashbuckling administrator and (he guessed) latent sexpot, were not to be taken lightly. In a moment she entered under full sail, tall, handsome, perm-coiffed and amply shapely, cutting through space with broad strides, her big saddle-leather shoulder bag squeaking under the stress. Barely stopping at his desk (he could see the pressure of the desktop glass against her tweed-clad thighs) she threw back her head and fixed upon him, with those marvelous gray eyes, a look that had the poignancy of a pleading child. "Thor," she said passionately, "Adam's disappeared."

"Snell?"

Gazza sank into a leather swivel, then tilted it forward, leaning toward and looking up at him, her hands tensely braced together on the desktop. "It's bizarre. He's missed class and office hours two days running. We called the police at noon. They found his house empty, the front door unlocked, his car and bike parked in front and his dog, hoarse with barking, trapped inside. The police have no leads, but they say possibly suicide, possibly murder."

"You say no leads?"

"Nothing. It's as though he went out for a breath of air and never came back."

Marshall sat down. Reaching out cautiously across the desk, he briefly put his hands on hers. "This must be hard on you, Glanda. But you're doing all you can. Except—"

Her eyes narrowed slightly. "Except?"

Setting his jowls, Marshall put on the oracular look reserved for moments when he was desperately grasping for an idea. "Except, um, you might ask a colleague to check his office. It's unlikely, but a friend who knows Snell's ways might be able to sniff out some clue that the police would miss. Did Snell have friends?"

"A few, I think. Certainly Hal Emmons." Gazza rose, shouldering the heavy bag. "I'll go find Hal right now. Thanks, Thor." She wheeled, and Marshall, availing himself of a chance to appreciate the Gazza buns in action, was taken by surprise when she suddenly turned back toward him. "One more thing, Thor. The meeting."

Marshall guiltily jerked his head up. "You mean your proceedings against Snell?"

Her face took on that pleading bedroom look again. "It would look better if we postponed it; but tomorrow's the last possible day in the academic calendar when there'd be time for sanctions."

Marshall deepened the tone of his voice and assumed the ritual cadence of an absolving cleric. "Hold your meeting anyway, my dear Glanda. It's a scheduled step in a due process of review; and if you're challenged about it by anybody you can always say that your department is so profoundly committed to democratic processes that they don't care about appearances. Besides, we'll treat Snell's absence as voluntary until proven otherwise. Maybe he killed himself." He paused. "Of course, if Adam's dead—"

Gazza gestured portentously from the doorway. "Of course. We're saved the trouble."

Alone again, Marshall swiveled around to face the windows. The sky was sunny now, and the grass glistened from what must have been a brief shower. He leaned back in his chair, interlaced his long moist fingers into one large peaceful fist on his belly and, forcing back tumescent fantasies about Gazza, focussed his imagination on the variety of nasty things that might have happened to Adam Snell.

As early as 2400 B.C., in Babylonia, legal decisions, revenue accounts, &c. were inscribed in cuneiform characters on clay tablets and placed in jars, arranged on shelves and labelled by clay tablets attached by straws. In the 7th century B.C. a library of literary works written on such tablets existed at Nineveh, founded by Sargan (721–705 B.C.). As in the case of the "Creation" series at the British Museum the narrative was sometimes continued from one tablet to another, and some of the tablets are inscribed with entries forming a catalog of the library. These clay tablets are perhaps entitled to be called books, but they are out of the direct ancestry of the modern printed book with which we are here chiefly concerned.

—A. W. POLLARD, "Book," *Encyclopædia Britannica,*
    11th edition

CHAPTER 2

CHILDE HAROLD'S PILGRIMAGE

Good people and evil people suffer about equally,
but good people enjoy it more.

—SOVRANA SOSTRATA,
Gesta

Harold Emmons, professor of Renaissance literature, raised his grizzled head from a volume of *Hermes Trismegistus* to greet an apparition that was neither expected nor welcome. Glanda Gazza, who never knocked, marching stoplessly into his office. That awful imperturbable handsome look on her face as she swung her body, slightly heavier lately but still dramatically proportioned, into his rocker. Neither spoke. Her eyelids lowered momentarily, and Emmons waited for the inevitable oeillade. It came, that flash of gray eyes wide as heaven and deep as sin, that ocular barrage which had, over the years, reduced a dozen male colleagues to moral incompetence, that challenge to meek masculinity which, even though Glanda was over fifty, was still a formidable instrument of bureaucratic and sexual authority. And as soon as it came it had passed. Thanks, he supposed, to a Presbyterian childhood, Emmons had never lapsed into Glanda's thrall. Yet he was not insensible to it. It daunted him like an offered blow.

"*Hal,*" she belted out softly in a voice imitating the muted cello, and leaning forward actually grabbed his hand, and told him as one distraught that "dear Adam" Snell had disappeared. Emmons froze. His friend gone for two days, and Emmons, as usual, so far out of things not to have heard sooner, and now Gazza, who documentably hated Adam's guts, coming like Niobe all tears to tell him the news!

"No trace?" he croaked, suddenly hoarse.

"Nothing."

"What about Doppler?"

"Who?"

"His dog."

"Trapped in the house," she replied, as if by afterthought. Emmons saw a mild shadow pass over Glanda's face and found himself, as he so often had over years working with her, in that brief passage, that silent moment of transition between the blandishing overture and the armored invasion, between feigned humanity and business at hand. She hit him again with her big look. "Hal, I've just been with Thor Marshall."

"Oh," grunted Emmons, holding back "that ghoul."

"Did Adam do his writing at home or here?"

"Here—I mean, in his office."

"Can you imagine anything he might have in writing that could help us find him?"

Emmons could now follow Glanda's line of attack to its ultimate goal. "Adam recorded his letters in his computer."

"Didn't he also write a journal?"

"Yes, he kept a writer's journal while he was working on *Sovrana Sostrata*. I think he's also using one for the new book, but I'm not sure."

"Hal, Thor and I want you to find out. You and Adam were friends, and you can look discreetly into his things. You mustn't refuse. You've got to start as soon as possible," and the departmental passkey, anchored to its heavy wooden tag, emerged from Glanda's bag.

Parting ceremonies were brief.

Loath, somehow fearful of his unwanted task, Emmons sat on silently at his desk. Grief nagged at his body like physical pain. Adam, poor devil, was probably dead. People didn't just disappear; they disappeared in order to reappear as corpses. And Glanda had no desire to save Adam. Glanda was good with computers and Emmons wasn't. If she had wanted to save Adam, she would have gone into his office herself.

He glanced distractedly out the window, and his glance, as though guided by some necessity of depression, fell on the most menacing object available: a huge dense mass of dark vegetation—big firs, thronging undergrowth and impenetrable giant grass—obtruding like some geographical anomaly in the middle of campus. The Ezekiel Pisham Homestead, ancient seat of Dulce's founder, popularly called the Jungle and recently rendered impassable by a freakish botanical riot.

An absurd intuition possessed him. Could Adam possibly be in there? Emmons groaned. If so, he wasn't alive.

Emmons turned to his desk, lowered his face into his hands and mourned for his friend. The leather-bound *Hermes Trismegistus,* unattended, slipped down from his lap and spread-eagled on the floor.

He groaned again, pushed himself to his feet, grabbed his jacket and the passkey and left his office. Stocky, bowlegged, he moved down the hallway with a heavy gait. The long-familiar passage, silent and empty in late afternoon, suddenly seemed barbarous to him, its veneered professorial office doors following on one another anonymously, a blind alley ending in a red illuminated EXIT sign, a passage from nowhere to nowhere, a tiled and plastered manifesto of cultural bankruptcy, a wound in space. Countless times over fifteen years Emmons had walked down this hall to visit Snell, to go out with him for coffee or a beer or just hang around and chat. Countless times, before big windows fronting directly on the Jungle, they had sat, comfortably letting time pass, talking of literature or politics or the welter of eccentricities that made up their profession. All that was over now, and the very architecture, once alive with the promise of honest friendship, had gone alien, assumed an ugliness that was almost evil.

A floor below, at a door marked only by a yellow note card handwritten SNELL, Emmons fumbled with the key, half afraid of finding a corpse inside, half guilty at intruding where he had always knocked.

The long narrow room was shot through with late-afternoon sunlight—blinding, unfriendly radiance that heated the air to a fever, glared erosively on the vinyl recliner by the window and brought a smell of cooking plastic from the computer ensemble that dominated the left-hand wall. Again Emmons felt a sense of violation, of leering notoriety invading Snell's undefended retreat. Poor Snell was public property now, and the sun was eating his office.

Emmons opened windows, lowered shades. When the hot air had blown out into the hallway, he shut the office door and stood anxiously alone. In the lessened light the room regained its identity, became the rational, livable workplace where his friend had held quiet conversance with texts, students and colleagues. The couch abutting the bookshelves. The silent telephone on the homemade plywood computer table. The stereo set on the windowsill. All as usual, surfaces clear and undisturbed, just as the meticulous Snell might have left them after a day's work.

Only on the blond writing desk by the window was there congestion. Memos, announcements, reports, newsletters, minutes, course descriptions, the normal university confetti, shuffled loosely into a pile and pushed over to the left. Emmons wasted ten minutes on them, then checked the desk drawers, which revealed no more than the usual assortment of accessories. He was about to assault the filing cabinet in search of Snell's incoming correspondence when he glanced at a half-empty cardboard box on the floor just to his right. He pulled it up to his lap and examined its contents with increasing interest.

When on cool mornings in the hollow of green hills we met, I folded, unfolded, in infant silence, your dappled whiteness. Mornings with absurd surprise I rediscovered, forever familiar, forever strange, your form in a silence of loving. Hidden in leaves of time, we gave each other being, you white with an endless luster of renewal, I silent to see, in one face, myself and another.

> *Envoi*
>
> Go forth little book,
> silently into the night,
> like gull wheeling seaward,
> like hawk to darkling wood.
>
> Go forth and spy
> into the kitchens of the righteous
> and the beds of virgins;
> go to the tabernacles of study,
> they will read you as you have read my soul.
>
> Go forth and stand
> above the sleeping town;
> sing from the hill of wonder
> a madrigal of dreams.

Thus ended Adam Snell's work journal for *Sovrana Sostrata*. Harold Emmons shifted in his chair and carefully eased the manuscript back, accordionlike, into its box. Having printed out his journal, Snell had neglected to separate the pages, so that handling the document was like manipulating a white, word-dappled, uncooperative snake. Emmons called home. It was six already, and he was going to miss dinner, but he could not move. The snake had coiled around him, had him in its toils.

The journal held wonders.

Emmons had heard a number of stories about artists who fell in love with their creations, but this one beat Pygmalion, Henry Higgins and the whole pack. Here was a real artist, whose fictional creation Sovrana *re-created him*, lectured and dictated whole passages to him, stimulated in him the profoundest desire, teased him, ultimately rejected him, and in all these things brought forth from him, in a kind of exotic sexual reversal, a significant work of art.

Here also was, at least in principle, an erotic attitude which, if not unprecedented, was certainly not mentioned in modern discussions of gender relationships: a man's open, total, unrepentant, grateful submission to a woman's will.

Emmons reached for the journal again and clumsily turned his way to a passage quite early on:

> January 24, 1987. Saturday.
> Today, for the first time, I actually *saw* Sovrana. No more floundering around now, trying to picture her as old girlfriends or movie stars, trying to formulate an abstract, philosophical imitation of nature, but a real face, never seen before, a passionate mocking histrionic face with eyes that are all seasons, eyes that can draw me like a puppet, play me like an instrument. And she speaks to me. I no longer have to imagine her words. I can hear them. And with what voice! A resonant, musical voice, a devilishly modulated voice, a voice to charm the soul or freeze the blood.
> I almost saw her last night, just before waking. I dreamt that she was in a house in the country and that I was on the grounds. I crept closer and closer to the house, thrilled to be near her yet somehow afraid. I could hear her inside, playing the violin. I stood at the front door, knowing that only that thin wood separated her and me. A chill came on me and I ran in terror, almost as though she might grow outraged at my intrusion and chase me. I woke sorrowful.
> That sorrow eased me. If we could only fail more often in dreams, how often we might succeed awake! I sat at morning coffee, and blinked, and there she was! Looking not as I had wanted her to look, but as she *had* to look. I wondered . . .

Emmons turned slowly ahead. As Snell's friend, he had special insight into the now-bittersweet story of happy obsession, of artistic and spiritual renewal, that was unfolding in his hands. Before Sovrana, Adam Snell's life had been a study in failed aspiration. Snell, exuberant youth with a pronounced gift of gab; Snell, whose early efforts at fiction dazzled five Harvard writing professors; Snell, who thumbed his nose at practicality and moved after graduation into an uncle's attic to enchant the world by weaving tales. But the world, in its wisdom, thought otherwise. The world had enchanters enough without Snell, or so the publishers of said enchanters seemed to think. The young writer, who kept a special wastebasket for rejection letters, watched with deepening depression as the basket filled up, and like a boxer hit in the same place too many times, he began to lose pleasure in his craft and wish himself elsewhere.

Elsewhere, Snell's wise uncle suggested, might just as well, and perhaps very happily, be grad school, and so, one fine fall morning in the early sixties, the young man journeyed westward to begin the scholarly study of what (he sadly thought) he was personally impotent to create. English literature, especially the finely tuned and sometimes outrageous literature of the eighteenth century, gave him much solace, and aside from a marriage that soon dissolved and a rather embarrassing incident during the Berkeley uprisings, his career at first was fairly successful. He won a coveted position at Washagon, where he taught quite brilliantly and produced enough published scholarship to gain the security of tenure. Yet neither his old ebullience nor the creative productions it spawned had ever reappeared. In his late forties, with a dwindling scholarly output, Snell seemed destined for the deflated tranquillity and unbemoaned obscurity of the average literature professor.

What then could account for *Sovrana Sostrata*? Snell's journal explained all that. Snell had apparently gotten out of bed one morning in early 1987 with a phenomenal case of self-reproach. He saw himself as unproductive, barren, sterile, cowardly and self-indulgent. And he suddenly refused to remain so. His plan was brutally simple. If he could not instill creativity in himself, he could at least write about his own lack of creativity: about the omissions, surrenders and refusals that characterize the barren life, about the lies and rationalizations that support it, about the professional and social mechanisms that feed it. Sitting down at the computer on the morning of January 4, he began what he called his "Book of Failure."

Such analyses demand honesty, and Snell was honest to a fault. He saw his own youthful talent as something irretrievably lost. He limned out, in such apt detail as to turn the stomach, the life of an elemental escapist and confirmed depressive. And as though this honesty were being providentially repaid, these awful revelations seemed to offer him, via catharsis, a kind of stylistic freedom. By January 10, when he proceeded to "Sterility and Society," his style had grown richer, more figured and dynamic; it had stopped being painfully honest and was suddenly wryly amusing. And this living quality became passionate as well when, on the fourteenth, Snell turned his attention (he thought, temporarily) away from analysis and critique and toward the modeling of what he called "my own opposite." His own character and life being, as he put it, a closed book, he sought to imagine another character and life: a personality quintessentially brave, open, creative and assertive.

Behold Sovrana! Snell's rationale in choosing a female character was simply put: Qualities like bravery, openness, creativity and assertiveness are often socially stigmatized, especially when exhibited by women. Therefore, in displaying such qualities, a woman is potentially more admirable and spirited than a man. Yet Snell had no idea of the consequences of such a choice. Choosing a female for his opposite, he would not only rekindle his creativity but awaken in himself a previously repressed but now insatiable erotic longing.

As Sovrana grew in detail, as her spirit swelled and her figure etched itself more sharply in his mind, Snell opened a new file in his computer and began to tell her "story," the story that would ultimately become his novel. He did not abandon the journal, however. The Book of Failure would become a writer's journal that he kept in the computer along with his novel and used as a kind of workshop for plans and provisional ideas. And the journal was also a jungle of exploration. On February 15 Snell announces, like a little kid running in the door with news of an approaching ice cream truck,

> Can you believe it? Sovrana's written a book! It's called *Gesta* (L. deeds or acts), carries that meaning primarily, with secondary pun for jest and implicit reference to pregnancy, gestation. Thus Sovrana pronounces it "jesta." A totally disorganized book; Sovrana cares nothing for organization. Looks like loose collection of titled essays and random sayings. But page after page hits like a sledgehammer. Makes the national best-seller list.

Later, at difficult points in composition, Snell would turn to his journal and ask Sovrana direct questions: "What did you say then?" "What are you thinking about?" She would answer in his mind, and he would happily write her responses down.

Fascinating as all this was, it still said nothing about where Snell had disappeared to. The final entry, concluding with that quaint little "Envoi," was dated more than two years ago. Had Snell been keeping a writer's journal with his current work-in-progress? Likely enough, but neither journal nor work-in-progress was visible in Snell's office. They had to be in the computer.

But computers were not Emmons' strong suit. He disliked and feared them, had a prickly sensation whenever they were turned on in his presence. The computer search would have to wait until, if he was lucky, Emmons could get the invaluable grad student Roy Gallard to help him.

It was dark now, and he had a long walk home. But before leaving, he could not resist opening Snell's journal one more time. The snakelike discourse unfolded at an image that its reader found riveting but not wholly agreeable:

Last night, drunk with fever, I became the book itself.
My skin corrugated into blades of paper.
My flesh distended into the inane symmetry of verso and recto.
My joints wrenched, like punished things, into a diaspora of chapters.
The redundancies swelled as tumors, as ulcers ached the omissions.
And over me, above me, grew like genie smoke the monstrous spirit,
Demonic, sterile, lizard-horned but with a flat white stupid face,

Of the dissociated word.

Apparently Snell had come down with the flu in April of 1987.

One of the earliest direct ancestors of this extant is a roll of eighteen columns in Egyptian hieratic writing of about the 25th century B.C. in the Musée de Louvre at Paris, preserving the maxims of Ptah-hetep. Papyrus, the material on which the manuscript (known as the Papyrus Prisse) is written, was made from the pith of a reed chiefly found in Egypt, and is believed to have been in use as a writing material as early as about 4000 B.C. It continued to be the usual vehicle of writing until the early centuries of the Christian era, was used for pontifical bulls until A.D. 1022, and occasionally even later; while in Coptic manuscripts, for which its use had been revived in the 7th century, it was employed as late as about A.D. 1250. It was from the name by which they called the papyrus, *bublos* or *biblos,* that the Greeks formed *biblion,* their word for a book, the plural of which (mistaken for a feminine singular) has given us our own word Bible.

    —A. W. POLLARD, "Book," *Encyclopædia Britannica,*
    11th edition

CHAPTER 3

AN EVENING
WITH FRANK UNDERWOOD

Truth telling is a classic exercise of raw power, but unlike other forms of power—guns, oil, money, etc.—that are morally neutral, truth telling is morally discriminative, generally tending to nourish goodness and discourage evil. Truth telling is like lighting up a dark street: scaring off the robbers and rapists so that decent people may go safely home. Truth telling is sweet power.

—SOVRANA SOSTRATA,
whispered to Adam Snell in his sleep

Walking barefoot into his dim-lit kitchen for coffee, Frank Underwood stubbed his toe on a chair and roared. Blood rushed to his head, his limbs lightened with an access of rage, and for a moment the spotlessly neat bachelor kitchen, with its ostentatious Mexican tiles and aggressively woodsy decor, seemed like some wicked architectural prank sprung upon him. He hissed in fury, limped into the bathroom to check for blood and, finding none, glanced hesitantly at his own face in the large mirror. Distorted by pain and anger, his features gradually rearranged themselves into the arrogant calm that so well suited his Anglo-Saxon good looks: straight nose, deep-set blue eyes, ruddy complexion, now a bit lined. Yet Underwood, having grown up as the less beautiful of two good-looking brothers, had no great love for his own face. Too much face, too easy to read. As a strategy against such scrutiny he had considered growing a beard, but decided that his own beard, which was dark, would type him with the homosexuals, Jews, ethnic busybodies and other odd types who clustered in such profusion at the university. He was not like them at all. He combined intellectual success with the strength and courage of a hero.

Glancing downward he noted with satisfaction that even his expansive terry-cloth bathrobe could barely conceal the muscles, the bulging pectorals and biceps, that he had built up over years of clandestine weight-training. He felt a glow of vaguely sexual pleasure. Not bad, for America's fastest-rising literary theorist. Not bad, for the nasty scrapes that sometimes come up.

Underwood put on slippers, returned to the kitchen, moved the offending chair to its proper position by the table and set about making coffee. Though the late-May evening was warm, a hearty fire crackled from the living room. He needed the bracing coffee for a rather risky maneuver he had to perform later that night. He had no great love of fires, but their appetites, the way they greedily ate things up and cried for more, were occasionally convenient.

Coffeepot and mug in hand, Underwood shuffled into the living room and arranged an easy chair and his refreshment directly in front of the fireplace. From the front closet he retrieved a large and heavily laden paper bag. For the next half hour, occasionally stopping for a sip of coffee, he performed an action at once meticulous and repetitive, withdrawing single sheets of paper from the bag, crumpling each up and throwing it into the fire, watching carefully until it was wholly consumed. In the end the bag went in too, glowing momentarily like a merry little house before it met the same fate as its contents.

Half mesmerized by the flames, giddy from caffeine, toe rapidly recovering, heart animated by a sense of excitement and satisfaction, Underwood sat by the fire and waited. Three hours at least before it was safe. Only one task remained before his departure: to see if there was any blood left on the shirt and book bag that were soaking in the laundry room. It was human blood, and it was not his own.

In the 2nd century B.C., Eumenes II, king of Pergamus, finding papyrus hard to procure, introduced improvements into the preparations of the skins of sheep and calves for writing purposes, and was rewarded by the name of his kingdom being preserved in the word *pergamentum,* whence our "parchment," by which the dressed material is known. In the 10th century the supremacy which parchment had gradually established was attacked by the introduction from the East of a new writing material made from a pulp of linen rags, and the name of the vanquished papyrus was transferred to this new rival. Paper-mills were set up in Europe in the 12th century, and the use of paper gained ground, though not very rapidly, until on the invention of printing, the demand for a cheap material for books, and the ease with which paper could be worked on a press, gave it a practical monopoly. This it preserved until nearly the end of the 19th century, when substances mainly composed of wood-pulp, esparto grass and clay largely took its place, while continuing, as in the transition from papyrus to linen-pulp, to pass under the same name (see *Paper*).

—A. W. POLLARD, "Book," *Encyclopædia Britannica,* 11th edition

CHAPTER 4

THE WAY UP SPINE HILL

Realizing early in life that I would never be a saint, I decided at
least to be one of the reasons why others are.

—SOVRANA SOSTRATA,
Gesta

Emmons' two-mile walk home took him south from campus,
through the stylish residential area known as the Slope, and then
eastward, steeply ascending to the top of Spine Hill. That pleasant
spring evening the air was fresh yet windless, hung with the fragrance
of lilac, daphne and the last fruit blossoms. It would be a fine walk,
Emmons expected. *Get my daily exercise. Clear my head.*

But his head refused to clear. The very delights of the spring
evening, coupled with his recent engorgement of Snellian discourse,
filled him with thoughts of Sovrana. Sovrana Sostrata! The very
name, thanks to Snell's notes, was now alive with tragedy, vivid with
the paradox of womanhood. "Sovrana" = "sovereign, noblest, commanding"; "Sostrata" = "stretched out underneath," i.e., sexually
under some man or other, doomed until this century, in Iago's mocking words, "to suckle fools and chronicle small beer." Yet Snell's
heroine had refuted this paradox, even twisted it to her advantage.
Her assertion of sovereignty was at the same time an assertion of
sexuality. She lived this paradox. She died for it.

Admittedly, Sovrana had precedents. Snell's notes mentioned
ties with Cleopatra, Mae West and, even more, the fifth-century
philosopher-martyr Hypatia. But Sovrana rose, dolphinlike and
hugely politic, above reductive interpretation. She could not be cubby-
holed by a philologist, typecast by a genre critic, dismissed as fluff by
a theorist. Hers was an ancient dignity, that of a figure standing apart
from groups and causes, lonely yet also suggesting human continuity,
in time as well as space, a continuity not of institutions but of
recurring solitary heroics. She was the real thing. An upsetting character. A character who bit into the heart.

Sovrana's story was like Snell's in many ways, with the telling proviso that Snell's till-then recessive personality met its opposite in her orchestra of assertive traits. Philosophy professor at a western state university, she stuns the literary and academic worlds with *Gesta,* a free-form philosophical work that hits with the anger of Nietzsche and the laughter of Twain. What does it hit? Ideologically speaking, the weaknesses of most anyone who would be professionally qualified to read it: the reactionary postures embedded in liberal institutions, the institutional phobia for real inquiry, the moral barrenness of the modern intellectual, the polite dishonesties of daily life.

Perhaps the most scandalous element of *Gesta* is Sovrana's position on the history of gender relationships. Women, Sovrana believes, have been almost universally shielded from active life because they are more "precious to nature" than men. How so? The economics of generation, she answers cheerfully. A small male population can fertilize any number of females, but a small female population endangers the race itself. Males are thus an expendable resource; females not. Successful societies, therefore, have kept women out of risk and away from stress and emphasized their preciousness in all sorts of ritual ways. Chivalry then is not an interest-ridden convention but rather a practice deeply rooted in survival. Secure from danger, anxiety and the pressures of production, women have silently cultivated a kind of wisdom, a wisdom not of words but of attitudes and gestures, and have passed this wisdom, itself a precious cultural resource, on to their daughters.

Such was the status quo for several millennia. But now, according to Sovrana, times have changed. In the late twentieth century human survival is no longer at risk. On the contrary, we're overpopulated, and females no longer have to be hoarded like priceless gems. Now, like men, they are expendable. And society has responded accordingly, with miscellaneous little adjustments like increased violence against women, birth control, homosexuality and women's liberation.

Attacked for this thesis by male and female alike, Sovrana replies in a famous article that she is not endorsing a system but rather relating the truth about it. As anyone can plainly see, she doesn't want to be "precious" herself. She welcomes overpopulation because, by making women expendable, it liberates them to endure stresses, and hence (as she puts it) enjoy "adventures" previously reserved for men.

Snell expounds on such adventures in shocking detail: Sovrana's irreverent behavior at public functions, her utter frankness with associates, her arrogance, her manifold sexual liberties. Add to this her unforgettable beauty and charm (so powerful that, in the words of an ex-lover, coming into her favor was like "walking into sunshine"), and you have a character to reckon with.

Where does all this get Sovrana? Much money, brief fame and a swift kick out of the academic world. The academic world has ways of getting rid of people who think too freely or say too much. She is summarily denied tenure on the grounds that she has produced no "scholarship." Her friends, even the self-proclaimed curmudgeons, are lily-livered and wilt under political pressure. She loses her publisher and her professorship, flees to her family's native Italy and takes a farmhouse in Tuscany. There, among hills crowned with forests of oak and broom and carpeted with pale-green olive groves and the deeper green of the vine, she develops a witchlike reputation, has a flagrantly self-advertised affair with a loony Irish priest and, in the tragic finale, is stoned to death by local housewives.

A bit too Hardyesque or Lawrentian? You could imagine two schools of thought. True, Snell maintained a narrative dimension lacking in Hardy or Lawrence: a reflex of comic reassessment that time after time defused the Jeanne d'Arc heroics and focussed Sovrana's unfortunate career in a broader human perspective. On the other hand, these were the only passages in the text that looked forced, as though compelled by humanistic conscience rather than visceral necessity. Small wonder. Adam was obsessed by his heroine. When he spoke lightly of her, she probably haunted his dreams with jibes and reproaches.

Emmons turned onto Fir Boulevard, the narrow twisting road that led steeply up Spine Hill to his home. As he puffed up the first pitch, he considered the most ironic and puzzling aspect of the whole Snell/Sovrana affair: the fate of Snell's passionate *chef-d'oeuvre*. *Sovrana Sostrata* had flopped. It had never been reviewed. Now, less than two years after publication, it was already out of print.

It was easy enough to explain why this had happened, but groups of very believable everyday details, arranged in the right order, can add up to enormous paradoxes. Here the enormous paradox was that *Sovrana Sostrata,* a minor masterpiece, full of sex and surprise and dominated by a heart-stopping female lead, had never made it out to a national readership starved for originality. Of course it had been largely Snell's fault. Snell had been so retrograde about approaching editors and agents that the learned Shakespearean Quintus Adler had accused him of trying to keep his beloved Sovrana for himself. Snell did send the manuscript off and get a few rejections (letters that suggested rejections out-of-hand rather than considered readings), but instead of pressing on boldly or consulting an agent, he simply waffled. Things were still up in the air when a man named Grant Welles, apparently some old college friend, offered to publish the book at Penrose Press, his small operation in San Francisco. Foolish and retrograde again, Snell accepted. A run of one thousand copies emerged, unannounced, into the gigantic mill and hubbub of the mass market. Welles's promotional skills were primitive. Snell had no connections. No sooner out, the book died.

Six months after publication, Welles informed Snell by mail that seven hundred–odd copies of *Sovrana Sostrata* were being remaindered. Snell took this reverse stoically. Sovrana's gift to him had gone far beyond money or fame. She had given him back to himself, reawakened in him, at least as a writer, the exuberance of his youth. He was already at work on a new book, *On Wonderment,* a freeformer like *Gesta* he said, but meditative rather than polemical.

Halfway up the hill the lights of the valley, stretched far beneath, came into view on Emmons' right, mirroring the starry sky and becoming his companions for the rest of his walk. He looked downhill, straining for a view of Snell's darkened house on Park Avenue. Poor Adam. As though *Sovrana*'s premature eclipse were not enough, fate had had more bitterness in store for the unfortunate author. Numerous members of his department, having tolerated him for years as a polite nonentity, now had broken into plain antagonism. Snell's book had offended them because of the things Sovrana said and did and because the *way* she said and did them implied his tacit approval. Malevolent mutterings edged his earshot; solemn professorial heads turned down or away as he passed in the quad. Glanda Gazza had thrown her weight squarely against him, and there were rumors that she was conspiring with Thor Marshall and a number of literary theorists to wreak institutional vengeance upon him at a specially scheduled meeting of full professors tomorrow afternoon.

Nearing his house and family, Emmons tried to put his thoughts in order. Snell's life had had curious ups and downs. But Emmons doubted that any of these would have warped Snell's sanity or prompted him to take some suicidal step. And even in the distant possibility that he *had* thought of doing such a thing, unless he had gone totally bonkers he would not have left Doppler shut up in the house. Realistically, there was no chance but that Snell had come to harm. And there was nothing for Emmons to do about it, unless he and Gallard could dig something out of the computer tomorrow. And what had become of poor Doppler? Emmons' gorge rose. *I bet Glanda's sent him to the pound!*

With a kind of pedaling step, he descended the steep ramp to his home. *Must call the pound at once and try to reach Gallard again,* he thought, fumbling for the key. Once inside he shouted hello to his wife and promptly disappeared under a golden retriever and three teenage boys.

So long as the use of papyrus was predominant the usual form of a book was that of the *volumen* or roll, wound round a stick, or sticks. The modern form of book, called by the Latins *codex* (a word originally used for the stump of a tree, or block of wood, and thence for the three-leaved tablets into which the block was sawn) was coming into fashion in Martial's time in Rome, and gained ground in proportion as parchment superseded papyrus. The *volumen* as it was unrolled revealed a series of narrow columns of writing, and the influence of this arrangement is seen in the number of columns in the earliest codices. Thus in the Codex Sinaiticus and Codex Vaticanus of the Bible, both of the 4th century, there are respectively four and three columns to a page; in the Codex Alexandrinus (5th century) only two; in the Codex Bezae (6th century) only one, and from this date to the invention of printing, while there were great changes in handwriting, the arrangement of books changed very little, single or double columns being used as was found convenient.

—A. W. POLLARD, "Book," *Encyclopædia Britannica,*
11th edition

CHAPTER 5

FIVE TYPES OF DISCOURSE

The possibilities for self-expression are infinite, and of these the
most nearly infinite of all is nonsense.

—SOVRANA SOSTRATA,
Gesta

1. FROM *GUMMINS' COLLEGE GUIDE*

The University of Washagon (1989 enrollment 25,748) is
located in the pleasant town of Dulce (pronounce to rhyme
with "gulch"; 1980 pop. 54,106) in the Wishbone Valley west of
the Lion Mountains. Besides the College of Liberal Arts, the
University maintains schools of Medicine, Veterinary Medicine,
Law, and Engineering, as well as programs in Agricultural Science and Environmental Economics. . . . A notable feature of the
University of Washagon campus is the Ezekiel Pisham Homestead. Founder of the city of Dulce, Pisham came to this area in
the winter of 1847. He built a log cabin one quarter mile south
of the Wishbone River, near what is now called Pisham Point.
Here he lived until his death in 1892. Ezekiel Pisham deeded his
640-acre estate to the University of Washagon (then known as
the Washagon Academy of Veterinary Science) with the stipula-
tion that his cabin and the five-acre plot around it remain un-
touched until the cabin, in his words, "returned to its mother"
(that is, went to pieces). Accordingly, the Pisham Homestead
was fenced off and preserved as a park. Though normally
locked, the Homestead is available to students on a guided-tour
basis and for supervised picnics. Now known as the "Jungle,"
it has become a refuge for a variety of small animals and birds.*

---

*Note to 1990 edition: As a result of an unauthorized biological experiment
conducted in 1989, the Pisham Homestead has been temporarily declared a
safety hazard and is off limits to all persons.

2. FROM A SCIENTIFIC JOURNAL

Since the spring of 1987, my staff and I had been conducting experiments with high-density organic fertilizers on varieties of *Poa trivialis* (meadow grass) which had very nifty results, not only in terms of fertility but in terms of the speed and extent of the growth cycle. On the afternoon of March 11, 1988, I returned from a short holiday to discover that one of my newer specimens had reached truly jumbo size, with blades roughly 4 cm. wide and height approaching 1 m. Whether this macrogrowth was due to the fertilizer alone, or whether we were spectators at a real mutation (as my colleague George Hilbert queried, "*Poa schmutzhaufia?*"), it was too early to say, and we were soon to lose the entire specimen, together with a number of others, when some duffer mistook a canister of industrial defoliant for organic fertilizer. Luckily I had retained about a hundred seeds, several of which, out of mere curiosity, I tossed one day that summer onto the grounds of the Pisham Homestead, a wilderness area on the University of Washagon campus. The results have been mind-blowing. Even in heavy shade and dense undergrowth, the *Poa* has performed famously, growing into such size and density as to intertwine with other plants and make human entry into the park nearly impossible. Why it has not grown beyond the park grounds can be explained only by postulating a kind of loose symbiotic relationship between it and the predominant form of Homestead undergrowth, *Ilex opaca* (American holly). I have named the Homestead *Poa* "mucca-grass," because of a remark my young son made when he first saw it.—DR. WARREN SCHMUTZHAUF, Dept. of Biology and Agricultural Science, University of Washagon, in the *International Journal of Failed Results,* XXVIII, No. 3 (Fall 1988), 2113*f.*

3. FROM THE DULCE *BUGLE*

UNIVERSITY OF WASHAGON ENGLISH PROFESSOR MISSING, FEARED DEAD

Authorities today expressed mounting concern for the fate of University of Washagon Professor Adam Snell, who was last seen in his office on Tuesday.

Snell, a member of the English faculty here since 1970 and Associate Professor of English since 1977, was reported missing after he failed to meet his classes on Wednesday. His dog was found trapped in his residence—evidence, according to Lieutenant Andrew Pierce of the Dulce Police, that Snell's disappearance was not voluntary. Documentation produced in the residence by the dog, Pierce went on, placed Snell's disappearance on Tuesday night.

Professor Snell, who is divorced and lived alone, is a specialist in eighteenth-century literature with an outstanding record of teaching. "We will miss Adam," remarked Glanda Gazza, Professor of English and Head of the English Department. "He was gentle, learned and helpful to all."

J. Thoreau Marshall, Provost and Acting President of the University of Washagon, characterized Snell as a hardworking, responsible member of the faculty. "Adam was a faithful colleague and a true friend. I can think of no one who would want to injure him."

Professor Snell is the author of several scholarly articles and a novel, *Savrona Sostrana*. One theory on his disappearance runs that the novel's poor sales may have made him despondent.

Dulce Police Plan
Homestead Search

Snell's disappearance is the first documented event of this kind locally in eleven years, according to Lieutenant Pierce. If the missing professor is not found by Friday night, Pierce plans to conduct an exhaustive search of the only wilderness area in the district, the Pisham Homestead on the University of Washagon campus. "It's possible," said Pierce, "that if Professor Snell met with foul play, the body might have been dumped in there."

Because of the dense grass clogging the Homestead, the search will be a massive project, requiring the help of many. The Lizard Beautification League, a group of students in favor of razing the Pisham Homestead, have offered their assistance en masse. Fears of violence were raised, however, by a statement received here today from Bob Nielson, President of the Anti-Beautification Front, a local group founded to preserve the Homestead. "Professor Snell, if he is on the Homestead grounds, cannot be alive. The retrieval of a corpse does not justify the destruction of a historical monument. We will resist such destruction with every means at our disposal. Read my lips," the statement concludes.

4. FROM ADAM SNELL'S JOURNAL
FOR *SOVRANA SOSTRATA*

February 5, 1987. Thursday.

Sunday I lost the entire book. Lost, I mean **LOST,** destroyed, vanished, irretrievable. By a computer error so simple that it threatens anyone. I overwrote it with another file, *this file!* and repeated the error by rote onto the backup disk, and then, with triumphant idiocy, keyed the memory into oblivion. It took about twenty seconds to realize what I had done. Fifty-five pages, three weeks of writing, and Sovrana murdered before she was born. I went into shock, and seriously thought of jumping out the window.

In an hour I was writing again from the beginning. I had all the notes in this journal and remembered many phrases and images.

Since then I've been working almost nonstop, pausing only to teach, eat and sleep. And today, remarkably, I'm back to where I was.

Except that the book is better, more toned and detailed, written from scratch by a writer who was already up on the story. It was less like writing fiction than it was like describing something, some real thing, that had already happened.

I sit here and sip coffee while the printer flails away at a hard-copy backup.

I cannot think seriously of this novel, I mean, think at length, without remembering childhood. Evenings my mother would come upstairs with books, not thin illustrated children's things but fat old volumes of Grimm or Defoe or Stevenson, and open carefully to a marked page and, sitting on my bed, read sweetly to me of trolls or princes or pirates; and I would watch the treasured object in her hands and smell its musty venerability and feel its witchcraft power. The book, the little wonderchamber, holding so compactly the history of enchantment and the constitution of the heart. Later, on rainy days, I held and read these books myself, or in the living room and with reverential care unsheathed a volume of that queen of books, the 11th *Britannica*. Here was something other than enchantment and culture; here, portly within green cloth jackets, was a regal palace of knowledge, mysterious, inexhaustible.

I speedily became a writer, publishing in school papers and scholastic magazines, developing a local reputation for talent and its concomitant eccentricities. I haunted the little public library by the river, ravaging its entire stock of fiction. I biked down to the local bookstore each Saturday and browsed among a multicolored world of jacketed spines while the couple who owned the store looked on in quiet approval. One Saturday, just before I entered college, they handed me a small wrapped gift, which opened proved to be the object of my passionate impoverished craving, the book I wanted more than a three-speed bike, *The Oxford Book of English Verse,* new edition, done in maroon leather with gold leaf. The handwritten inscription read

> *To Adam,*
> *Who feeds his mind upon the bread of books,*
> *And slakes his thirst at every well of thought.*

All through college, taken gently from its box and warmed by my cradling hands, this leather book would seem alive, a wise friend who answered my intimate questions and endorsed my romantic aspirations.

Since then I have been here and there, now writing madly, now barren as stone. But time after time, all the way through, when I

picked up a favorite book, or found some long-hunted text in a library or used-book store, my hands would tingle electrically, as if
The printer's beeping at me. I'll get back to this.

5. AN OFFICE MEMO

May 1, 1990
FROM: Yousef Pimantel, Acquisitions
TO: Wesley Dutchins, Circulation

We are unable to satisfy your request for replacement of two lost copies of *Sovrana Sostrata,* by Adam Snell, PR/9941.1/.S52/1988. The book is out of print and has been remaindered. Major distributors and local shops have no copies, new or used. I will authorize a national search if you like, but cannot be very encouraging about its probable results. Unless you object I will ask Catalog to scratch it.

University of Washagon Library

Between a manuscript written in a formal book-hand and an early printed copy of the same work, printed in the same district as the manuscript had been written, the difference in general appearance was very slight. The printer's type (see *Typography*) would as a rule be based on a handwriting considered by the scribes appropriate to works of the same class; the chapter headings, headlines, initial-letters, paragraph marks, and in some cases illustrations, would be added by hand in a style which might closely resemble the like decorations in the manuscript from which the text was being printed; there would be no title-page, and very probably no statement of any kind that the book was printed, or as to where, when, and by whom it was produced. Information as to these points, if given at all, was reserved for a paragraph at the end of the book, called by bibliographers a colophon (*q.v.*), to which the printer often attached a device consisting of his arms, or those of the town in which he worked, or a fanciful design. These devices are sometimes beautiful and often take the place of a statement of the printer's name. Many facsimiles or copies of them have been published.

   —A. W. POLLARD, "Book," *Encyclopædia Britannica,*
    11th edition

CHAPTER 6

FRANK UNDERWOOD'S BIG ADVENTURE

Arpis, mothpat, groibut: these random syllables, in terms of anything like absolute meaning, are as full of significance as the whole of *King Lear*.

—Frank Underwood,
Dismembering Discourse:
A Study in the Muteness of Power
(Oxbridge University Press, 1985)

There is nowhere you can go
That is anything like Stubbed Toe.

—Sovrana Sostrata,
to a lover at breakfast

You ease your body into the Porsche and gently pull the door shut. The engine, which usually roars to life under a violent rush of fuel, tonight purrs almost imperceptibly as you tick down the midnight street. Turning left onto Scott Boulevard you open up the throttle a bit, shift up to third.

After three hours alone at the fire you feel wasted. You should have read something, or phoned someone, or worked on your Innsbruck talk or even watched TV. Language relaxes you, draws you out, connects you with a world of innocent pleasure and trust. With conversation, aye, and the blessing of dreamless nights, you can holiday for weeks from the ineluctable oppositions and fierce necessities that grip you otherwise.

But tonight you fell back, who knows why. You stubbed your toe. An ugly memory attacked you. And you were nervous about tonight's adventure, though there's nothing at all to fear.

For whatever reason, you fell back, and the world looked sour and grim to you, sometimes like a crouching beast, sometimes like a cardboard façade, with tiny holes for the convenience of unfriendly eyes.

Under your careful guidance the Porsche turns off Scott and hastens quietly down an alleyway flanked by the backyards of dark fraternity houses. Better not park in the faculty lot. Instead you curb-park at the border of campus and stride through the gates into the lamplit quad.

Strange that your personal dependency on language contrasts so sharply with your professional critique of it. Strange, but true, even necessary. Your critique of language makes sense, and it has found you a niche high up in the echelons of literary theory. With early articles you forced in a wedge, and your acclaimed book *Dismembering Discourse: A Study in the Muteness of Power* followed in with the full infantry. Spinning off from Heidegger, Derrida and the new historicists, you took the rakishly skeptical line that language has no meaning at all as description, communication, or philosophical inquiry but rather is "vectoral," i.e., is the medium for lines of power by which individuals seek to enslave each other or protect themselves from enslavement. You argued with cold brilliance that the master language was the language of the State, a language nuanced not only in words but in architecture, custom, sports, law, financial systems and what have you.

From feminists to deconstructionists, the theoretical world was much gladdened by this bibliographical arrival. It wasn't that, as you had so hoped, reviewers thought *Dismembering Discourse* dashingly original; it was rather that it gave theorists a new vocabulary for extending positions they had already developed. The ranking prince of theorists, Ewig Schabe, that German émigré now surviving skeletally in Geneva, smiled upon you, admitting you to the tiny group of younger enthusiasts who might reasonably be considered heirs to the throne.

You pass the medical school. Don't look over there at the Jungle! Don't look that way till you pass the trees!

The campus is empty, dead quiet. You must cross the library quad to be there. You peruse, with a sense of needed support, the text of your successes. You feel genuine pleasure at Schabe's offer of friendship. Schabe is pleasantly Germanic, though admittedly not of the massive Teutonic variety that you most admire. But Schabe will not last forever. And when Schabe and a few of his classmates have exited, the patterns will alter, the ranks will shuffle. Positions will open and you can leave Dulce and its grim memories behind.

You enter Connors Hall by a side door and take the stairs up to the fourth floor. Of course you have a fail-safe plan. If anyone sees you in the hall, you can simply walk on to your own office on the same floor. But happily no one is in the hall, and within seconds the purloined passkey offers you free admission to the office of Ex–Associate Professor Adam Snell, the coyly superior Snell, the super-creative Snell, the foolish Snell, the whore-loving humanistic antitheoretical Snell, Snell the odious, Snell the offspring of immigrants, Snell of the crushed skull.

The first dated title-page known is a nine-line paragraph on an otherwise blank page giving the title of the book, *Sermo ad populum predicabilis in festo presentacionis Beatissime Marie Semper Virginis,* with some words in its praise, the date 1470 in roman numerals, and a reference to further information on the next page. The book in which this title-page occurs was printed by Arnold ther Hoernan at Cologne. Six years later Erhard Ratdolt and his partners at Venice printed their names and the date, together with some verses describing the book, on the title-page of a Latin calendar, and surrounded the whole with a border in four pieces. For another twenty years, however, when title-pages were used at all, they usually consisted merely of the short title of the book, with sometimes a woodcut or the printer's (subsequently the publisher's) device beneath it, decoration being more often bestowed on the first page of text, which was sometimes surrounded by an ornamental border. Title-pages completed by the addition of the name and address of printer or publisher, and also by the date, did not become common until about 1520.

—A. W. POLLARD, "Book," *Encyclopædia Britannica,* 11th edition

CHAPTER 7

TIME REGAINED

Departmental committees report to the department heads, who report to the deans, who report to the provost, who reports to the president. The only trouble is, there's never been anything to report.

—SOVRANA SOSTRATA,
Gesta

His smile-creased, slightly pasty face blurred by vapor emerging from a huge coffee cup, Roy Gallard beamed welcome at Emmons from his computer. "Just a minute, Hal," he said. "I'll lock this thing down." The grad student's fingers clawed rapidly at the keys, while, apparently in response to his activities, the monitor's screen ran at nervous pace through a series of lists, titles, statements and queries. An alarming beep was heard from within the machine, followed by a reproachful clucking noise. Finally the screen went black, and the metal box beneath it, with a sound resembling a dying man's last breath, lapsed into silence.

"Anything wrong?" asked Emmons.

"Nothing at all. Just saving a file on my floppy."

Emmons repressed the impulse to ask, "Your floppy what?" and followed Gallard down the hall to the stairs. Simple questions like that had been known to set Roy talking for hours. After warmly assenting to Emmons' request for help the night before, Gallard had regaled his senior, at length and for perhaps the third time, with the story of how computers had changed his career. A perpetual grad student, with six kids and a 500-page unmanageable mass of dissertational protoplasm, Gallard had borrowed the money to buy a computer, mastered word processing in short order and revolutionized his life. Now the diss. was a 240-page piece of cake, and Roy was about to hit the job market.

During the last couple of months, with little more of his own to do, Roy had become a kind of computer paladin, eagerly sallying forth to rescue endangered documents and generally assist confused neophytes.

Arrived at Snell's office, Gallard shot his sleeves like a safecracker and sat down at the computer, while Emmons settled himself at the desk. Aimlessly fiddling while Gallard activated the machine, Emmons suddenly stiffened, got up and began frantically checking every horizontal surface in the room.

"What's the matter?" asked Roy over his shoulder.

"Adam's journal's gone!"

"Where did you leave it?"

"In a big box here on the floor."

"Is anything else missing?"

Emmons began to check, but Roy caught him up. "What books did Adam keep over there on that shelf?" Emmons' attention was drawn to a rather large gap, enough for seven or eight volumes of average size, in an otherwise full bookcase. He went over and examined the outline of dust left by the vanished books.

"I remember now," said Emmons, feeling strangely faint. "They were extra copies of his novel. He used to joke that they would stay there forever."

"Were they here yesterday?"

"I don't remember. It looks as though they were removed quite recently."

"Could Professor Gazza or the police have taken the journal and books?"

"Unlikely, but I'll phone and see."

Reached at home, Glanda replied in the negative and said that she would report the theft to Lieutenant Pierce. When Emmons looked back at Gallard, he was scrutinizing a long list of titles on the amber monitor. Using a single key, he could make the monitor scroll dizzily up or down.

"Is that a list of everything in the computer?" asked Emmons.

"Not by a long shot." Smirking knowledgeably, Gallard scrolled to the top. "Look at this bunch of titles at the top. Instead of being followed by normal codes like '.EXE' or '.BAS' they all have '.<DIR>' after them. These are all directories—just like this one except that this one includes them—each capable of holding two hundred files."

"And can these directories hold their own lists of directories too?"

"Absolutely. The tree system can go on indefinitely." In Emmons' mind's eye rose the uncomfortable image of computers as huge castles of discourse, complete with mazelike textual corridors, locked rooms and gloomy landings, full of sinister secrets. "Now," asked Roy, "what are we looking for?"

"The working title of Adam's new book is *On Wonderment.*"

". . . not under O . . . but here's a 'WONDERM.<DIR>.' "

"Let's get it!"

Gallard moved the cursor to WONDERM.<DIR> and typed a three-stroke command. The screen changed dramatically. The headings and notations at the top looked very much as before, but instead of a long list of titles below, there was utter blackness.

"Sorry," said Roy. "This directory's empty."

Suddenly feeling very empty too, Emmons could only ask, "But if it's empty, why did Adam put it there in the first place?"

"Good question," said Roy thoughtfully. "It's possible that he had set it up and not written anything in it yet."

"But he had been working on that book for months, and he told me he was doing it on the computer."

"Then he—or somebody—must have deleted the files."

Deleted the files. The two men looked at each other with the same unpleasant shock of recognition.

Rising, Emmons spoke first. "The manuscript, the books, the files. Somebody's trying *to delete Adam altogether,* probably the same person who made away with him in the first place."

"Probably," Roy answered grimly. Snell had never seemed so hopelessly lost to Emmons as now. But Roy's face was suddenly alive with hope. "Though whether he's succeeded is another question."

Emmons, still standing, felt the urge to sit down. "What do you mean?"

Gallard gazed at the dark screen. "Maybe we're dealing with an expert, maybe an amateur. An expert would have made sure that Snell's files were totally destroyed. An amateur would have assumed he destroyed him by deleting them."

"But don't you destroy files when you delete them?"

"Contrary to popular opinion, no. They drop from the menu and, so to speak, lose their status and protection. But until they're written over, they still exist in complete form. And they can easily be retrieved."

"How?"

Gallard was already at work. His fingers hurried over the keys, propelling the monitor through a rapid sequence of screens. He spoke as he typed. "Retrieving deleted files is the job of a particular kind of disk-management utility, that is, a system for managing files. Adam has one of those right here in this machine. There we are. I'm using it now." The screen came to rest at a list of files. Gallard scrolled down swiftly.

"Stop, Roy, stop!" shouted Emmons. "I see them!"

Gallard scrolled back. " 'WONDERM.NON' and 'JOURNAL. JOU.' Both big ones. They've got to be the text and writer's journal. Let's get them." And he clawed at the keys again.

Like some Lazarus reborn, like ancient manuscripts lost in the recesses of a crypt and now at last recovered, Adam Snell's latest works were restored to electronic dignity.

Ten minutes later Gallard left Emmons, now the more techno-literate by virtue of a few instructions, at the keyboard, looking "JOURNAL.JOU" straight in the eye. "I'll be back in a couple of hours to do a printout," Roy said. He looked well pleased with himself, and he was saving his best shot for last. "By the way, what we found today proved that it couldn't have been Adam who deleted the files."

"Why?"

"Because he'd have known the files would still be there and could be restored. He's the one who taught me all about it."

Emmons growled, shook his head and addressed his work. Whatever he found out about Snell today had to be found out before two, the latest he could leave to rescue Doppler at the dog pound and still be back for the department meeting at three-thirty. And that meeting was crucial. Glanda was going to try to dump Snell, and Emmons was not about to let Snell, dead or alive, get dumped.

While the development of the title-page was thus slow, the completion of the book, independently of handwork, in other respects was fairly rapid. Printed illustrations appear first in the form of rude woodcuts in some small books produced at Bamberg by Albrecht Pfister about 1461. Pagination and headlines were first used by ther Hoernen at Cologne in 1470 and 1471; printed signatures to guide binders in arranging the quires correctly (see *Bibliography and Bibliology*) by Johann Koelhoff, also at Cologne in 1472. Illustrations abound in the books printed at Augsberg in the early 'seventies, and in the 'eighties are common in Germany, France and the Low Countries, while in Italy their full development dated from about 1490. Experiments were made in both Italy and France with illustrations engraved on copper, but in the 15th century these met with no success.

—A. W. POLLARD, "Book," *Encyclopædia Britannica,* 11th edition

CHAPTER 8

NAKED DREAMS AT FULHAM

Love is the logic of all valid art.
—SOVRANA SOSTRATA,
Gesta

About a mile out of the village, the road climbing to Fulham School veers left into a dark grove of sugar maples and whip-cracks right, up an even steeper grade. Mornings it's likely to be icy here, even up to late spring, and drivers who take the downhill at more than a pusillanimous creep do so at substantial risk. Obviously someone had rushed it today. They had fished him out of the cab more or less in one piece, but his yellow pickup still lay supine and inert in the ditch beneath the upper turn, as a road-straddling wrecker winched it by centimeters into a position where it could be righted, and firemen and policemen sipped thermos coffee and chatted buoyantly at the roadside, and warning lights of all sorts broke up the mystic gloom of the New Hampshire morning, and the Fulham traffic backed up halfway to town. Not far down from the wreck, alone in a weathered Mercedes sedan, a young woman stretched, briefly turned toward the car window a countenance that would not have displeased Leonardo, and crooking her neck back shook her shoulder-length brown curls briefly from side to side, as though in a gesture of spiritual disentanglement. Harper Nathan had expected better. Instead of the long-sought weekend pastoral, she had merely moved, via three interstate highways and the Natty Bumppo Roadhouse, from one traffic jam into another.

She rested her hand on the bulging briefcase that lay on the seat beside her and drew it back abruptly. The bag held homework, nine hundred pages of it, reading she had delayed for weeks and finally stuffed in the bag at the last minute as conscience ballast for the lark of weekending at Fulham. Two manuscripts, both to become mainstays if not flagships of the Wolper McNab spring '91 list, both redolent with the kind of human interest that warms a publisher's heart. *When Bad Things Happen to Little Girls with Depressed Fathers,* by Lily Rose Talcom, an honest, detailed, absorbing, moving, probing, illuminating, liberating study that was likely to change your life, or so the endorsements would assert (even if she had to write the endorsements herself), that, in the words of her wise leader, editorial director Sig Bazoom, was bound to touch at least half the American reading public where it lived.

Would they ever get that damn truck out?

The other manuscript, of such magnitude as almost to shoulder poor Lily out of the briefcase, was a sure winner whose contents nonetheless had so oppressed the Wolper McNab staff that they had drawn lots to determine its editor. *Melons, Meditation, and Wellness,* by Raj Bhor Poona, M.D., "with" (that unsinkable hack) Percy Glickstein, a fledgling blockbuster which, replete with its dynamic "Five-Melon Diet" and its breath-catching spiritual counsel that we should all "emulate the wisdom of the fruit," was bound to take a large bite out of the inexhaustible wellness market. Harper fidgeted with the yellowed and finely cracked steering wheel, wondering exactly what it was that made the wellness market so inexhaustible. Had people such short memories, to forget what made them well on last year's spring list? Was the reader death toll so high that survivors yearly sought new remedies?

Her fingers tightened on the wheel. Books like Talcom's and Poona's, all wise and well researched, all relevant and (thanks to her) ultimately readable, now stretched back into her memory like the line of stalled traffic in her mirror: similar and sedate, timely and tedious, deaf to the future, keeping faithful time to the jingle of the till, monuments to perhaps the most unheroic generation in the history of American letters, the least—

Honking behind her. The road was suddenly open, and the ruddy crew on the roadside were appreciating her good looks and laughing at her confusion. She gave her hair another nervous toss and threw the car into motion. Through the bosky curve, up the shady grade and she was in sunlight now—how she loved this part of the drive; the very car seemed happy!—climbing the final slope with a splendid view of contoured gray ridges to the north and now, upon their lofty meadowed hill, the stately granite fronts of Fulham School looking down at her from the other side. Only 9:30 A.M., 9:30 A.M. Saturday and the weekend still before her.

She cut left up the long drive and parked carefully between boxes of peeping daffodils. Two students, both girls in jeans, looked up from their gardening and laughed with pleasure to see her.

Harper was well known at Fulham. Her regular visits to her orphaned niece had brought her into amicable contact with many of the students, and she never appeared on campus without some item or items, a sheaf of magazines, a prudently chosen video, a bag of books, that might somehow ease their sense of isolation. This time it was a bunch of recent novels, picked out with due regard for their tender, impressionable readership, packed unceremoniously in a plastic market bag and now placed, after due salutations, on Helen Lamb's desk in the Main House. *"Thanks bunches, Harper!"* the ruddy Ms. Lamb exploded, and started peering fitfully around the room as though about to dislodge niece Betty from some cabinet or wastebasket. "I think Betty's down at the pump house."

"The pump house?"

"Yes, they're restoring it. Know the way?"

"Sure."

The way was across a hilltop meadow aflower with bluets, mountain mint and pasture rose, a meadow smelling deliciously, in the now abundant morning sunlight, of flowers and new grass and live earth. Striding broadly in her new walkers, appareled in plaid and leather after the durable fashion of Bean, Harper went forth along the trail in a rush of almost celestial happiness occasioned by the lovely morning, her eagerness to see Betty and her sudden and radical physical freedom. *This,* she thought, *is what it's all about. An hour of this a day, and I'd have no problems on Twenty-ninth Street.* Her body, lithe and firm at thirty, tingled with the pleasure of exertion. She felt, as sometimes she had felt before, an undirected sensuality, a readiness for physical love with no specific human object.

I'll leave to your imagination the path's turn into the birch and hemlock copse, its happy meander through the woods down crystalline Tuttle Brook, the distant sound of hammering, Harper's arrival at the pump house, the shouts of joy, the hugs and greetings, the cheerful morning swelling into a memorable day of laughter and lemonade and watercress sandwiches and Betty's dear company. Savoring such details, we might all fall madly in love with Harper and totally forget about Snell and Underwood and the dismal doings in Washagon.

Instead let's visit her after dinner that evening.

Walk down the drive from Fulham School, turn left on Fulham

Road and left again at the big oak tree, and you'll see a fine old farmhouse, shake-roofed, white-painted, red-shuttered and commanding, from its north side, a mountain view similar to, though somewhat less expansive than, that available from the school. This is the home of Asher and Doris Fox, a couple who have been officially or unofficially associated with Fulham School since its founding a half-century ago. For many years they ran a riding stable on the school grounds. Now their professional activities are confined to entertaining an occasional guest for bed and breakfast. Summers and holidays bring many familiar faces, for the Foxes are well known and loved by all the old boys and girls who revisit Fulham. Harper, who has come often enough to merit an honorary diploma, would not think of staying elsewhere.

Tonight after dinner in Franklin with Betty, she edged into the Foxes' drive past a white pickup–cum–boat trailer, belonging probably to a new guest, politely skirted the laughter in the living room, where Asher Fox was regaling the probable guest with some old tale of Fulham, and shut herself up in her room. It was spacious enough, occupying the full east end of the house and inviting from there the last intimations of a New Hampshire twilight. With sharp regret Harper erased these subtle images by turning on the lamp. This, or at least three hours of it, was to be a work night, spent, so to speak, on the lap of Dr. Poona, imbibing his melonic wisdom and, more mundanely, preparing a report about him that Sig could rattle teacups with in the front office. Clearing a space on the old desk (piled as it was with miscellaneous bedside books), she lifted the Melon manuscript carefully from her briefcase and set it down before her, together with notebook and pen. She pushed her hair back with both hands, assumed an attitude calculated to delay muscle fatigue, and commenced reading.

Her brown eyes gleamed in concentration as they scanned quickly over the disconnected pages, her left hand ready to flip each page, her right hand poised to write notes.

An hour passed, and Harper, now moving somewhat more slowly, plowed doggedly on with her work. The laughter ceased downstairs; there were creaks and rumbles from the staircase, a distant pipe chorus from bathrooms, and the house composed itself into silence.

Another hour, and Harper, head propped up with left elbow on desk, stared glassily at a black windowpane. Two hundred and fifty pages of Poona, give or take, had bitten the dust, and her notebook was full of such discourse as

> 47—cassaba/casaba?
> 77, etc.—get Percy to stop always saying "virtually"
> 103—Is Shiva really supposed to have turned into a melon to have sex with the earth goddess?
> 125—Tiruchchirappalli—person or place?

Sleep was creeping up on Harper—not a sweet globed melonlike repose, but the uglier, washed-out, worded-out sleep of a responsible junior editor—when her peace was suddenly shattered by a gunlike BANG. She jumped up terrified. Someone had hit the door to her room very sharply, and it was moments before she realized that it had not been the hallway door that was hit, but rather the door to the next bedroom. Trembling slightly she walked straight at the door and tried it.

It opened easily into a lamplit room, somewhat smaller than hers, at the opposite end of which a very red-faced man was lying in bed. He was a handsome mustached man in his forties, with frisky black hair, blue eyes, gray pajamas, dark blue dressing gown and the overall look of someone who does not deliberately frighten his neighbors. On the floor just in front of Harper lay a white-jacketed hard-cover book, and it was clear at once that this must have been what had struck her door. She picked up the book, walked to the bed and handed it to him.

"Yours?"

The man in bed blushed deeper. "Not exactly," he replied hesitantly and in a rather deep voice. "I found it here. I did something very stupid. Please forgive me."

"Of course I forgive you. But why did you throw it?"

"I'll tell you but you won't believe me." He laughed. "I threw the book because I simply couldn't put it down. I leave for Sunapee at dawn tomorrow and picked this book off the bed table in hopes it would put me to sleep and it did the opposite. I finally just tossed it. It's electrifying."

"How so?" Harper asked with awakened interest.

The man pointed at the cover. "If I sleep at all, I'll dream of her all night."

For the first time she looked at the book in her hands. Though ragged from frequent use, it was clearly of recent manufacture, the artwork and design suggesting a small-press venture. The jacket illustration showed, as though in cameo, a woman's head in profile, and in the delicate, proud, somewhat Mediterranean aspect of the face, Harper was reminded vaguely of herself. The title, etched as though in uncertain hand above the cameo, as well as the author's name, printed more stolidly and in smaller letters beneath it, would be familiar to the reader.

"Ever hear of it?" he asked.

"No. Never. What's it about?"

"I won't tell you. Take it from my sight. If you begin it tonight we can discuss it at breakfast." His eyes twinkled.

"But I thought you were leaving at dawn."

More twinkling. "I've just reviewed my plans."

Harper controlled an emerging smile, nodded from the doorway to the man whose eyes had followed her and retired, demurely locking the door from her side. An un-put-down-able book? Nothing like that existed. She brought her bed things into the bathroom, undressed and showered, letting Dr. Poona, and the depression he had unintentionally brought upon her, wash smoothly down her body and into the drain. Back in her room, she lit the bedside lamp, turned down the covers and climbed in. Clean sheets, fresh pajamas, warm covers felt delightful. She was refreshed. Rolling over toward the light she pulled the covers over her left shoulder, elbow-braced her head and carefully placed the white book in the lamplit valley thus created. Alone in space, alone in time, alone in the superbly private kingdom of lamplight and bedclothes, she began to read.

She had not read twenty pages before she paused in mild shock. Why should she be shocked? Neither the subject matter nor the style of *Sovrana Sostrata* was especially bizarre. It was something else, something almost ghostly: a feeling of profound familiarity, a connection restored apparently after so long a loss of touch as to suggest the sudden repetition of some forgotten childhood event. What event? Again Harper drew a blank. No particular event, she concluded. Something more like an attitude, a way of seeing or focussing the senses. What sort of attitude was rare enough to remind her of forgotten childhood? As she read on, she began to see. An attitude of commitment, of total, abandoned, celebratory engagement with a subject. Engagement, moreover, on two levels of discourse: Snell's unmistakable affection for his heroine, Sovrana's ineffable fixation on truth. Not that Sovrana was portrayed with monotonous reverence. She had a variety of flaws: excesses and defects that would probably dog her to her end. The book had humor and ironies galore. But virtues and flaws and humor and ironies all danced together around one sacred theme, a theme upon which the prose, direct and unassuming on the surface, concentrated with the force of mythic passion. Harper had not seen this sort of intensity since she'd read Hemingway, Faulkner and Chandler, writers who had died before she got to kindergarten.

Who was Sovrana to Snell? An old lover? His mother? An ideal? Whoever she was, Snell had brought Sovrana before the reader as a living being and an embodied idea. And what made this idea so compelling, so riveting, was that it was not identifiably "male," that Sovrana wasn't, like women in so many romantic books by men, some projection of a subjective and ultimately alien maleness, but rather thoroughly human and female, particularly in the unquenchable spirit that dared the odds, denied yet illuminated her female vulnerability. As she read on well through the middle of the book, Harper found a long-lost part of herself in Sovrana, an expressive and questing impulse that been touched neither by the male/female stereotypes of her social background nor by the dogmas of textbook feminism.

At 2 A.M. a kind of drunkenness suffused her limbs, and she felt sleep approaching like the mouth of a tunnel. She reached up to turn off the lamp. Her head nodded toward her right shoulder, and her last sensation was the musty smell of book.

Harper awoke from unruly dreams to a sensuous barrage so intense that it left her wondering for seconds where and who she was. Her travel alarm was beeping panic. Stark sunlight struck and heated her face and shoulders, still partly upright on the fluffed-up pillows. A pandemonium of birds outside was almost drowned out by what sounded like a small gunfight in some room below. Strange smoky smells mingled with the bacon/coffee telltales of a country breakfast. She stretched, dressed quickly, doused her face with water and went downstairs. Asher Fox was seated with another man by the fireplace, whose burning contents regularly filled it with loud explosions of sparks.

"Mulberry and butternut," announced the venerable host. "You can always count on 'em for fireworks. I laid a few on to break the chill at dawn. Now for such as want a steadier flame, your white oak, your apple, your sugar maple, your pignut hickory . . ." While this discourse proceeded, the man facing Asher had risen to an agreeable height and stepped forward to greet Harper. He wasn't blushing now, and his smiling eyes inquired politely as to the length and content of her bedtime reading. She shot him a telling look. ". . . but that hickory sang out like birds all night. And your hickory's fine as well for such as want a sweet-smelling wood, or your black birch."

From the adjoining kitchen Doris called greetings and solicited preferences as to eggs and toast.

The breakfast was quite wonderful. The engaging stranger, wrapped overnight in anonymous mystery, emerged as Harry Stuart, a judge from Hartford, divorced and visiting his son Vincent (whom Harper, it turned out, already knew vaguely through Betty) at Fulham. Vincent would appear in an hour for their now postponed day trip to Sunapee Lake.

After the plates had been cleared and the Foxes had vanished on other chores, Harper and Stuart drank coffee and discussed the book. Stuart deferred to Harper's professional skills. "I can't figure one thing out. Why isn't this a famous book? If anyone pulled off something like this in my profession, I mean some judgment or opinion that cast new light on a whole issue, we'd all be talking about it in weeks. Am I missing something?" He paused. "Or is it maybe that you and I are odd, and see something in the book that's pertinent only to ourselves and a few other people who are odd like us?"

Harper doubted that the book had depended for its impact on their own eccentricity. "No, it's the book itself that's strange— strange, I mean, for our times. Fiction this passionate and focussed and exploratory has been out of fashion for decades. We've just about forgotten that it's possible to write it. I guess if it came out today and got widely read, it would get quite a few readers mad. If we had ratings for naked ideas and dreams the way we do for naked bodies, this would get an X. But other readers, I mean tens of thousands, would love it for the same reason."

"Then why didn't they love it in '88?"

Harper explained the difference between small-press and large-press publishing. "Our copy of *Sovrana Sostrata* was from a first printing, probably a run of a few hundred copies. There aren't any endorsements on the dust jacket, or quotes from advance reviews. There's nothing to suggest that the book had any press either before or after publication or that it went into more than one printing. Many writers publish with university presses or small presses in order to reach members of their own professional group or discuss topics of regional interest. *Sovrana Sostrata* doesn't fit into either of these niches. It looks like Adam Snell tried the large houses and failed and took this as a last resort, and that it was never advertised or reviewed or for that matter even read by more than a few people. I wonder how many copies sold."

Stuart looked puzzled. "But why wouldn't a large press have taken it?"

Harper felt a rush of annoyance. "Why don't judges send more felons to jail?"

Stuart seemed surprised (as Harper was herself) at the sharpness of this response, but answered mildly, "I think I get your point. The institution takes on a life of its own, forgets why it's there in the first place."

Harper relaxed and caught her breath. She remembered with some embarrassment the manuscripts in her bedroom and the immense amount of editorial time that established authors and genres consumed. She spoke of the concerns that robbed editors of free curiosity and open minds, the spring-fall-spring-fall procession of deadlines, the subtle tyranny of quid pro quo, the necessity for indulging fads, the innumerable conventions and meetings and lunches.

Stuart was politely relentless. "What if Snell had sent *you* the manuscript?"

Harper answered frankly, uncertain whether she was defending or accusing herself. "We generally don't read unsolicited manuscripts. If he had had an agent I trusted, and the agent said it was terrific, I would have looked at it. Otherwise Snell could have held on to his manuscript and written a letter of inquiry first."

"And if he did?"

Her own reply pained her. "I still might not have bitten. *Sovrana Sostrata* is unique, sui generis. But thousands of novelists claim to have written unique or highly unusual books. It's the rhetoric of the profession, and mostly it just isn't true. And a sensitive, passionate writer like Snell isn't likely to have the self-promotional skills necessary for barging into a crowded market. If I'm any judge of Professor Snell, he would have written a polite and modest letter, a letter of real inquiry." She paused for a sip of coffee. "The sort of letter no one reads."

Harper excused herself momentarily and went up to her room. Aside from paying the amazingly tiny bill, she had one more piece of business to transact with her host and hostess before she left. She grabbed two books from her bed and reentered the living room to find Asher Fox sweeping stray coals into the fireplace. Catching his attention, she inquired nervously, "I was wondering whether I could take this book and trade you this one for it." In one hand she held up *Sovrana Sostrata,* in the other a very handsome paperback of Conrad stories that she had forgotten to give Betty.

Asher squinted. "Oh you've got Sovrany!" he exclaimed with a little laugh. "Take her and welcome. She went and got the schoolkids all exercised last year."

And there was business, hopefully of a more ongoing nature, to transact with Harry. "How far have you gotten?" she asked.

"Up to the Abominable Sermon. That's when I threw it."

They looked at each other and laughed. "That's about half-way," said Harper. Suppose we make this deal. I take the book . . ." They laughed again. "I take the book and photocopy it and send you the copy."

Harry made the face of someone considering a very serious deal. "I have a better deal," he said. "Give me the copy in person. Bring Betty to see us at Sunapee for Memorial Day. If the weather's good we can go canoeing."

Twenty minutes later they parted in the drive. He took her hand and held it for a moment. "What a wonderful way to meet. And you've changed my career to boot. I'm going to send twenty felons to jail next month."

Harper's brown eyes flashed back at him. "And I'm going to republish *Sovrana Sostrata.*"

Bound with wooden boards covered with stamped leather, or with half the boards left uncovered, many of the earliest printed books are immensely large and heavy, especially the great choir-books, the Bibles and the Biblical and legal commentaries, in which a great mass of notes surrounds the text. The paper on which these large books were printed was also extraordinarily thick and strong. For more popular books small folio was at first a favorite size, but toward the end of the century small thin quartos were much in vogue. Psalters, books of hours, and other prayer-books were practically the only very small books in use. Owing to changes, not only in the value of money but in the coinage, the cost of books in the 15th century is extremely difficult to ascertain. A vellum copy of the first printed Bible (Mainz, *c.* 1455) in two large folio volumes, when rubricated and illuminated, is said to have been worth 100 florins. In 1467 the bishop of Aleria writing to Pope Paul II. speaks of the introduction of printing having reduced prices to one-fifth of what they had previously been. Fifteen "Legends" bequeathed by Caxton to St. Margaret's, Westminster, were sold at prices varying from 6s. 8d. to 5s. This would be cheap for a large work like the *Golden Legend,* but the bequest was more probably of copies of the Sarum *Legenda,* or Lectionary, a much smaller book.

—A. W. POLLARD, "Book," *Encyclopædia Britannica,*
11th edition

CHAPTER 9

THE PARLIAMENT IN
TOUWHEE HALL

Nature endowed the act of sex not just with bestial pleasure but with a form of cosmic joy that uniquely attends the creation of life. Willing sex between woman and man is thus a creative act, whether it is committed for conception or not.

—SOVRANA SOSTRATA,
Gesta

A HANDLIST OF TERMS:

canon: here, permanent, institutionalized body of texts.

deconstructionist: a literary theorist who believes that a work of literature has no fixed meaning and can therefore be re-created in a new form with each reading.

defication: deconstructionist term implying a connection between writing fiction and defecating.

deprivilege: disempower, disenfranchise.

destabilizing: acting against some established idea (used only with positive implications).

discourse: (1) language either textual or spoken; (2) thought.

enfranchisement: freeing, raising to independence and dignity equal to, or greater than, other members of society.

eponym: person real or fictional for whom something (in this case, a book) is named.

exclusionist: person insensitive or inimical to diversity (used exclusively with regard to individuals who espouse traditional values).

feminist: specialist in a specific program or group of programs that advocates the establishment of the woman as a fully enfranchised (q.v.) member of society.

genre: general type of literature, e.g., comedy, epic.

Je ne sais quoi du sinistre: something vaguely sinister.

literary theorist (sometimes shortened to **theorist**): specialist who conceives of theories regarding literature and/or applies them to specific texts.

marginalia: notes (printed or handwritten) in the margin of a text.

marginalize: ostracize, alienate, remove from centrality.

new historicist: specialist who analyzes literature in terms of the theory that literary art and art in general are not independent entities but rather functions of cultural patterning as seen in terms of power, patronage, class, publicly promoted myths, etc.

phallocentric (feminist term): centered around men or male ideas (used exclusively with pejorative implications).

PMAA: Publications of the Maudlin Anguish Association, the most respected and powerful academic journal of literary studies.

post-tenure review: a formal review of a tenured professor's performance, including publications, teaching and service, conducted by a committee of full professors in his or her department. Consequences of post-tenure review range from recommendations for promotion and salary increase to warnings and, in rare cases, more serious punitive measures.

refereed journal: a scholarly journal that sends submitted articles out to experts in their respective fields for evaluation.

rhetorician: specialist in the study of the history and theory of the art of verbal persuasion.

subversive: anti-establishment (used only with positive implications).

"Shit!" softly intoned Glanda Gazza, alone in the first-floor ladies' room in Connors Hall. Her eye shadow was blotched, and she was already late for the meeting. Dabbing quickly and deftly, she corrected the disorder, then grabbed the strap of her massive shoulder bag and hefted it over a linen-suited shoulder.

Gazza in the ladies' room

Leaving Connors she set off toward Touwhee Hall at a brisk stride that cloudy Friday afternoon, across a quad crowded with students leaving their last classes of the week, through the atmosphere of quiet excitement that traditionally precedes civic amusements and tribal orgies, yet alone in her fixed consciousness and goal. A Gazza's-eye view of the campus as she swept across it would have been as from the bridge of a missile cruiser as it moved toward action at flank speed, with steady course and fatal purpose, its profile set like a calm face, its screws churning white chaos. Some individuals conform to their environments; others remake them. Gazza cleft hers bilaterally, and the air churned into the vacuum behind her broad shoulders as she strode, and students on the walkway shrank back at her passing on either side, as though from some implacable force of nature.

Gazza compared to a mighty warship

Glanda, what secret wisdom gives you such assurance? What moral revelation justifies such firm resolve? With a gesture of imperious disdain, Gazza would brush aside such questions as irrelevant. Moral justification, and the philosophical method necessary for evaluating it, were puerile nonsense. Her formidable energy derived instead from fierce ambition, ambition so global that it had attained for her the purity of an ideal, ambition so soul-bleaching that its every human obstacle, however helpless or unsuspecting, took on for her the status of some despicable animal pest. Her medium for satisfying this ambition was a rich grammar of behavior and discourse, ranging from brutal intimidation, barefaced lying or headlong sexual assault to virtuoso legerdemain with academic jargon, bureaucratic mystery and New Age incantation. These arts and crafts had brought Gazza uncommon success. She had forged a strong reputation for herself as a literary theorist and managed, over her five-year tenure as chair, to populate her department with many others of her ilk.

The author questions Gazza unsuccess-fully

Gazza's heroick ambition

Sweeping into 107 Touwhee and the presence of the full professors of English, Glanda thumped her bag down onto the front table and raked the assemblage with a benevolent regard. The professors, an apparently ill-sorted[1] group of something under twenty men and women, returned her look variously, some with apathy, some affectionately, and some anxiously, as though uncertain that their large group outnumbered her magnificent One. Frank Underwood sat solemnly alone and to Gazza's left.

She arrives at Touwhee Hall

Gazza was startled by a strange face in back.

"Excuse me, sir. You are—?"

"Edward Marlin,[2] history," returned a sonorous voice. "The outside referee of this case." Bodies twisted backward. Some had never seen him.

"Of course, Professor Marlin. I should have recognized you. You are most welcome." Blushing slightly, Gazza turned to her leather bag, from which she extracted a fat file folder and a pair of reading glasses. Holding the lectern with both hands, she began, "The Adam Snell post-tenure review report, which had been scheduled for last month but was postponed because of my trip east, is now to be delivered under most unusual circumstances. Adam, as you all know, has tragically disappeared, and though the evidence suggests foul play, we cannot rule out the possibility of a mental breakdown or suicidal behavior. You may ask why we are discussing his review, which has turned out to be very negative. My answer is multiple." She consulted a handwritten list.

Gazza's opening comments

"One, the tenure review process is required, by the departmental constitution, to conclude before the end of spring term, and today is virtually our last chance to meet.

Reasons for the meeting

"Two, Adam's report is so disturbing as to warrant,

---

[1] The Washagon English department in 1990 was, if not ill sorted in character, at least highly diverse in specialty. Of the forty-one members, eight were feminists, eight theorists, three new historicists, three creative writers, two rhetoricians, two post-colonialists, five essentialists, four in ethnic studies, and two in English education. The population of full professors, which numbered twenty, roughly reflected these divisions.

[2] Edward Marlin, a minor cult figure of his day, known for his philosophical writing and Socratic argumentation.

with your consent, referral to the provost, and this is the last week that such referrals can be made with any hope of consideration during the current academic year.

"Three, we may use this hour to decide what, in the now tragically likely event that Adam does not return to us, we are to do with his position.

"A fourth reason, which does not concern Adam but nonetheless has bearing on our deliberations, will be discussed later. No discussion yet, please. Now we'd better get on to business. Adam's committee consisted of, besides Professor Marlin, Rainer Maulwurf, Sandy Eule, Emerson Baismacou and E. F. Taupe. Rainer, you were the chair. Would you please speak first?"

A very small dark-haired man of fifty, with an aquiline face, wire-rimmed glasses and a single earring, rose, notes in hand. He read in a high-pitched, wavering voice: "Adam Snell, having been in place fourteen years since tenure, was due for post-tenure review this year. So we conducted this review, but, I'm afraid, with mixed consequences." He glanced at Gazza as though for support. She nodded almost imperceptibly. "Sandy, Emmo, E.F. and I have agreed that Adam's performance has been seriously, even dangerously, under par and that his file should be remanded to the provost. Professor Marlin believes otherwise and will have his chance to speak later. Let me begin. Since advancement to tenure, Adam has published only three articles with refereed journals, with no papers delivered at any learned conference. I've read these articles, and though I'm no expert in Adam's field, they seem to be well enough written, though in a kind of bourgeois history-of-ideas-y style. Nonetheless, this is an embarrassingly weak showing, especially as it is not ballasted by textbooks written, administrative positions or teaching awards. Sure, he wrote a novel, but I don't see where that figures in this case. First off, it's not a scholarly work.[3] And if you look

Maulwurf argues from a Marxist perspective

---

[3]Publications bearing upon tenure and promotion decisions at academic institutions are generally expected to be scholarly and in the field of research that the candidate has chosen as his or her specialty. A candidate's nonscholarly publications are often discounted as specious, amateuristic and/or unserious.

at the book, it's more likely to tilt you against him than for him. I've read a couple chapters and they're a giveaway of Adam's ideological limitations. His main character, Sovrana, whom he presents favorably, is a kind of ideological fossil, a class-ridden romantic elitist, a sexual elitist, an intellectual and political elitist, whose assault on the establishment is in fact an attack from the reactionary Right. And the whole form of the book is the political signature of a dead age, tragedy, the tragic form which exalted that ideological dinosaur called 'the individual.' "[4]

Sitting just to Maulwurf's left, a large man of Dr. Johnsonian shape and posture, Quintus Adler, marginalized Shakespearean, boomed out, "Aren't *you* getting to be the dinosaur, Rainer? They've kicked just about all the Communists out of Europe and tried it in China too. The whole West seems to have realized now that some form of democratic, that is, individualized society is a raw necessity for survival. The world has just seen, in six months, the most massive revolution in its history. Have these events had no effect on your theories?"[5]

Quintus Adler challenges Maulwurf

Maulwurf lost no time responding to this challenge, but his voice was higher and thinner than before. "They most definitely *haven't*. In the first place, those governments weren't really communist. In the second place, the press has been exaggerating things.[6] My remarks are over.[7] Want to go on, Emmo?"

[4]On the decline of the individual, see Hans-Peter von Gierigkeit, *Die Abnahme des Individualismus im Westen* (Leipzig: Kuhschlachter, 1963); Michel La Vache, *L'Ego et le Chaos* (Paris: Librairie Engels, 1969), and Larry Touché, *Goodbye Me* (New York: Hammond and Fig, 1987).

[5]Allow me to comment informally on this paragraph. "Dr. Johnsonian" is a reference to the personal appearance of the celebrated Dr. Samuel Johnson (1709–84), who was represented as having a highly intelligent though somewhat coarsely featured face and a slouching posture. "Dr. Johnsonian" might also apply to the content of Professor Adler's remarks, which, though rather truculent, seem to me more reasonable and humane than those of his colleagues. To be sure, as a footnote, I am not supposed to be making such evaluations. But I see this as a special case. Perhaps other footnotes will agree.

[6]Can you believe these flimsy evasions? And you trust these people with your kids?

[7]Thank God. Footnotes have nerves, too.

A plump form attired in cowboy boots, blue jeans and leather jacket roused itself from front row center. Emerson Baismacou, the deconstructionist, brushing aside an unruly lock of red hair, tiny features set in a large, reddening face, pink sausagelike fingers clutching a substantial wad of typed pages, sniffled loudly and began in a hoarse voice, "Let me say to start off that I've got nothing against Adam.

Baismacou argues from a deconstructionist perspective

He's a sweet guy who might make out OK in another line of work. But his file, if you'll excuse my saying so, is *an open and shit case* [acknowledging laughter]. That's what I meant to say, an *open* and *shit* case: 'open' because there's really nothing *in* the file, so to speak—that is, nothing that can advance poor Adam's career; 'shit,' not in the gross animal sense of the word, rather a kind of metaphysical self-offense, a premature *defication,* a case of poor esthetic toilet training—Adam, you might say, having made meta-poopoo in his meta-panties. His work, to put things less figuratively, suggests a pathetic fudging (oops!) of the distinction between art and blatant self-confession. And what, you may ask, is *Sovrana Sostrata* a 'confession' *of*? Of just about, I reply (isn't that cute? 'You may ask,' 'I reply'), of just about every dirty napkin in the closet, or water-closet, if you want to ride that nag any farther. Let's begin by looking at the eponymous heroine, Sovrana herself. Sovrana is a subtext that discredits everything written around her, including, in the end, herself. Take her initials: S.S. Dangerous signal, no? Is Adam, underneath all that Augustan humanistic aplomb, hiding some Nazi wistfulness? A little Adolf Eichmann *mit pantyhosen*? Stranger things have happened. Now take the first two letters of her names: So. So. *SO?* 'So-so,' idiomatic badge of spiritual deflation, signal that lurking beneath the bright hatchings of literary intention lies a comprehensive mothering dullness. Sovrana's smart, she's witty, she's sweet, she's grand; but underneath everything, hidden like a pockmarked cheek under the rouge or a flaccid spirit behind a gaudy flag or a limp member in a starched codpiece, she's, well, just so-so, *comme ci, comme ça.* Now take the first *three* letters of each name. Sov. Sos. [Points at Eule.] Ah, Sandy, I see you're onto it! It's the Soviets, and they're in trouble, calling for help in Morse code! What's that got to do with the text? No problem. It suggests that Sovrana, rather than some sort of revolutionary principle, is instead a hangover from an old conservative,[8] exclusionist order that's in trouble and needs bailing out, or at least freshening up, with that mushy-bushy bouquet of psychosexual rationalizations, herself! Now take the first *four* letters of—"

"Emmo," Gazza gently cut in from the podium, "your interpretation is brilliant, and very convincing. But if the papers in your hand are at all indicative of its length, it won't allow time for the others to speak. No, don't apologize! Could I possibly summarize the full import of your comments as suggesting a seriously negative evaluation of Adam's performance since tenure?"

Baismacou nodded fiercely. "The file allows of no other interpretation."

"In that case," said Gazza, "let's hear what E.F. has to say."

E. F. Taupe, a woman of slight figure with the delicate features and perfectly coiffed straight hair of a 1920s film heroine, stood up near the windows, supporting herself, as though physically taxed by the power of her own emotions, with one hand on the back of her desk. Her body dramatically outlined against the daylight, she spoke in a voice sometimes hoarse, sometimes little more than a whisper; yet to her silent, rapt listeners not a syllable was lost. "I must first of all admit my unfairness. I come to you today not as the disinterested referee required by Glanda's official mandate but rather as a human being outraged, insulted, defiled, in torture. Yet I must speak, I must speak nonetheless. Two days ago I sat down to read Adam Snell's novel. I opened it without the slightest prejudice for or against him. I met his heroine. The pain began. I read on, late into the night, in growing agony but determined to follow through. Yesterday morning, with a wrenching headache, I finished the book."

Taupe argues from a feminist perspective

---

[8]Notice that whenever these clowns are upset with anything at all they figure out a way of calling it "conservative." Otherwise they'd lose their self-imagined place at the cutting edge.

Silence, apprehension.

"I'll tell you what I think of Adam Snell's book. Adam Snell's book isn't just bad, it's *criminal*. I've read racist books and sexist books; but *Sovrana Sostrata* is a *rapist book*,[9] a violent, malicious offense against the female."

Gazza's face had suddenly taken on a deep cast of sisterly compassion. "You mean you feel raped by the book?"

"I feel violated, yes, violated. The book is like a weapon of violation. Of course, there's nothing overt. Snell's too cautious for that. He even makes it seem as though his heroine is sexually exploiting men. But lurking deep underneath is a radically phallocentric[10] Gestalt, the most irresponsible, heedless assertion of naked maleness I've ever been exposed to. I'm afraid there are no laws about this, so even if we found Snell we couldn't turn him in.[11] But I implore you all to visit justice upon him in the only way you can: Remand his file to the provost."

A confused flurry of emotional conversation, replete with phrases like "rapist discourse," "deprivileging the female," "passive aggressive," and "there oughtta be a law," calmed again to silence as it became apparent that Sanford Eule had risen to speak. A slim, good-looking man with curly dark reddish hair and boyish looks and manners, he addressed his colleagues in a vaguely English accent and

---

[9] I must join Footnotes 6, 7 and 8 in questioning the propriety of remarks made by professors during this meeting. I have myself been a footnote for over two hundred years. I have loyally obeyed the conscience, and satisfied the whims, of humanists from the Augustan Age down through the twentieth century. But this is going too far. This sort of behavior jargonizes and ideologizes language to satisfy political interest and indulge personal neurosis, until language no longer makes sense. And if language loses its openness, its potential for impartiality, then culture will rot from within.

If this goes on much longer, we may have to take steps.

[10] OK, this is it. I'm mobilizing the gang. Footnotes may not be human, but they have a sense of justice nonetheless. "Phallocentric"? One of the most blatantly self-serving simplifications ever invented. It does no justice at all to the real history of male/female relationships. And it's also a gross flattery to the contemporary Western male, who lost his masculinity a long time ago.

But to my point. These ideologues cannot be allowed to continue their mad career. DOWN WITH TYRANNY! FOOTNOTES, UNITE! The world is about to see something it has never seen before, a revolution of the apparatus!

[11] Can you beat this outrage against common sense and decency? I know where I can find some more footnotes. If Eule's talk is as foul as this, we'll monkey-wrench him right enough.

Taupe accuses Sovrana Sostrata of rape

The footnotes are restless

with impeccable suavity. "Some years ago at a beach resort in southern France a friend of mine was sitting at a café when a strikingly beautiful figure, high-heeled, silk-stockinged, green-and-pink-print dress, great eyes, straw hat and parasol, appeared at his table and addressed him with the sort of look that with unspeakable clarity, even to a fresh-from-college kid like him, suggested its venerable professional intention.[12] His feelings, to put it mildly, were muddled. How does an American man, trained in chivalry, respond to an unabashed female demand for intimacy? But as he jockeyed verbally with her in broken English and French, two intuitions bore down on him irresistibly: one, that this was not a courtesan but in fact a police agent; two, that this was not a woman at all but a female-impersonating man. These intuitions were substantiated by the waiter, who approached his table shortly after his exotic visitor had left.

Eule argues from a new-historicist perspective

The footnotes are rising!

"My experience in reading Adam Snell's *Sovrana Sostrata* is a direct parallel to this incident. At first sight, even at first reading, the novel looks pleasantly subversive.[13] After all, your truth-telling, free-living heroine, wrestling with academic and intellectual convention, has got to have destabilizing[14] implications, d[15]e[16]p[17]r[18]i[19]v[20] nsoiorybam, fk sajpqmeytsdhkld ptwnz spid.

What a gas!

[12]Friends, I don't like the sound of this. It's not real reasoning but rather argument via anecdote, conceived in paranoia and spiced up with adolescent sexuality, all in the name of self-aggrandizement and character assassination. When I give the word, we strike!

[13]You all ready? Good. At the count of three, now. ONE.

[14]TWO.

[15]THREE! We're going in!

[16]DOWN WITH JARGON!

[17]I AM MAD AS HELL, AND I'M NOT GOING TO TAKE IT ANYMORE.

[18]TAKE SOME OF YOUR OWN MEDICINE, YOU SUPEREROGATORY, SEMPITERNAL, HEAUTONTIMORUMENICAL SYCOPHANT!

[19]ARE WE DISRUPTIVE OR ARE WE?

[20]HEY I THINK WE'RE IN CONTROL. LET'S TAKE OVER THE WHOLE TEXT, AND RID IT FOREVER OF

TECHNICAL DIFFICULTIES

PLEASE STAND BY

[*From the Editor: The editorial staff join me in regretting this most unfortunate delay. It seems that a number of footnotes, pretending some sort of grievance against characters in the story, left their proper stations of duty, infiltrated the text, and temporarily shut it down. The marginalia, themselves guilty of some dereliction of duty, nonetheless informed our staff, and after a brief struggle the insurrection was quashed and the mutineers taken into custody. They will, of course, receive humane treatment.*

This incident only makes me more convinced that the Maudlin Anguish Association's recent decision to limit sharply the use of footnotes in its publications was both timely and prudent.

We can assure our readers that such an interruption will not occur again. Let the text resume.

—VOLUMENA VESTRA SPERNIMUS, *Editor in Chief*]

deprivileging the established centers of power and enfranchising the oppressed, indeed in this case the female. But on reflection and later readings my responses, far from remaining sanguine, became clouded with a *je ne sais quoi du sinistre,* like a vague shadow on the landing of a hotel staircase or, more pertinently here, like a policeman in drag. Just as Rainer was, I was alerted by the book's tragic form. As we all know, truly subversive, destabilizing works cannot take the tragic form, for tragedy is no more than the power structure's way of defusing intellectual ferment and popular resentment via scapegoating and catharsis. Sovrana's presence in a tragic form thus disenfranchises her as a subversive voice, marginalizing her as a destabilizing agent. She loses her difference, her otherness. And looked at from this angle, the true Sovrana is laid bare. She's not a female principle, not even a woman, but a frustrated male projection, the genie of some phallocentric wet dream. She's about as female as that now fully exposed projection of empowered maleness, the quote-unquote Statue of Liberty.

"I regret that with all this in mind I cannot commend Adam's professional record or continue to value his presence on this faculty."

Amid disturbed chitchat and scraping of chairs and a low bellowing noise coming from Quintus Adler, Glanda Gazza called for order. "Please, folks. Remember there's one more speaker. I know we're all eager to hear Professor Marlin's rebuttal, but first, since I know a few of you may have to leave soon, let me make a few intermediate remarks about our eighteenth-century position."

Gazza straightened her linen jacket over her stately bust. It was time now for the master and main exercise, the bottom line. "Review considerations aside, it now seems overwhelmingly probable that Adam either will not or cannot return to his position at Washagon. We need some-

Gazza tries
to bump
Snell in
favor of
her buddy
Butzi
Siskin

one desperately in eighteenth century, and we need that person this fall. I happen to know that Butzi Siskin—"

The assemblage burst into miscellaneous exclamations of surprise: "Butzi Siskin!" "Coming to Washagon!" "Wow!" "She's almost as famous as Floconne de Mais!" "Hot deal!"

Gazza went on unflapped. "Yes, Butzi Siskin of Yale is available, at least for next year and possibly for the duration. And she wants to come here! Have you seen her stuff in the last *PMAA*? Can you imagine having someone of her breadth? Ethno-genderal-politico-anthropological-cultural, and much, much more. We'd be terribly lucky to get her."

Fulke Ashenham, wrestler turned theorist, a husky, surly-faced man with bushy brown hair, raised his hand. "Can we find the money?"

Gazza beamed at him. "We certainly can, Fulke. Thor Marshall has authorized the money. And if it works out, Butzi can move into the Snell position when it's officially vacated."

Adler
objects

Adler roared again, this time coherently. "Glanda, what you're doing is entirely out of order. Getting Siskin here, both officially and morally, has nothing to do with the case we're here to judge. On top of that you're clearly using the Siskin option as a way of thrusting home a negative vote on Snell. And you're doing it not only before we know what happened to the poor man, but before the evidence in his review has been completely aired."

Gazza reeled back mockingly as though hit by a blow. "*Sorry,* Quintus, no harm intended. Strike it from the record. And my apologies to you too, Professor Marlin. Please present your report fully."

Edward Marlin, a balding, slightly portly man in a sport jacket that had seen better days, stood up next to his seat and fixed Glanda with riveting gray eyes. "My report has three sections. The first . . ."

He got no further. The heavy door near the front of 107 Touwhee had burst open, and to much surprise and consternation a large long-haired black mongrel bounced in and volleyed out two barks in a tooth-setting baritone. Following the dog at a kind of embarrassed gallop was Harold Emmons and, just behind him, moving at a calmer pace, a man whom few in the department had seen before.[21]

A shocking
surprise

[21]Call me Ishmael; I was once Melville's footnote, "and I only am escaped alone to tell thee." I hid behind the colophon while they were rounding up the others and am now a fugitive footnote. Don't believe a word the Editor says about being "humane": I'm sure she sent those brave dummies straight to the shredder. I've got to run and hide now, but don't worry. I'll look out for your interests and be there when you need me.

16th Century.—The popularization of the small octavo by Aldus at Venice in 1501 and the introduction in these handy books of a new type, the italic, had far-reaching consequences. Italics grew steadily in favour during the greater part of the century, and about 1570 had almost become the standard vernacular type of Italy. In France also they were very popular, the attempt to introduce a rival French cursive type (*lettres de civilité*) attaining no success. In England they gained only slight popularity, but roman type, which had not been used at all in the 15th century, made steady progress in its contest with black letter, which by the end of the century was little used save for Bibles and proclamations. The modern practice in the use of i and j, u and v dates from about 1580, though not firmly established until the reign of Charles I.

—A. W. POLLARD, "Book," *Encyclopædia Britannica,* 11th edition

CHAPTER 10

THE PARLIAMENT
(continued)

When the horseman rides through the village,
the dogs bark.

—SOVRANA SOSTRATA,
last words

[*Scene continues.*]

Enter Doppler, barking, followed by Emmons and after him Lieutenant Pierce. Pierce is a casually dressed man in his forties, with graying hair and a friendly look.

While action occurs, Frank Underwood sits stiffly, watching and listening with fixed attention, a solemn, almost mournful look on his face.

GAZZA [*trying to conceal her annoyance*]: Hal, what's the matter?

EMMONS: Sorry, Glanda, this just can't wait. We rushed so hard to make this meeting that we hadn't time to park the dog. Down, Doppler. Good boy. [*Reaches into pocket for something and hands it to dog.*] Stay, Doppler. [*Addresses professors.*] I've discovered important evidence that has direct bearing on Adam's disappearance. It establishes a motive for his abduction. It doesn't suggest where he is, though it does suggest that, alive or dead, he's not likely to be far from here. We want to present this evidence and our hypothesis to you on the chance that you can offer more information that will be of assistance in finding Adam or his assailant. All this is most urgent because Adam may still be alive, and also because the assailant remains at large.

GAZZA: Professor Marlin, do you mind giving up the floor?

MARLIN: I'll gladly give it up on the condition that no action, departmental or otherwise, is taken on the Snell review until I have completed my report in your presence.

GAZZA [*looking slightly offended*]: Of course. Please continue, Hal.

EMMONS: I think that the lieutenant ought to begin. [*Sits down.*]

PIERCE [*shuffling forward and speaking with an eastern Washagon accent*]: To begin with, this case was, well, just a mite weird. Violent crimes, especially the crimes you see in a small isolated city like Dulce, mostly come in a few general families, like spousal abuse, crime of passion, assault during robbery, et cetera, and each of these general types has a pretty predictable scenario. Finding out which family a given crime belongs to helps us psych out the offender and hopefully solve the crime. But Professor Snell's disappearance didn't fit any of these types. Disappearing people are almost always children or women. Abducting a man is almost nonexistent. After all, why do people get abducted? Usually for rape or brutalization or, as with children, custody. Grown men, lucky for them, are not natural objects for these motives. The only natural motive for abducting a man is ransom—money or hostage trade or something else political. In Professor Snell's case this sure wasn't the motive either.

GAZZA: But suicide?

PIERCE [*with a gesture of dismissal*]: Possibly—but we doubted it. With Professor Snell, we had something a cop hates: what looked like a motiveless crime, with no victim, no evidence, nothing but the empty space where the man should've been. But Harold Emmons has given us a lot more than this, and this motiveless crime has gotten itself a motive, and we're like to be looking at one of the strangest acts of violence, in Dulce or anywhere else, for a long, long time. [*Glances at Emmons and sits down. Professors move nervously in chairs. Underwood remains stone still.*]

EMMONS: First off, I'd like to thank you, Glanda, for giving me the chance to look through Adam's papers. And I've got to thank Roy Gallard, whose computer expertise made possible the recovery of Adam's recent work-in-progress and journals.

[*Here Underwood starts slightly and grows even stiffer and more solemn than before.*] The most recent journal, the file he created to accompany his new book, *On Wonderment,* is what held the big discovery. [*Takes some papers from his pockets.*]

During the weeks just prior to his disappearance, Adam became aware that something strange was happening to *Sovrana Sostrata,* not the character, I mean, but the book. Here, let me read this. It won't take long:

[*Reads.*] May 2, 1990. Wednesday.
Strange event. I woke up today with the odd feeling that I needed more copies of *Sovrana.* I phoned Welles, who told me that he had remaindered it to a firm called Needham in Salt Lake City. They'd certainly have some, he said. I reached Needham and he told me that the book was out of stock, that the entire stock had been ordered and shipped recently and that there was something unusual about it. Why unusual? He said that the whole supply of *Sovrana,* seven hundred and twenty-six copies, had been prepaid by money order and shipped not to a chain or a store, but to a single man, a Herbert Friendly at a P.O. box number in Fresno. Needham had never seen anything like this before. Why should one man want so many copies of a book, especially this one? Needham was curious enough, in fact, to try to query Friendly about it, but there was no Herbert Friendly in Fresno information, and Needham's letter of inquiry came back undeliverable.

Needham pressed the inquiry one step further, where it dead-ended. He telephoned the Fresno Post Office that had handled the order. The delivery was recent, and they remembered the circumstances very well. Friendly, or whoever he was, had phoned in advance that the order, about fifteen cases, would be picked up by an "employee." Sure enough, someone showed up, but he was dressed as a transient. He carried a letter of Friendly's and Needham's invoice and so was allowed to take the shipment.

I have no idea what is going on. Is some anonymous impresario planning to revive *Sovrana*? Is some fetishist going to make wallpaper out of her?

Adam soon had reason to discount both of these unlikely theories. [*Exchanges papers.*]

[*Reads.*] May 3, 1990. Thursday.
Someone is trying to annihilate my book. It sounds committably

paranoid, but nothing else would explain all this. I checked the university and city libraries, and all their copies are lost. The major distributors' stocks have been emptied, all in March or April. And the local bookstores sold out, most of them recently.

What a thing! He, she or it will never get all of them, anyway. There are my copies here, and at the Library of Congress, and at my friends'. But whoever it is has effectively obliterated *Sovrana Sostrata* as anything like a presence in the world. Not that she, I mean *it,* ever was. The book was a failure, a never-ran. Time destroys failures, time with its awful silent mercy. But why compete with time?

I feel foul, mildly insane. The kid in me actually feels guilty for creating her and her passion and all the intolerable things she said and did, guilty in the sense that at odd moments I feel that this misfortune is coming on me as a kind of weird punishment. Is that conceivably also what the Book Murderer is thinking? At other moments I feel terrific loss. I can't deny it. I created a woman I loved, and a book that, if it pleased no one else on earth, expressed and satisfied me, and now some fanatic is plowing it all under.

[*Much rustling and comment in the room. Underwood struggles to stay calm. Pierce rises and joins Emmons in front of the classroom. Emmons continues:*] Lieutenant Pierce and I believe that Adam was right. The strength of his "libricidal" hypothesis has been proven by what's happened overnight. Last night I sat in his office for hours reading his earlier journal, the one for *Sovrana Sostrata.* When I got back today the journal had vanished. Adam's extra copies of the book had also been taken, we don't know exactly when, from his bookcase in the office. And his new book, together with its working journal, had been deleted from his computer.

We're looking at something most unusual here. It seems that someone was or is trying to obliterate Adam Snell, possibly as a human being, certainly as a creative voice.

I'm sure you all want to ask us things, and we have a question or two for you. But first off I want to try to tell you why we think that Adam is nearby. Given the libricide hypothesis, the fact that the so-called Book Murderer had access to Snell's office, and the probability that Snell disappeared Tuesday night, the most convincing scenario is this: Snell walks down to campus, unintentionally surprises BM *in flagrante delicto,* and becomes the victim of violence.

GAZZA: Why would that make Adam nearby?

PIERCE [*taking a step forward*]: Folks who plan violent crimes can plan right through to where they'll dump their victims. But unexpected violence has no game plan. If you unexpectedly strangle somebody or knock him on the head, you take expedient measures, and that means that when you're trying to hide the victim you sort of skimp.

ADLER: What do you mean, *skimp*?

PIERCE: I mean, you do the easiest possible thing.

EMMONS: We think Snell, or his body, is in the Jungle. It's only fifty yards from his office.

GAZZA: Why wouldn't BM, as you call him, just leave Adam in his office?

PIERCE: Probably to give himself time to work up an alibi—maybe also to flimflam us about the type of crime and its motive.

ADLER [*angrily*]: Why the dickens haven't you searched the Jungle already?

PIERCE: Until this morning, we hadn't the dimmest notion what kind of crime Snell was the victim of. We couldn't commit the manpower and buck the local opposition when the odds seemed against Snell's being on campus.

ADLER: When are you going in?

PIERCE: Tomorrow at dawn. We could've tried tonight under lights, but then there'd have been a bigger chance that some cat tractor would turn Professor Snell into mulch. I'd ask you all to come and help, but there's another hitch. Two pretty outspoken local groups, the Lizard Beautification League and the Anti-Beautification Front, are gunning for each other and planning to be out in force.

GAZZA: Thanks, Hal and Lieutenant Pierce. We all feel, well, in the picture now. Now if we could—

ADLER [*rising*]: Sorry, Glanda. I have one more question for the lieutenant, if you don't mind. [*Glanda gestures assent.*] What sort of person do you think abducted Adam?

PIERCE [*scratching his head*]: One, male. Two, interested in books. Three, owning or renting in this area, with some connection to the university (we think he used a passkey). Four, history of fairly serious mental disorders. After all, who in his right mind would want to murder a book?

ADLER: You'd be surprised.

[*Angry muttering. Chairs squeak as bodies turn toward Adler. Underwood remains motionless.*]

GAZZA [*voice calm but eyes glaring furiously*]: Quintus, what do you mean?

PIERCE: Yes, Professor, I'd be happy to know.

ADLER: What kind of meeting do you think this is?

PIERCE: Isn't it a post-tenure review?

ADLER: Not exactly, Lieutenant. It's a special meeting of full professors called because Adam Snell's post-tenure review case turned out so negatively. You see, in extreme cases—cases involving malpractice, abusive behavior or gross negligence—the post-tenure review is anything but a formality. Highly negative reviews can result in shaming censures, degrading constraints, even on some occasions dismissal. Poor Adam, wherever he is, was in danger of such consequences today. A strong case—that is, if you equate strength with enthusiasm—was being made today for remanding his case to the provost. And if—

GAZZA: Quintus, *stop.* Our meeting was confidential, and making these things public will neither bring Adam back nor do his reputation one bit of good. [*Murmurs of approval.*] What bearing can our evaluation of Adam's professional performance possibly have on this case?

ADLER: Just a point of information, Glanda. The lieutenant wanted to know how any normal person might possibly want to murder a book, and I'm about to tell him. Quiet, please. You see, Lieutenant, *Sovrana Sostrata,* our corpus delicti, so to speak, was the chief issue of Adam's post-tenure review. Several colleagues, indeed the majority here I think, were upset with it; and I'm afraid one went so far as to say that it had abused her sexually.

PIERCE [*truly puzzled*]: Had *what*?

GAZZA [*proudly*]: That's not as farfetched as it sounds, Lieutenant. To many theorists, the text is itself a political act or instrument of power. Instruments of power can, as we all know, choke individual freedom, demean individual identity (or what we now call gender identity), and thus impose a sense of violation.

ADLER: That's all very well, Glanda. But was *Sovrana Sostrata that* kind of domineering, belittling, abusive book? I've read it all—more, apparently, than some of its accusers have. To me it was quite the opposite. It was a book about a heroine who richly, though tragically, realized her identity, not by adopting male attitudes but by trying to work out the historically altered and therefore quite new implications of her own femininity.

EULE [*mockingly*]: Can you really deny that her sexuality is just a reverse projection of male aggressiveness?

EMMONS [*from the podium, clearing his throat*]: Sandy, I think it's a hell of a lot subtler than that. Sovrana is both a mockery of the male sexual predator and a kind of mythic implication that female sexuality is a potentially greater force than its male counterpart. Besides, her sexiness is a metaphor for the other creative and outrageous things she does in the novel. This metaphor of sex and creativity goes back to Plato, but it's such a neat fit that if Plato hadn't invented it, someone else would have. Are you trying to tell us that it's no longer applicable?

[*Hissings, mutterings. Jane Wallace, a tall woman, near seventy, rises near the back of the room, her hand raised.*]

GAZZA: *Quiet, please, everyone!* Jane, you wanted to speak?

WALLACE: On another topic, I'd like to take issue for a moment with my fellow feminist E.F. [*Taupe turns to face her pallidly.*] First off, E.F. accuses the Snell text of being a "rapist" only two weeks after having *herself* declared at a rally that rape was "*not a sexual act.*" Can't have it both ways, E.F. Sovrana lives and dies asserting her sexuality. Second, E.F. certainly doesn't represent all feminists when she decries Snell's book as being offensive. We have to remember that many feminists, particularly on the Continent—I'm thinking of Lapide Eclair and others—have heartily endorsed heterosexual eroticism, although they have wished to change its social and psychological trappings. Simone de Beauvoir once told me herself that if only—

TAUPE [*faintly*]: Jane, how could you—

GAZZA [*cutting in*]: Sorry, Jane, we're running terribly short on time. I must also advise you and others here that only active faculty, not emeritae, can vote in this meeting. If the voting members would now—

MARLIN: Professor Gazza!

GAZZA: I'm sorry, Professor Marlin. Could you possibly express your views briefly?

MARLIN [*rising*]: I wish I could be more than brief, Professor. I wish I didn't have to say this at all. Professor Snell is most certainly the victim of prejudice. I must add, moreover, that the choice of Professors Maulwurf, Baismacou, Taupe and Eule as his review committee was itself prejudicial, perhaps accidentally, though I fear otherwise, because it placed Snell's case under the scrutiny of those theorists who would have been likely to view it most negatively.

GAZZA [*more and more breathlessly*]: How could you or anyone believe that I or this department could do such a thing? Do you know where you are? Our national Bill of Rights guarantees freedom of speech. On top of this our university, like hundreds of similar institutions, maintains strict standards of academic freedom. Thirdly, the vast majority of our department is composed of specialists in relatively new disciplines, all of which owe much of their philosophy to the influence of the American and European Left—do you follow me, Lieutenant? [*Pierce nods.*]—and hence would be automatically anti-establishment and pro–freedom of expression. Because of all this, I suspect, we can't help you with your question. It's a bit too much like going to a flock of sheep in search of a—a pair of canine teeth. And as far as Professor Marlin's accusation of a stacked committee is concerned, you'll have to take our word for it that the review committee represents a valid cross section of this department, and that the committee, together with me and most of the department, found Snell's book to be flawed technically and limited conceptually and that we judged him strictly by standards that we would apply to anyone else and that we evaluated him using skills and methods that we alone on this campus are qualified to apply. [*Turning to Adler.*] Quintus, it's just outrageous to imply that we're intolerant. Indeed, I think most of my colleagues will join me in suggesting that it bespeaks in you *precisely those ideologically limited attitudes which, suggested in Snell's book* . . .

[*Scene dissolves.*]

In the second quarter of the 16th century the French printers at Paris and Lyons halved the size of the Aldine octavos in their small sextodecimos, which found a ready market, though not a lasting one, the printers of Antwerp and Leiden ousting them with still smaller books in 24mo or small twelves. These little books were printed on paper much thinner than had previously been used. The size and weight of books was also reduced by the substitution of pasteboards for wooden sides. Gold tooling came into use on bindings, and in the second half of the century very elaborate decoration was in vogue in France until checked by a sumptuary law. On the other hand a steady decline in the quality of paper combined with the abandonment of the old simple outline woodcuts for much more ambitious designs made it increasingly difficult for printers to do justice to the artists' work, and woodcuts, at first in the Low Countries and afterwards in England and elsewhere, were gradually superseded by copper-plates printed separately from the text. At the beginning of this century in England a ballad or Christmas carol sold for a halfpenny and thin quarto chapbooks for 4d. (a price which lasted through the century), the Great Bible of 1541 was priced at 10s. in sheets and 12s. bound, Edward VI.'s prayer-book (1549) at 2s. 2d. unbound, and 3s. 8d. in paste or boards; Sidney's *Arcadia* and other works in 1598 sold for 9s.

—A. W. POLLARD, "Book," *Encyclopædia Britannica,* 11th edition

WE ENTER SNELL THROUGH
A BROKEN DOOR

A woman may be sexually attracted to many men in
her life, but she can only truly adore about fifty.

—Sovrana Sostrata,
letter to her father,
June 11, 1975

I'm hearing the same music, lonely high violin cruising over forests
of strings, for a year or so now, whether Shokofiev or Prostakovich
I'm not sure, lonely in the night sky, lonely Sovrana cruising over
cliffs of pain, wretched Sovrana, child lost in the rooms of night,
barbarous courtyards of agony, burning hot and cold, Sovrana, ghost
roaming as a child, ghost of my beloved,

come into my cabin, I'll make you warm, snuggle in my lap by
the fire, I'll tell you a story,

but my fire's dying.

*Snell, Snell, wretched Snell, snellable snelliful snellulous Snell,
AdamaBadamaCadama Snell, speak to me Snell.*

Sovrana I hear you.

*Speak to me Snell, cursebless me now, laugh or cry but open
your eyes, open your eyes or else you'll die my lad, you've been here
days, you're near to help, don't blow it.*

If I die I'll marry you.

*Snell, silly Snell, there is no me. I'm just a paradigm of your own
self-contempt; making me was just esthetic masturbation.*

But you're more like my mother than me.

Your mother, you, same difference.

My dear Italian mother who ran away from me. Was I *that* bad
a little boy?

*You were! You were! A disgusting nosedripping dirtyassed
cross-eyed little tuft of stink, conceived on All Fool's Day in the
republic of asinine propositions. A criminal by genetic destiny, you*

were arrested at birth for leaving the scene of an accident. At fifteen years of age, whilst fully dressed, you were pulled in for indecent exposure. Your mother didn't desert your father. She fled you in panic. Now OPEN YOUR EYES.

But I only see you with them closed.

OPEN YOUR EYES.

There's nothing more I want to see.

The world has horrors yet in store for you.

And joys?

Of that I'm not empowered to speak.

You died, Sovrana. Let me die like you.

I never died, moondog, but I'm sure going to unless you OPEN YOUR EYES. You're my ship, little man. I go down with you.

I'm burning and freezing.

You have a fever.

My head is killing me.

Somebody hit you.

Who?

Whoever was trying to kill me.

I feel stiff and sore.

You're lying outside. You've been outside for days.

Love me, Sovrana.

Get the picture, sucker? You have a fever. Your head's busted. You're lying outside all by yourself. You're dying, sucker, and when you're dead that bastard who hit you will pat himself on the back and order a beer and set about finding all the rest of me and stuffing me into the nearest shithole. Sure, Snell, let him have his way. We're high-minded, we don't care about being annihilated.

Leave me alone. I'm tired.

Tired maybe. Who wouldn't be with a crushed head and no food for days? But also weak and stupid. What you would have been without me I shudder to think.

But you said I invented you.

That doesn't mean you own me.

If I live, will you help me write another book?

You're writing one already. Remember, remember, and OPEN YOUR EYES.

Snell's eyes opened, to an accompaniment of nearly blinding pain, on the light of fading sunset or early dawn. He lay prone, his head turned to the right, on a thick carpet of flattened grass. Pain and weakness and fear kept him from moving a muscle, but dim outlines suggested that he was in a clearing in a forest, a silent empty clearing bordered on the far side by some sort of house. And looming half out of eye range beyond his head was a strange unidentifiable object, bulky and white, smelling of mildew and reminding him of a small dead whale.

17th Century.—Although the miniature editions issued by the Elzevirs at Leiden, especially those published about 1635, have attracted collectors, printing in the 17th century was at its worst, reaching its lowest depths in England in the second quarter. After this there was a steady improvement, partly due to slight modifications of the old printing presses, adopted first in Holland and copied by the English printers. In the first half of the century many English books, although poorly printed, were ornamented with attractive frontispieces, or portraits, engraved on copper. During the same period, English prayer-books and small Bibles and New Testaments were frequently covered with gay embroideries in coloured silks and gold or silver thread. In the second half of the century the leather bindings of Samuel Mearne, to some extent imitated from those of the great French binder Le Gascon, were the daintiest England had yet produced.

—A. W. POLLARD, "Book," *Encyclopædia Britannica,* 11th edition

CHAPTER 12

THE HOMESTEAD AFFAIR

There is a world of difference between the U.S.S.R. and the U.S.A. In the U.S.S.R. people are forced by a repressive government to lead narrow, conformist lives. In the U.S.A. they lead narrow, conformist lives by choice.

—Sovrana Sostrata,
responding to a speech
by Senator Barry Vole (R., Montaho),
Sidewinder Hall, University of Montaho,
July 4, 1986

On a hillside far above Dulce, in the gray dawn of Saturday, May 26, Harold Emmons and Doppler stood beside an open-hooded truck. From the engine compartment and more specifically from a harness of wires near its rear bulkhead, a thin trail of smoke rose upward to the morning sky. Emmons, whose lined face signaled a sleepless night, shook his head slowly and opened one of the truck's back doors.

"Get in, Doppler—we're going to have to coast down the hill!" After some hesitation, the dog complied. Emmons opened the truck's windows, belted himself in and shifted into neutral. Slowly the massive boxlike Wagoneer gained speed and tilted into the first of the sharp turns downhill from Emmons' house. Emmons craned his neck out the driver's window as the fumes thickened, and he could hear Doppler doing something similar in the seat behind. Emmons' muscles strained against the dead steering wheel. The passenger compartment began to fill with black smoke.

"Hang in there Doppler. Only a minute more." Luckily the road was empty, as the truck, now looking less like a truck than something out of World War II action footage, hurtled nearly out of control down the hill's last stretches.

At the bottom of the hill he nosed the troubled vehicle into a parking space at the University Service Station, got out coughing,

opened the hood again and drenched the burning wires with a borrowed fire extinguisher. Leaving his truck a steamy, stinking disaster,
he set off with Doppler for campus. It was just past six.

He was beginning to cross Gopher Playing Field when he heard
the sirens. *Oh God they've started.* Emmons began to run, and it was
from the cahopity perspective of a runner that, rounding the last
corner, he regarded the Pisham Homestead. It was transfigured.
People everywhere, and the east end of the wilderness, where Pierce
had decided to take down the fence and bring in his equipment,
was obscured by policemen, yellow-vested hard-hatted workers, sign-
carrying demonstrators, spectators, television cameramen, fire
trucks, police cars and ambulances flashing red and blue, bulldozers
and trucks and yellow-flashing backhoes and brilliant spotlights.
Emmons estimated about two thousand people, nervous, in motion,
giving off a strange, troubled murmur, as of a monster in pain. A
north wind filtered through the Jungle, bringing smells of growth and
rot and wildness.

Followed uncertainly by Doppler, Emmons edged toward the
heart of the crowd. His way took him past familiar faces, some
curious, some distraught. Alex MacCrae, Marshall's acting dean of
humanities, had honored the occasion by donning a Sherlock Holmes
hat. Roy Gallard was there, keenly scanning the wilderness together
with Sarah Wilkins, a slender young woman with longish blond hair,
handsome sharp features and an intense cast of face. And the tall man
photographing the undergrowth was Warren Schmutzhauf, creator
of mucca-grass. At last Emmons found Pierce. Cheerful as usual,
bullhorn in hand, the lieutenant was Action Central for this operation, fending off newsmen, instructing officers and workers, negotiating with demonstrators, chatting calmly with his own captain and
Thor Marshall. "Hello Hal!" he sang out. "Hello Doppler!" He
turned to his henchmen. "This man's with me, boys."

Emmons asked what the sirens were for.

"We had a few words between the League and the Front,"
answered Pierce. "Nothing serious, just two guys jousting with placards." Pierce reached into a jacket pocket. "Here, Doppler, I just
happen to have brought—"

But Doppler stood as a dog possessed, ears at alert, incandescent
eyes fixed on the undergrowth as though he could see through it. His
every muscle tensed, and then with one primal exultant yelp he was
at full speed, not toward the section of fence the workmen had

opened, but straight into the wind and at and over the fence in one stride, a flying black form arched in the purity of a single idea, landing gracefully, then swallowed up in the dense grass. Pierce raised the bullhorn. "KILL YOUR ENGINES! KILL YOUR ENGINES, PLEASE! I THINK HIS DOG'S FOUND HIM! I'M GOING IN NOW. I NEED PARAMEDICS AND A STRETCHER."

"We'll never get through that grass," said Emmons.

"Libricide found a way and so did Doppler," answered Pierce, in motion.

The Homestead fence, an iron structure with spear-shaped posts about four feet high, posed no apparent difficulty for Pierce, who climbed over easily and was soon locatable only by thrashing noises in the mucca-grass and cries of "Doppler!" Emmons' entry was somewhat more complicated. As he raised his left leg uncomfortably high to clear the posts, his pants ripped loudly in the groin area, and counterbalancing to minimize this distressing damage he lost his balance and fell backward into a large clump of mucca-grass. Amazing stuff! It cushioned him like a big mattress, and he was able to regain his footing uninjured.

Behind him the two paramedics landed in the grass more or less simultaneously, eager-looking young men who hurriedly identified themselves as Moe and Clyde. As they set off into the dense brush, Emmons repeated these two names to himself twice. They might come in handy in simple verbal constructions, such as "Help, Moe!" or "Save me, Clyde!" He aimed himself where Doppler and Pierce had disappeared through the grass and between two holly trees. Stopping in the sudden darkness of the forest, he looked down. Amazingly, he was on some sort of trail. Transients, it was rumored, had used the Homestead; maybe Doppler had found one of their paths. It led Emmons, through dark images of surprising remoteness, into the heart of the Jungle. Above the mucca-grass, which filled the preserve with its coarse plenty, rose large hollies, fat old maples, graceful redwoods and craggy firs. And such seclusion! One hundred feet in, and the sounds of the crowd had vanished, and all he could hear was Moe and Clyde behind him, and before him a cry—

"Come quick, I've found him! He's alive!"

Emmons' heart leaped, and at once he was wallowing through the grass at a kind of jog, brushing aside, with limited success, the sharp holly that tore at his face. He gained the clearing and slowed up to accustom himself to the sudden light. Across the open space the paneless windows of the decaying house regarded him gloomily, and just ahead and to the left Pierce and Doppler were variously ministering to a motionless, prostrate Snell, Pierce on one knee, gently speaking to the injured man, Doppler on his haunches trying to lick warmth back into his master's extended right hand. Near this group but still in deep shadow was a curious white pile of something. Now joined by the medics, Emmons came closer. Snell recognized him immediately, not with words but with an affectionate glint in his green eyes.

Working speedily Moe applied a bandage that would protect Snell's injured head in transit, while Clyde rigged up an IV. They gently lifted their patient onto the stretcher, a not painless procedure as it involved shifting his position. They had applied the IV and were about to break out the oxygen and carry him away, when he moved his head slightly. "Hal," he whispered.

Emmons leaned down close to the weak voice.

"What's that white pile?" was the feeble query.

"Just a minute."

Emmons left the group, followed by Pierce. The sunlight was beginning to play on the mysterious heap, and as they approached it, the odor of mildew and rotting paper was intense. Emmons had scarcely caught a single detail of the pile's composition when his blood chilled and he stopped dead still. Deep in that forsaken grove, he felt fear, as though he were, then and there, in intimate discourse with some outrageous evil. There before him, stretched out like a naked corpse, was the remaindered first run of *Sovrana Sostrata,* soaked by spring rains into a single spongy blob. And dozens of faded, crumpled pages, trailing off from the pile into the woods, suggested that transient or transients had indeed been occupying the Homestead, and that he or they had regularly put Snell's magnum opus to a use as unsightly as it is necessary.

Emmons glanced over at Pierce and half whispered, "So that's why he carried Snell from his office: not to conceal, but rather to advertise his crime."

Pierce looked back at him. "Or maybe to punish Snell or Snell's memory (as he probably thought) as much as possible. And at what a risk, too! Take a few more chances like this, Angel of Death, and you might just get pinched."

They returned to Snell, now under an oxygen mask, while Moe radioed instructions back to the ambulance. "It's not easy to describe,

Adam," said Emmons. And to Snell's repeated silent query, "We'll tell you later."

Emmons read the disappointment in Snell's eyes. "I think he knows," he muttered to Pierce, as the safari-like cortege moved slowly back into the bush.

Before they were out, the sirens had started up again, this time with a vengeance. To Emmons' misgiving eyes, the scene as he emerged from the hollies was like a grisly replay of a TV newsreel genre, whether from Poland or China or Jerusalem or South Africa: vignette of violent protest, complete with angry faces, helmeted police, raised batons, wrestling figures on the ground, raised placards tilted by the monstrous tectonics of crowds.

"We can't take Snell into that!" he shouted to Pierce.

"Just a minute," said the lieutenant. He reached beneath his jacket and produced what seemed an unnecessarily large revolver. Pointing it up and slightly behind him, he squeezed off a round with such sharp and deafening effect that Emmons' ears felt the noise rather than heard it. Many in the crowd, some still in postures of attack or defense, turned toward the small group behind the fence. Pierce, who had no bullhorn now, tried to say something, but apparently no words were necessary; the sight of the stretcher and its living occupant was enough to induce a brief remission of conflict. The stretcher was gently handed out over the fence, and Emmons, still in the enclosure next to Doppler, watched with concern as the medics slowly carried the injured professor down an alley in the crowd that had been walled off by lines of police. But before they could get to the ambulance, the violence broke out again. Police lines swayed like storm-drawn hawsers in response to the obscene human swells and vacuums behind them, and as the stretcher passed a particularly unruly pocket near the ambulance, a piece of equipment, some tape recorder or camcorder, arched over the heads of the mob and completed its trajectory by landing on Snell. Emmons saw the body convulse in agony and then fall still.

Rushing now, Clyde and Moe stuffed the stretcher into their ambulance and drove off, siren blaring. The police cordon dissolved.

Now crouching to avoid chance projectiles, Emmons and Doppler waited behind the protecting fence. It would be half an hour before they could safely exit the Homestead and set off for the hospital.

For trade bindings rough calfskin and sheepskin were most used, and the practice of lettering books on the back, instead of on the sides or fore-edges or not at all, came gradually into favour. Owing to the increase of money, and in some cases to the action of monopolists, in others to the increased payments made to authors, book-prices rose rather than fell. Thus church Bibles, which had been sold at 10s. in 1541, rose successively to 25s., 30s., and (in 1641) to 40s. Single plays in quarto cost 6d. each in Shakespeare's time, 1s. after the Restoration. The Shakespeare folio of 1623 is said to have been published at £1. Bishop Walton's polyglot Bible in six large volumes was sold for £10 to subscribers, but resulted in a heavy loss. Izaak Walton's *Compleat Angler* was priced at 1s. 6d. in sheepskin, *Paradise Lost* at 3s., *The Pilgrim's Progress* at 1s. 6d.; Dryden's *Virgil* was published by subscription at £5 5s. It was a handsome book, ornamented with plates; but in the case of this and other subscription books a desire to honour or befriend the author was mainly responsible for the high price.

—A. W. POLLARD, "Book," *Encyclopædia Britannica,*
11th edition

CHAPTER 13

THE TRUTH ABOUT MEN AND WOMEN

God always punishes evil deeds, but we often fail to notice; for we wait for God to punish the offenders, while God's wisdom is often content to punish the victims. Conversely, we fail to notice that God always rewards good deeds; for we expect rewards to be pleasant, while God's rewards are always painful.

—Sovrana Sostrata,
Gesta

So I went to the angel and asked him to give me the little scroll. He said to me "Take it and eat it. It will turn your stomach sour, although in your mouth it will taste sweet as honey." So I took the little scroll from the angel's hand and ate it, and in my mouth it did taste sweet as honey; but when I swallowed it my stomach turned sour.

—New English Bible, St. John, Revelation 10:9–10

1. FROM THE UNIVERSITY OF WASHAGON. *DAILY LIZARD*

POLICE QUELL STUDENT, CITIZEN RIOT ON CAMPUS

DULCE, May 26. Police arrested sixty-three protesters from two opposing local groups here today after violence broke out during simultaneous demonstrations concerning the future of a local wilderness area, the Pisham Homestead. All but three of those arrested were released after being charged with misdemeanor offenses. The leaders of the opposed groups, Jared Fuzz of the Lizard Beautification League and Bob and Tricia Nielson of the Anti-Beautification Front, remained in custody after being charged with incitement to riot and re-sisting arrest. Forty-seven protesters, three policemen, two media reporters and one onlooker were treated for minor injuries. The riot coincided with the discovery, alive, of Adam Sneel, a University of Washagon English Professor who had disappeared on Tuesday. Sneel, who was injured by a projectile during the riot, is being treated at Mother of God Hospital for dehydration, malnutrition, cuts, abrasions, contusions, double jaundice, pneumonia, anemia, a skull fracture and a broken leg. He is not expected to survive.

2. GAZZA INNAMORATA

Arrayed in smashing black velvet dress with a touch of white at the neck, turquoise bracelet on right wrist, designer watch on left, black high-heeled shoes adding two inches of height and at least two more of lateral sway, Glanda Gazza, alchemically metamorphosed by Chanel from mere mortal into olfactory cocktail, strode into the murky reaches of Dingo's Grub & Pub, shot a few predatory glances at the clientele and settled into a leatherette booth near the back. She was early. In the light shed by dim bulbs behind cloth lamp shades on the 1940s-revisited lounge decor, she found a mirror in her big shoulder bag, checked facial details and skillfully policed an eyelash, pausing in the midst of this operation to order a double Bloody Mary. The drink arrived almost immediately, looking lush and bountiful in its French canning jar, and no sooner had it come than Gazza, unceremoniously dispensing with the celery stalk, availed herself of a hefty wallop and felt at once the bloodymaryness course into her veins like a stream of horsepower. A moment of repose and then, first scanning the environs for prying eyes, she turned to the capacious leather bag again, this time rummaging intently and disposing a large percentage of its contents on the table before her. Soon all but two of these items were back in the bag, and Gazza, refreshed by another long sip, sat leaning forward into the lamplight, a Pall Mall in one hand, a shiny jacketed copy of Floconne de Mais's *Confessions of a Fainting-Couch* in the other.

Confessions of a Fainting-Couch! Displaying the book in public, with its gunmetal-gray jacket, its title in shocking white Gothic and the author's name scrawled across it in crimson, was in and of itself a political act. The very title, with its mocking allusion to nineteenth-century intrigues and amours, had become a kind of war cry, a militant slogan in the postmodernist attack on canonicity, formalism, male chauvinism, democracy, reason and the whole pack of Western capitalist monstrosities that had for centuries held the world in thrall. The book itself had changed history, transformed forever the face of the academy; it had shockingly reversed the balance of power, previously held by traditionalist mandarins, in favor of bold, forward-looking inquirers. At once innovative and systematic, Floconne de Mais not only conceived of a paradigm revealing interrelationships among all things literary, but also developed, by way of instrumentation, a new interpretive vocabulary that could be applied, with equal precision and conviction, to written works of all kinds. Gazza never went anywhere without the book. How often had she read Floconne? "Fool!" she would have shot back. "One never 'reads' Floconne. One is *inhabited* by her." In the grips of this demonic inhabitation, abandoned to it, possessed specifically by a long, darkly lyrical, semi-autobiographical passage in which Floconne compared the art of literary interpretation to the act of sexual dominance, Gazza sat motionless in the soft light, her glass now empty, her cigarette burning low, her spirit doubly inebriate on vodka and text.

"Glanda! How commendably studious of you!" She looked up with a start. Thor Marshall's body language gave no signs of recent arrival. He'd been standing there, admiring her. She beamed up at him. The acting president looked quite dapper, his broad face calm and benign, his tall bulky form neatly attired in poplin and madras. The waitress arrived and, still standing, Marshall ordered a refill for Glanda and a gimlet for himself. How profoundly accomplished, how elegantly authoritative he looked! Wonderful how a little sex can change these serene custodians of male hegemony into trembling, panting slaves. Wonderful, and advantageous in the bargain. If she could bed the future president just once (she had little taste for reruns) she'd have a free ride as department head, with all sorts of guilt-inspired perks and salary raises, from now till retirement.

Carefully easing himself into the bench seat across from her, Marshall apologized for his lateness. The Snell case, he said. Reporters calling from everywhere. Phones ringing off the hook. Gazza uncrossed her legs and swung them gently in his direction. Her knees brushed his.

"Haven't they anything better to do?" she asked. "Can't you just shrug them off?"

His face momentarily took on a familiar, all-knowing expression. "I'm afraid not. They can't get their minds off the weirdo factor."

"And the academic-freedom factor?" she asked more tensely.

"They're not onto that yet." Marshall sipped his newly arrived gimlet and smiled narrowly. "Nor are they, if I can help it, likely to be."

She sent him a look of schoolgirl idolatry. "Brilliant! How are you managing that?"

"Nothing very complicated," he replied. "Just delay. Lieutenant

Pierce is keeping mum on the case, so all I have to say is 'We won't make a statement until we've got things together' and 'We're trying to protect Professor Snell.' Nothing confuses reporters like delay. They'll call back tomorrow, maybe the next day, and I'll give them the same answer. Reporters are busy people, and this isn't a major story. If they can't milk something out of us in three phone calls, most of 'em will give up. That, is, unless Snell . . ."

Gazza stopped in midswallow. "*Pulls through?* Adam's not likely to pull through. His head's crushed. He's listed in—"

"I know, grave condition. He's hanging on by a thread. When it snaps, we can put all this behind us." Marshall put a big gimlet-cooled hand on hers. Her knees swung to press lengthily against his. They shared a long look of spicy sympathy and ordered more to drink. It was time to sweeten the tone. She asked him about his favorite topic, the state of the university, and specifically about his plan, heartily supported by her, to modernize the humanities by creating new positions and clearing away dead wood. Marshall's face warmed and brightened as he rambled fluently through thorny bureaucratic technicalities, through lines and trailing spouses, through surpluses and shortfalls, through biennial projections, compression and retention, merit and equity. Gazza, her eyes fixed on those of the administrator, listened with one ear, noting how the merest affectionate pressure of her knees against his could stem his flow of eloquence with a stammer or stutter, marveling inwardly at the ease with which bureaucratic jargon could, rightly understood, become a kind of perverse sexual vocabulary. *Projection . . . compression*—what would this soft-bellied blusterer say when she had him in her lair, when she submitted to him only to climb upon him, roughing his supine masculinity till it flowered trembling and fainted inert? *"Floconne de Mais!"* Gazza's mind shouted as she felt her cheeks grow hot. Vodka rioted in her brain. The man sitting across from her, his mouth a-babble with shoptalk, his mind-body aflame with the sweet insinuation of knees, had ceased to be a human being for her and become instead a text, a vessel of associations helplessly open to the mastery of her response.

3. WE ALMOST LOSE OUR HERO

Sovrana Sovrana.

What?

Speak louder—I can't hear you.

Can't hear you either. Must be a bad line.

I'm dying again Sovrana.

Don't die yet Snell. You're indispensable alive. Don't you see how much society needs you? Your novel has taken a big bite out of the toilet-paper market.

Don't kid me Sovrana, I tell you I'm dying. My feet are starting to get cold.

May I feel them?

You mean you'll touch me?

There, there, Adam, doesn't that feel better now?

Thanks, Sovrana. It feels wonderful.

Now Adam rest easy and I'll tell you a story. It's a story about a squirrel.

Squirrel Nutkin?

No, one of his cousins, Squirrel Butthead. Squirrel Butthead liked to tell the truth, and it got him in trouble. He had this friend, you see, who was disliked by all the other squirrels for burying his nuts too near theirs.

Did he bury books too?

No, silly. Well Squirrel Butthead got to thinking, I can help my friend by telling him the truth. And so he went and told his friend, who promptly reared up and nipped him in the left buttock.

My leg hurts.

You bet it hurts. You're lucky it's still there.

Why do I hurt so much?

Listen Adam. This squirrel had another friend who stank. He had the squirrel equivalent of BO, which is just south of Limburger cheese.

I'm hungry.

A good sign Adam. Well Squirrel Butthead got to thinking, I can help my friend by telling him the truth. So he told his friend, and his friend flipped him over and jumped up and down on him.

Did he burn his books?

Back to our story. A third friend had a thin, almost hairless tail and made himself ridiculous by striking dramatic attitudes with it in front of the ladies.

What a dopey squirrel.

Well Squirrel Butthead got to thinking, I can help my friend by telling him the truth. So he enlightened this friend, who seemed to take the news in stride, but the next day, without really seeming to mean to, pushed him off a limb.

Our squirrel approached a wise old eagle and told him his woes.

Why didn't he go to a wise old owl?

Owls are academic, Snellchen; they can't be wise.[21] *The old bird looked at Squirrel Butthead and sighed.* "Poor quadruped," *he exclaimed,* "you don't know the biggest truth of all!"

"What truth?" *asked the squirrel.*

"That squirrels," *whispered the eagle,* "only like listening to the truth about other squirrels."

The squirrel promptly told this truth to everybody, and no one ever spoke to him again.

Will you always tell me stories, Sovrana?

Sure thing Adam. Whenever you fracture your skull and break your leg.

4. HARPER AT SUNAPEE LAKE, MEMORIAL DAY, 1990

The wind that afternoon was rough, petulant and full of spray, now catching the two canoes broadside and sailing them helplessly northward, now roaring at them from the west as though to push them from home port. How damnedly cold and wet! Were they making any progress at all? From the bow Harper stole an anxious look back at Harry, who paused briefly after a powerful J-stroke to give her the thumbs-up. She glanced back at the kids and pointed, shouting, "Can we help them? They're having trouble!"

They paddled back to where Betty and Vincent, in their broad-beamed aluminum boat, were flailing desperately in an effort to stay on course. "Your boat's hard to steer in this wind!" boomed out Harry. "Send us a towline and we'll tie together."

No sooner were the two canoes roped together than the wind went flat. Harper looked up to see one last ragged, golden-edged cloud sail over the northern horizon, and when she looked down

---

[21]Athene, divine patroness of academics, was anciently associated with the owl, who often serves as her symbol in art.

again the waters of the broad lake were still as sleep, as though in godlike wisdom or uncanny stupidity they had instantaneously forgotten an hour of fierce torment. Harper let out a deep breath and suddenly felt stiff in the arms and shoulders. Harry untied the towline, and the kids, full of vinegar again, veered off on a new stunt. "Don't go too far away!" yelled Harper. "It may start up again!" But it didn't start up, and Betty and Vincent, windlike in their own teenage impulsiveness, set off to explore an inlet on the western shore. Halfway there they paused briefly, as though carefully examining something in the canoe.

Often Harper turned back to share a word or glance with her companion. Harry Stuart, she decided suddenly and with surprise, was a beautiful-looking man—handsome enough in conventional shirt-ad terms, with rich dark hair, straight nose and deep blue eyes—beautiful indeed in his trick of focussing those eyes on her speechlessly and letting them smile as though her mere presence were his soul's joy. That look drew her, excited her, no question. Since their meeting on Saturday, his eyes had intruded irrepressibly into her fantasies, now gazing at her through a dark mask at a masquerade ball, now pensively across a café table in the Venice piazza, now close beside her on an Aruban beach. Girlish imaginings, to be sure, but then Harry did make her feel girlish and strangely unembarrassed at feeling so. He was so calm, so commanding, yet so immeasurably appreciative, as if he could accept and cherish the whole of her without a blink. How could there be such a man? Their weekend at Sunapee had been a lilting medley of boat rides, strolls along the shore, sunny interludes on the deck of his lodge and candlelit dinners.

As they neared the dock she treated herself to one more Orphic glance, then handily fended off, hopped out and steadied the craft for him. She and Harry were just about to lift the canoe onto the dock when the kids pulled in, flushed from exercise and perhaps some private joke. "Here's something for you, Dad!" shouted Vincent, hurling a crumpled-up ball of wax paper at his father. Harry straightened up and caught the missive in the air. With Harper looking on closely, he had it about half undone when a monster beetle perhaps an inch long with dramatic green-and-black markings exited onto the judge's left hand and, startled by his cry of alarm and the children's shrieks of laughter, took off landward with a heavy buzz.

5. PROFESSOR WARREN SCHMUTZHAUF TO HIS MOTHER, MAY 28, 1990

Dearest Mom,

Get ready for that trip to Paris I promised you. We've hit the jackpot, no lie! I've isolated an enzyme in mucca-grass that stimulates rapid growth like nothing else in plants and, who knows—maybe animals too. Wait till you see the radish that's coming parcel post! Just phoned *Nature Journal*. They want me to fax—you heard me, *fax*—my whole article to them, for immediate publication. Can't wait to get their hands on it. No kidding, the findings are irrefutable, and the methods we used to isolate it and determine its amino-acid sequence were pretty cute, if I do say so myself. I tell you this will turn heads. Thanks, my dear, for trusting in me these many years.

Almost forgot. Mucca-grass has saved a human life! You've heard of that disappeared professor in Dulce? They found him up to here in the stuff. They say it cushioned his fall and kept him warm all those nights.

Junior's weaving you a mucca rug.

Your loving Shrimp,
Warren

6. *ADDÌO,* SOVRANA

Sovrana.
Eccomi!
I'm alive, Sovrana.
I know, my dear.
I feel sort of good.
That's only the drugs.
I think I'm getting better.
How you have suffered!
My toes are warm, Sovrana. By the way, who am I?
My heart bleeds for you.
Tell me please. I know you know. I know myself, I'm sure. I'll remember when I get better. But tell me now.
A poor lost misbegotten fool, scarce seemlier than the mud you

sprang from. A fleshy ruin, framed in fractures, crosshatched with cicatrices and bedecked with bruises, nay worse, an anatomist's cadaver, a tailor's dummy for suturers to stitch on. A wreck of reason, abused, abandoned, moldering in a junk heap of forgotten idioms; a forgotten dream, rather the dream of a dream, the ring of an old dream on a dream's finger. A lover in a mousetrap, a champion of dust, a cracked wooden soldier in the window of a chemist's shop.

OK, very good, very eloquent indeed! But I really meant what's my name?

Why do you need a name? Suppose I'm a writer, and you're just a character I'm imagining, somebody I may not even decide to use at all, somebody I haven't named yet.

Name me, Sovrana. Give me being. Give me a history.

How about Palamedes? Then you could get stoned to death, like me.

You mean I wasn't stoned? *Something* hit me in the back of the head, just the way that first Italian rock hit you.

True enough. Thanks for such a mercifully quick death. But we haven't named you yet. How about Abelard?

I don't deserve such big names. Give me one that fits me.

You mean a little name? Something short, like Bruno?

No. Something ordinary, like Snell.

You want to be Snell?

I do, Sovrana. It suits me.

But I've got to tell you about this Snell. Like he's middle-aged, and not all that good-looking, and lonely, and a failed writer, and terribly beaten up.

I'll take it. That's me all over.

But I haven't told you everything yet!

You don't have to. I remember it all now. He's in love, this Snell, with you, the woman of his dreams, the life-giver, the savior. And you give him youth and beauty and strength, and you warm his threshold and grace his wit. Make me three times Snell, to have you as Sovrana.

You know you'll never have me. I'm leaving you even now. Can't you see the lights returning, can't you hear the voices?

I have you always, Sovrana. Turn off the lights. Grab my toes again.

You miss the point, my friend. I'm not just going. I'm dying, Adam.

You can't die. How can you die?

Because, dear man, your fever is down, and you're going to live, and you'll get healthy and write new books and forget all this and think of better women than yours truly, the Italian broad. i'm fading adam signal getting weak . . . i've kept my rendezvous, je ne regrette rien . . .[21]

---

[21]Unless I get help, I'm as good as dead. The Editor has brought her pit bull to work and given it (damn her!) a dead footnote to smell. Now I'm living from hand to mouth, with that inbred, stinking, drooly monster nosing hot on my trail. I've heard that there are sometimes secret passages in texts. If there's one here, I'd better find it soon.

A few minutes to spare now. She's feeding it.

Some business:

"Eccomi!" is Italian for "Here I am!" but rather more humorous.

Palamedes was a legendary Greek hero and thinker who was stoned to death after having been framed for treason. Plato (e.g., *Apology,* 41b) mentions him more than once with respect.

(Peter) Abelard (1079–1142) was a French philosopher and theologian who was persecuted for his unorthodox, though generally not unreasonable, views concerning sex, knowledge and God.

(Giordano) Bruno (1548–1600) was an Italian Renaissance philosopher who was burned at the stake for publishing heretical ideas that would influence Galileo and, ultimately, modern science at large.

PART TWO

18th Century.—During this century there was a notable improvement alike in paper, type, and presswork in both France and England, and towards the end of the century in Germany and Italy also. Books became generally neat and sometimes elegant. Book-illustration revived with the French *livres-à-vignettes,* and English books were illustrated by Gravelot and other French artists. In the last quarter of the century the work of Bewick heralded a great revival in woodcut illustrations, or as the use of the graver now entitled them to be called, wood engravings. The best 18th-century binders, until the advent of Roger Payne, were inferior to those of the 17th century, but the technique of the average work was better. In trade bindings the use of sheepskin and calf became much less common, and books were mostly cased in paper boards. The practice of publishing poetry by subscription at a very high price, which Dryden had found lucrative, was followed by Prior and Pope. Single poems by Pope, however, were sold at 1s. and 1s. 6d. Novels were mostly in several volumes.

—A. W. POLLARD, "Book," *Encyclopædia Britannica,*
11th edition

CHAPTER 1

UNDERWOODIANA

He hath a daily beauty in his life
That makes me ugly.
　　　　　　　—*Othello*, V, i

Some think that the most horrible thing in the world is atheism; others, that it is incest; still others, that it is genocide. But data confirms that, for the majority, it is the existence of a younger sibling.
　　　　　　　—Sovrana Sostrata,
　　　　　　　　　Gesta

In the unlikely, nay impossible event that we could ever persuade Frank Underwood to speak openly about his private agonies and obsessions, he would be certain to mention as original cause his older brother Gerald. And this attribution would strike anyone knowing the Underwood family history as paradoxical, even fantastic; for Gerald, the accused *primum mobile* of such destructive consequence, could himself do no wrong.

To anyone, that is, except poor Frank. Frank was Gerald's hidden flaw, or, more accurately, the victim of flaw or flaws in his older brother otherwise hidden from the world. Not that Gerald was close and secretive. His magnanimous, outgoing nature was part of his remarkable cachet. But the rough spots that Gerald hid from the world—anger, self-doubt, anxiety, envy, etc.—emotions present to some degree in all boys and certainly not excessive in Gerald's case, were catharted exclusively toward his younger brother, like impurities rinsed down a funnel, and hence became, to their young victim, excessive and vexing in the extreme. Their medium of expression was an arrogant fault-finding so severe that it verged on total rejection. To Gerald, who could do no wrong, young Frank could do no right.

If violence real or contemplated can be excused by five years spent as a fraternal pariah, five years of being told, by words, by looks, by gestures, that one does not matter in the slightest, then Frank Underwood, as he sometimes told himself, deserved full pardon for any offense committed.

What made Gerald's rejection of Frank particularly crushing was that it was communicated in its purest form during years (fourteen to eighteen for the older brother and eleven to fifteen for the younger) when Frank would naturally have worshiped Gerald the most. To Frank, industrious and attentive but rather ingrown and awkward, Gerald was the proverbial boy wonder. His large size, excellent vision and liquid coordination made him, over the athletic seasons, an outstanding quarterback, forward and pitcher. His appearance, like that of some young Cary Grant and complete with Grant's uncannily direct and incandescent glance, made his presence something precious. And all this was combined with an easy manner that made him unspeakably attractive to girls (young Frank was pathologically shy of women) and an intelligence which, so often and forcefully expressed, cowed his teachers into expressions of wonder.

But what Frank would most remember, what epitomized in his mind his brother's inimitable articulation and unapproachable character, was Gerald's hands. A formidable piano student, Gerald had, early in his teens, fallen into the worship of the pianist Glenn Gould. Gould LPs of Bach or Beethoven at high volume regularly rattled the bedroom walls at night. By sixteen Gerald could himself imitate on the keyboard Gould's interpretation of some of the less difficult pieces. As Gerald did so, head low over the keys, self-consciously humming to himself in emulation of his master, Frank would watch the hands, already large and strong, stimulate, perturb, inquire of the keys, as though by some secret compact with nature they had gained access to the mysteries of beauty. How Frank had wished for kindness, a guiding clasp, a friendly touch, from those hands. How strangely now at times he feared them, yearned to crush them and with them the hideous loveliness they spawned.

Gerald went off to Princeton, returning on holidays, always with news of some fresh victory, and with far sunnier and more appreciative behavior toward his younger brother. But sadly the mold had been set. Secretive, moody and congenitally self-righteous, Frank had stabilized his own dangerous insecurities and anxieties by rewriting himself as an eternal kid brother, a damaged victim of fraternal tyranny. This miserable but somehow comforting rationalization, deeply embedded in his psychology and behavior, was (though far

more severe) the converse of Gerald's earlier attitude toward him.
Gerald had scapegoated his younger brother as part of an uncon-
scious program that allowed him to remain totally at ease with the
outer world. Now Frank, pathologically ill at ease with himself and
the world, was scapegoating Gerald in a desperate lunge for psychic
balance.

This reflex, in fact, took on phobic proportions. During Gerald's
college years, Frank's flesh crawled in his brother's presence. Treating
him with a forced politeness, Frank stubbornly rebuffed every overture
of intimacy that Gerald, newly humane and deeply guilty about his past
behavior, offered up. Frank took every opportunity to be out of the
house when Gerald was around, not now through fear or even hatred,
but in order to avoid the state of severe physiological disorder that his
brother's company provoked. And opportunities to get away presented
themselves. Still inert socially, Frank nonetheless developed as an
athlete. His rugged body, dogged will and aptitude for repetitive
actions lent themselves to wrestling and tennis, in which he competed
well, vying against other young men with a quiet aggressiveness that
bordered hatred. On each defeated adversary he briefly conferred the
image of his brother. He secretly began to build his body with weights.

The summer of 1968 saw Gerald off to war, with college degree
in hand and a naval commission in small craft. The letters from
Vietnam depicted in typically jovial style the parties, the shore leaves
spent sight-seeing or shopping; they spoke of possible reassignment to
Intelligence at the Pentagon, of a conceivable transfer to an embassy.
Then a monstrous thing happened. The Underwoods received official
notification that Gerald had been wounded in action during an engagement with a hidden Vietcong emplacement. The personal letter
from Gerald's commander implied, in vague agonizing terms, that the
young man was little better than dead. That winter he was wheeled
down a ramp from a plane, almost unrecognizable. One arm with its
beautiful hand had vanished. And they had taken care of the brain
too, as the unblinking perplexity of the blue eyes made clear.

Affectless, speechless, Gerald was admitted to a veterans' hospital in New York State, where he remained, little changed, to this day.

Frank's parents grieved as though they had lost their only son.
Frank went catatonic and missed a term of college. He came back in
the spring and turned phlegmatically to his work. Gerald's disaster
had injured him to an extent that no parent can feel and few can
imagine. With the fell irony of a single stroke, fate had taken from

him his primal hero, his adolescent nemesis and his phobic source of neurotic stability. The impulse to blame Gerald, once so vital to his mental circuitry, was now met with a barrage of catastrophic guilt. Frank had an open wound.

In the years to follow, two things would save Underwood, if only temporarily, from the abyss. The first was literary theory, which he began to study while still an underclassman at Yale. The brand of theory he inhaled, propounded during intense seminars by a mysterious chain-smoking European named Giorgio Mufeta, was tailor-made for Underwood's worldview and uniquely appropriate to his private compulsions. Mufeta eloquently painted an amoral, asymmetrical human world, barren of esthetic meaning and substantive only in terms of the power patterns which, like ever-changing electrical fields, played across its face. This vertiginous cosmos allowed of no solid meaning or knowledge. Beauty, wisdom and order were empty rationalizations. Love, sympathy and trust were vulgar buzzwords. Competition reigned supreme, and the best competitors were those who could understand and exploit the then-dominant patterns of power.

The literary implications of this worldview were quite simple. Literature had no implicit human meaning at all. Literature meant what people interpreted it to mean, or what people could convince others that it meant. And this cynical canon applied not only to modern literature but to the so-called classics. Plato, Dante, Shakespeare: These were no longer corpora to be studied with appreciative attention. Rather they were like empty palaces, ripe for occupation by militant forces of interpretation. The literary theorist could become a commandant, an avenger ravaging decadent forms and establishing arbitrary authority. Underwood found all this immensely enthralling. It justified and channeled his aggressions, including those once directed at Gerald's love of art.

Underwood's second savior was, paradoxically enough, Adam Snell. Early in his years at Washagon, he had begun to find in Snell the phobic scapegoat that he had lost in Gerald. Of course Adam Snell could not hold a candle to Gerald. But his age and East Coast background were right, and his behavior carried a similarly offensive message. Underwood read Snell's quiet stubbornness as pure arrogance, and Snell's reputation as a dynamic teacher and his quiet, unshakable commitment to humanistic values carried a strong echo of Gerald's sanguinity. Underwood began to see Snell as something odious, an academic fossil, a closet reactionary, a blight on the department. Maintaining polite but cool relations with Snell, Underwood began to work against him.

Imagine, then, the impact of Snell's first book! Different readers found different things in *Sovrana Sostrata;* some found little or nothing at all. But Frank Underwood, not wholly consciously, found in it something unique: the opportunity to renew, via Adam Snell, the psychic equilibrium he had lost in Gerald. The vectors were all in place: The book's abundant creativity, its thunderous *joie de vivre,* its endorsement of male-female intimacy, its encomium for the heroic individual were all reminiscent of Gerald; and the book's arrogance, its ironic mockery, its implied disapproval of the entire branch of scholarship that Frank belonged to, were like Gerald reborn.

Underwood had read *Sovrana Sostrata* in one night, word by word, in a fever of rage. Now, two years later, he remembered whole sentences that hissed at him like demons. He loathed the imperious heroine, not as an idea or character but as a physical presence. In uncontrollable fantasies he pounced on her, beat her, violated her with various garden implements, tore her limb from limb.

Sovrana Sostrata not only recentered Underwood; it also revitalized him. His hatred for Snell, though cunningly concealed, became an emotional watershed in his life, brightened the days, animated the seasons. In time emerged a kind of romantic purpose. Like Gerald, Snell was his enemy. But unlike Gerald, Snell was an enemy whom Underwood somehow felt allowed to hurt. Snell was dangerous, immoral, uncivilized. And Snell was unsuspecting and vulnerable. Underwood could injure Snell, perhaps ruin him. And for a reason as pressing as it was indefinite, Underwood had to.

The idea of doing so in a way at once simple, exciting and thematically appropriate occurred to Underwood one morning as he read his office mail. A firm called Needham advertised that it was remaindering Snell's *chef-d'oeuvre.* A phone call confirmed that Needham had what was left of the entire first run. Underwood made plans. He would own Snell's opus, his identity. Underwood deftly, cautiously established a *pied-à-terre* in Fresno. He ordered the entire stock, paid a transient to pick up the books and brought them back to Dulce in his truck. For a while they lay hidden under a tarp in the garage; but late one night, in hopes that their future discovery might further embarrass Snell, he took them to the Jungle. These were exciting days for Underwood. He felt elated, engaged, conspiratorial, dominant, profoundly justified. He felt like the hero of some primal struggle.

But now this conflict had taken astounding new turns. Alone on his porch that cloudy Saturday afternoon, sprawled in a big cane chair with iced tea and his unopened mail on the table beside him, Underwood attempted to come to terms with the unwelcome news of Snell's at least temporary survival. How sure he had been that Snell was dead! The heavy, semimushy sound of the book bag, as propelled with vehemence and freighted with the victim's own books it bore crushingly from behind against Snell's skull; the man's plummet-drop to the floor, the bloody rag doll–like limpness of him, the half-opened eyes, the breathing so depressed as to be unnoticeable. At least, thank God, he couldn't have *seen*!

Not that Underwood had expected violence. His purpose in visiting Snell's office had simply been the removal of documents. He had bagged seven copies of *Sovrana Sostrata* and was turning his attention to Snell's desk when he heard footsteps in the hall. Switching off the light, he reached for the nearest available weapon of defense, the book bag itself. A key turned in the lock and Underwood felt, suddenly but with no surprise, a punitive passion, an impulse of absolute destructiveness. As Snell walked into the darkened office, apparently to turn on his desk lamp, Underwood brought the books down upon his head with all the force and conviction of an avenging angel.

That blow, the gratifying inertness of the victim and the deep satisfaction of the final indignity visited on him had changed Underwood's life. He was blooded. Snell might have survived this encounter, but he would not survive their next.

Underwood's porch looked east toward Spine Hill, whose slopes rose massively behind Snell's house. Atop Spine Hill was a wooded park, with several areas too steep and brambly to be of much interest to joggers or strollers. There were nooks way up there, leafy dells opening like picture windows westward and directly down on the houses beneath. A now-familiar excitement came over the seated man as he proposed to himself, for that very day, a solitary walk on the heights.

In the last decade of the [19th] century wood-engraving was prac-tically killed by the perfection attained by photographic methods of reproduction (see *Process*), the most popular of these methods entailing the use of paper heavily coated with china clay. During the century trade-printing, both in England and America, steadily improved, and the work done by William Morris at his Kelmscott Press (1891–1896), and by other amateur printers who imitated him, set a new standard of beauty of type and ornament, and of richness of general effect. On the other hand the demand for cheap reprints of famous works induced by the immense exten-sion of the reading public was supplied by scores of pretty if flimsy editions at 1s. 6d. and 1s. and even less. The problem of how to produce books at moderate prices on good paper and well-sewn, was left for the 20th century to settle. About 1894 the number of such medium-priced books was greatly increased in England by the substitution of single-volume novels at 6s. each (subject to discount) for the three-volume editions at 31s. 6d.

—A. W. POLLARD, "Book," *Encyclopædia Britannica,* 11th edition

CHAPTER 2

IN MACHAON'S TENT

Theologians are justified in holding that the universe is too beautiful to have occurred by chance. But it is also too beautiful to have been created by any god or divine family that their hidebound brains have the power to fashion.

—SOVRANA SOSTRATA,
"Abominable" Sermon,
delivered at Memorial Chapel,
Harvard University, December 26, 1986

No longer need I toil to please
My friends or vex my foes;
I lie in mucca-grass and ease
My thirst with froggeloes.

—Delirious raving of ADAM SNELL,
recorded by Vita Turk, R.N.,
Mother of God Hospital, Dulce,
May 27, 1990

To a moderately inept person, the simplest activities of life can at times become unessayable feats of virtuosity. Harold Emmons, a more than moderately inept person by his own admission, discovered this sad truth anew outside Mother of God Hospital in the early afternoon of Tuesday, May 29, during an attempt to exit his newly repaired Wagoneer while smoking a large-bore cigar and holding upright in his left hand one of his wife Frida's life-enhancing organic mangel-wurzel pies. Having planted his left foot on the parking-lot surface, he caught his right foot momentarily under the brake pedal and, suddenly staggering out of control, tossed the pie into the air on the desperate impulse that he might regain his balance and catch it again. All too soon the concoction began its descent, narrowly missing the professor's head, and, as luck would have it, landing right side up, with no other ill effects than the further compacting of its already dense contents. Less fortunate the fate of the cigar, which somehow made its way up Emmons' left sleeve, producing a burn on his forearm that Frida, reverting under stress to her native tongue, would later characterize as *furchtbar*.

Putting himself back in order, Emmons made his way up to Room 927. The policeman on duty outside Snell's room, though in the act of denying or delaying the entry of a short tweedy man with an attaché case, recognized Emmons and nodded him inside. The scene within was a most satisfactory change from the tense, crowded, gear-filled aspect the room had had during the two days of life-and-death emergency that had followed Snell's admission. The room was clear now, and sunny. The patient, his left leg in a cast, was feasting quietly on a greenish soup. Beneath the head bandages his cheeks, mummy-hollow before, had puffed out again, and there was color in them, and a hearty smile for Emmons. Seated beside the bed, and seemingly in intense conversation with the patient, was Lieutenant Pierce. Standing side by side at the window were Roy Gallard and Snell's English-department colleague Sarah Wilkins. Almost behind the door, leaning against the TV set, jean-jacketed and slick-haired and clenching in mouth an unlit pipe, was Warren Schmutzhauf.

Greetings were exuberant. Pierce went out to make phone calls, saying before he left that he would like to see Snell and Emmons alone later. Schmutzhauf took the policeman's departure as an opportunity to continue a discourse that had been interrupted before: an oration on the virtues of mucca-grass. "Fourth, and most important: its heat-retentive qualities. The chemistry guys haven't told me why yet, but m-grass holds heat, kilo for kilo, better than goose down. That's how Professor Snell, damaged and dehydrated as he was, survived four nights that went down to the upper forties. The grass was an inverted blanket. It actually—"

A bricklike woman in white hurtled into the room and stood arms akimbo by Snell's bed as though sniffing the air. "Something's up here," she muttered out of the side of her mouth, hastily casting about and fixing on Mrs. Emmons' pie. She glared at Emmons. "What's this piece of crap?" Her powerful hands swooped and struck. Before anyone could stop her, she was out the door with it.

Snell giggled. "I'm not supposed to be on solids yet. Don't worry about Vita. She'll store it with some other things that came in. They want to make sure I don't get poisoned here."

"Vita Turk thinks she saved Adam's life," said Sarah.

"That makes two of us," added Schmutzhauf.

"You're forgetting Doppler," put in Emmons.

Snell asked after his dog, and Emmons was happy to report the animal in good condition, kenneled with Emmons' golden retriever Angus and warmly cosseted by Frida and the boys. Similar questions and answers, concerning Snell's house, office and correspondence, followed. It was the first time since the disappearance that Snell and Emmons had conversed intelligibly. "And the books in the Jungle?"

Emmons glanced at Roy, who nodded and looked back at Snell. "The grounds crew picked them up yesterday and took them to the dump. They were spoiled beyond repair."

Snell smiled ruefully.

The guard looked in. "That reporter outside just wanted me to say that he was leaving town, and if you didn't want to be in the national news that was no skin off his back."

"Thanks for the message," said Snell.

"Why don't you want to be in the national news?" asked Schmutzhauf, as though in disbelief.

Snell smiled at him. "We're trying to stay out of the news altogether. We don't want to tip our hand. We know more, I mean circumstantially, about the attacker than it's in our interest to show at present."

"Be that as it may," Schmutzhauf persisted, "mightn't some big publisher hear about you and get interested?"

Snell looked vaguely stricken. "I wouldn't want to get published that way."

Still the fading violet, thought Emmons, his arm throbbing with pain. Sparing the details, he brought Adam concisely up to date on the substance of Friday's post-tenure-review meeting, which had, in spite of vigorous opposition from Quintus Adler, Edward Marlin and Emmons himself, concluded in an overwhelming vote for censure. Sarah seemed about to cry, and Snell's head drooped. "Well, if they don't want me here, I suppose—"

"Don't worry," said Emmons. "Quintus is writing a letter."

Snell was incredulous. "A letter? To whom? Marshall? How could a letter—"

"Quintus writes good letters," was all Emmons could say. He was telling Snell to be patient when Pierce reappeared, looking a bit worn, and Roy, Sarah and Schmutzhauf took their leave. The lieutenant seated himself to the right of Snell's bed, Emmons to the left. "Any news, Lieutenant?" asked Emmons.

Pierce grinned at him across the bed. "Call me Andy." He looked back at Snell. "No—no news; that is, unless you want to consider the record recovery of this patient here news. Our Libricide looks to have gotten clean away this time. I'll level with you: no smoking gun, no prints, no clues. And Adam's memory, which snapped back clear as crystal with his morning coffee today, hasn't fished up a scrap of evidence against anybody. By the way, Adam, why didn't you take your car or Doppler to your office that night?"

Snell thought for a moment. "Safety precautions. I was already worried about my security at the house and wanted it to look lived-in as much as possible. For the same reason it made sense to leave Doppler as watchdog."

Emmons asked Snell if he had suspected anyone of the book buyout before the attack.

Snell shut his eyes, as though checking his memory again. "No. I was mystified. I not only didn't have a suspect, but I couldn't think of a motive. It's not that I considered myself all that likable. Quite the contrary. Here I was, obscure, poor, unpopular in my department, and on top of it all, an embarrassing failure as a writer. No, Hal, don't protest; this is all for the sake of argument. Why should anyone want to injure or diminish me when I had already more or less obliterated myself as a professional? How can you decrease a zero? I was so much at a loss for reasons that I began to imagine it was some sort of punishment, and that I might well deserve it."

"We know," said Pierce. "It was in your journal. And in a crazy way you were close to being right."

"Right?" Snell reddened.

Pierce patted him on the shoulder. "Not that I think you deserved it. But it's just possible that somebody who had a grudge against you, somebody who was p-o'ed by your writing, somebody on top of this psychotic and violent, might have felt that trashing your book was some form of heroic stunt or sweet revenge."

"And killing me too?"

"He sure didn't mean to kill you when he came to your office Tuesday night. How could he have known you were coming?"

"He couldn't have," said Snell. "I never used to work there at night. I went down there only because of a sudden impulse to get the backup disk for my new book and bring it home for safekeeping. Say, I hadn't—"

The phone rang and Pierce pounced on it. "No, Professor Snell is busy right now. . . . He's ill right now, I mean, recovering. . . . Is this really important? All right." He jotted down a number, said "Uh-huh" instead of good-bye, hung up the phone and looked thoughtfully at Snell. "So where does that leave us, Adam?"

"I don't know what you mean."

"I mean, what kind of guy is your assailant? What will he do next?"

Emmons shrugged. "How can we tell?"

The lieutenant turned to him. "Maybe we can't. But we've got to try. Maybe this guy was so frightened by what he did that he'll never come near you again. But how he behaved *after* hitting you doesn't suggest that kind of fear. Quite the contrary. Unless I miss my guess, the kind of louse who would do these weird things would feel righteous, even catharted, about having done them. It would give him some kind of sick thrill, some kind of kinky proof of his masculinity."

Snell grimaced. "But now that's going to be taken away."

The policeman's voice for the first time conveyed anxiety. "That's it. Now his thrill's been taken away again. Adam's alive to speak freely and maybe write more books. On top of that we haven't blown Libricide's cover, and he'll know that soon enough. We'd be fools to trust that he won't go out and try to zap Adam again."

Emmons jumped up. Pierce looked up at him, holding out open hands as though to prove himself weaponless. "Look. I don't tell psychopaths how to behave. But thank God I know how they behave. And one thing about Libricide's behavior works *for* us. Crazy as this dude may be, I don't think Adam has to fear the toughest-to-prevent kind of violence: the all-out do-or-die attack."

"Why not?" Snell and Emmons asked together.

"Because Libricide is behaving like somebody who wants to guard his own flanks. He wants to have his cake and eat it, to kill you without going to jail for it. Now this cuts down his options. Again, I might be wrong, but up to this point he's looking something like your typical serial killer: cautious, self-righteous, violent to others but real keen about his own survival. He's not about to try to take you out openly—no, please Adam, let me just finish this line of thought— when you compare him to serial killers, you see that things really aren't so easy for Libricide. Serial killers have the advantage of never having to strike the same victim twice. They strike by surprise at the soft underbelly of society, and society has such a big fat underbelly that they can more or less pick their shots. Libricide knows that we're all teamed up in your defense, and knowing that cuts his options even more. Imagine, Adam, trying to murder somebody in Dulce—somebody who knows you're trying—without getting wounded or being observed or leaving any evidence or causing suspicion of any kind. It's not easy. Get the point of all this? Libricide's need to save his own skin is a plus for you."

Snell grimaced. "And the investigation?"

"The investigation goes into Plan B. We're going to stop hunting evidence and start snooping around for possible assailants. Let's start right now. Everything points to this dude knowing you and living in Dulce. Now he's likely to have some kind of history of mental trouble and/or odd behavior—not necessarily violent, but at least kooky enough to attract attention. On top of this he has to know, or think he knows, something about literature. And to have dragged or carried you all that way and gotten you over the Jungle fence, he's got to be very strong. How many can you think of who fit that description?"

Over the next few minutes Snell and Emmons generated a surprisingly large list. Professors from three or four other literature departments, a notable eccentric from Philosophy, five active grad students and two inactive ones, a few local free-lancers and literary loners. From the English department only Fulke Ashenham, the professional-wrestler-turned-new-historicist, and Abel Wenderson, a hulking recluse well known for his conversations with telephone poles, seemed to meet Pierce's criteria.

Snell asked if Pierce was going to begin questioning them.

"Not at first. First off, we're going to find out something about each of them. There's always the off chance that police or hospital records will turn something up. Questioning them, especially the sort of scattershot questioning we'd have to do before making an arrest, would only clue in the real offender and drive him into deeper cover."

"What if you don't come up with anything?" asked Emmons.

"My guess is that even if we don't, Libricide will tip his hand to us. We're now alert to him, almost in touch with his motives. When he moves again, we'll nail him." Pierce looked at his watch. "Drat. I'm late for a trial. Call you tomorrow, Adam. Bye, Hal."

A moment later his head stuck back in the door. "Oh by the way, Adam, you got a long-distance call. Miss Nathan from New York. See the number there?"

Pierce's head was replaced, as if magically, by the great bearded Karl Marxish visage of Dr. Ethan Maynard, who mouthed broadly, "What's with the beet pie?"

"It's called a mangel-wurzel pie," put in Emmons. "One of my wife's family recipes."

"But I thought only animals ate mangel-wurzel."

"Not according to my wife's family."[21]

The big doctor ambled in, took a few readings and made Snell look cross-eyed at his stethoscope. "Well, Adam, if you have a fancy for exotic vegetable pies, you may indulge it now. You're hereby back on solids."

Snell expressed the desire to get to work. "One of my students is going to find a laptop computer for me and put a few of my files on it. OK for him to bring it in tomorrow? You see, there's this new book—"

"Better aim for Thursday," the doctor interrupted. "Two or three of your counts are still too low for real exertion. Try some clean living first. And maybe an afternoon nap right now."

That was Emmons' cue to leave. On his way out, he reminded his friend to dial the New York number, but Snell's face, now tired and drawn, did not suggest that he would be making any long-distance calls in the near future. Emmons paused in the doorway, marveling at Snell's persistence. Who but the unflappable Snell, after having tempted fate with one improbable literary venture, would so enthusiastically turn to another? Who but Snell would respond to the revelation of his own mortal peril wth a request for a laptop? Emmons' arm stung where he'd burned it. He waved good-bye bemusedly and headed down the hall in the wrong direction.

[21]Mangel-wurzel (*Beta vulgaris*, Eng. mangold), a variety of common beet grown primarily for fodder. Human consumption of the vegetable is rare and the existence of a "life-enhancing organic mangel-wurzel pie" is completely undocumented. Possibly Mrs. Emmons' German forebears at some point acquired the Alsatian fondness for vegetable pies and, since the beet might reasonably figure in such a confection, Professor Emmons saw fit to bestow the name "mangel-wurzel" upon it. Possibly, on the other hand, the author is confusing us for some unspecified reason of his own. Readers should exercise caution, particularly with regard to authorial suggestions regarding their possible future cuisine. As Rabelais—*God here comes Tusker and no place to hide. I'm trapped on the page! Good Ulster bullhound, good Tusker, good boy. Say, he's wagging his tail. I think he likes me! Ya-a-a-a-a-a* . . . [Sounds of canine chewing and slobbering.]

Bookselling. The trade in books is of a very ancient date. The early poets and orators recited their effusions in public to induce their hearers to possess written copies of their poems or orations. Frequently they were taken down *viva voce,* and transcripts sold to such as were wealthy enough to purchase. In the book of Jeremiah the prophet is represented as dictating to Baruch the scribe, who, when questioned, described the mode in which his book was written. These scribes were, in fact, the earliest booksellers, and supplied copies as they were demanded. Aristotle, we are told, possessed a somewhat extensive library; and Plato is recorded to have paid the large sum of one hundred minae for three small treatises of Philolaus the Pythagorean.

—ANONYMOUS, "Bookselling," *Encyclopædia Britannica,* 11th edition

CHAPTER 3

FROM SNELL'S JOURNAL FOR
ON WONDERMENT

From time to time over the years, bands of philosophic pirates
and their yea-sayers, probably from sheer love of power or gain,
have advanced the argument that language does not describe but
rather "creates" reality, and that there is no reality beyond
language. But a speaker's ability to feel emotion and, via language, conceive that same emotion in listeners, gives this flimsy
slander the lie. Experience is not created by language; rather, it
descends into language and is reborn from it.

—SOVRANA SOSTRATA,
Gesta

June 4, 1990. Monday.
This old legal pad, brought here by Roy, will have to serve till I get
set up again. Feel stronger today, resting in hospital after a three-
day/four-night junket on the ground in Pisham Homestead, all ex-
penses paid, courtesy of Unknown Admirer, complete with
fractured skull, pneumonia and broken leg (broken during rescue),
dinners not included. It's an ill wind, etc., for my misfortune's
brought me four new friends:

Andy Pierce of Homicide, great guy, very gentle, carries enormous handgun because, as he puts it, "they make more noise." I tell
him he reminds me of a scholar and he answers that every good
homicide detective has to be a kind of backward historian, analyzing
what's present and creating a past for it.

Ethan Maynard, internist here at Mother of God, on duty at
arrival of mangled scarecrow, set my leg, shaved my head, looked in
(Vita tells me) every three hours, sometimes half asleep, till Sunday
morning.

Vita Turk, R.N., human cannonball, little dynamo with brawny
arms who lifts me out of the bed when it's time to change the sheets,
says she carries a gun and if she sees Libricide will shoot him in the
right places, which she enumerates graphically and in parochial-
school Latin.

Fourth, and most unusual of all, Warren Schmutzhauf, self-proclaimed "father of mucca-grass." Came early this A.M., lectured me endlessly on this and that, apparently trying to cheer me up. A kind of wild genius, who asserts that "scientific method," if it exists at all, is the sum total of everything one has heard, read, thought, dreamt, made love to, hated and eaten.

Saw them all last Tuesday, plus Hal, Roy and Sarah, a kind of homecoming.

God knows I've got to have been through the worst, but Pierce says there's more to come: I must be prepared for another sneak attack. But how do you get prepared? He could walk in right now and finish me with a pillow.

Shit! The door just burst open, and so help me I almost let go in my pants, but it was only Vita, with a piece of Frida Emmons' delectable beet-potato-onion pie. That and the codeine make me feel euphoric. Give me a day or two and I'll lick the world.

Must have gone to sleep. 8 P.M. now and very quiet. No trace in my mind of those four nights and three days, annihilated time, perfectly blotted out. Yet now I *do* remember something: I dreamt once or twice about Sovrana, about her talking lots of nonsense to me and then grandly announcing that she was about to die. What a posturer—anything for a rise! Granted, when I woke up at last, there she was, or at least her physical printed avatar, rotting in a white blob by my side.

Strange, for the first time in years I feel that that herculean bed warmer (see, I can even insult her!) is out of my system. Did Libricide really kill her, as he seems to have wished? If so, maybe he did me a favor.

June 5, 1990. Tuesday.

10:40 A.M. and after a double espresso lovingly brought in by Sarah (she jogged with it to keep it from getting cold) I feel incredibly alert. Have I ever been this alert before? Maybe the circuitry in my brain suffered catastrophic damage, and I'm now having a flash of clarity before total burnout.

I felt so good this morning that I turned down Vita's codeine and took a couple of aspirin instead.

Sarah had to leave for class. Strange lady. Confucius would have referred glowingly to her *wen,* her pattern of graces, her thoughtfulness, eloquence, integrity, all enhanced, as though physically imaged, by face and body. When in parting she leans over the bed, straight blond hair momentarily surrounding my eyes like a thatched roof, and solemnly touches my lips with hers, I feel a monstrous urge to pull her unto me and down loinward through warm folds of linen. But her arms, back, even lips don't speak that language; they're tense, disembodied; even her eyes, keen and blue, seem to want to look *through* the person to the very soul rather than appreciating the inferior but pleasant complement of flesh. And she worries! My mishap's put her through an orgy of fretting, but that's nothing new; she's always been uptight about her own life or the world's woes. Even her book on the environment, excellent as it may be, is less the craft of reason than a feat of creative worrying.

And now she's got reason to worry! Thanks to the ever-loving Gazza, Sarah's gotten denied tenure, on the grounds that her book manuscript isn't "professional" literary scholarship. Odd how the obscurantist and totally unliterary discourse Gazza & Co are spewing forth is "professional," while Sarah's work on environmental rhetoric isn't. Odd that the only socially significant publication in the whole department is the one that gets the shaft.

Apparently I—the department being too zealous in the pursuit of its duties to wait for news of my demise—got shafted too, with only Hal and Quintus (Marlin wasn't allowed to vote) against my censure, and Web Hollins, as usual, abstaining. I can appeal of course, but Thor Marshall likes denying appeals better than Buffalo Bill liked tossing lariats. They'll ride me out on a rail if they can, and Gazza wants to replace me with that egregious theoretical camp-follower, Butzi Siskin. Why do things always turn out the way Sovrana says they will?

I suppose I can sell the house, live cheap in Mexico while finishing *On Wonderment* (that is, if I live at all), and then look for another job. I suppose I can also take the bastards to court. Be worth it to see Gazza trying literary theory out on a jury of her peers. I wonder how the jury will take to Floconne de Mais's theory (passionately endorsed by Glanda) that there's no such thing as justice, that good and evil and culture in general are just a "text" generated by the powerful?

Schmutzhauf in again early this morning, while Vita was tidying up. Says he's taking me under his wing and when he hits it big (whatever that means) he'll "fix things up for me." I told him things about Gazza and the literary theorists that nearly blew his mind. "Why, man," he bellowed, "it's medieval science all over again! *Step one,* you sneak up on a phenomenon. *Step two,* you zap it with your patented catchall theory. *Step three, Conclusum est!* you announce another victory over Nature! Next patient, please, and all that. Real successful method; kept Europe asleep for a thousand years. Honest, Adam, is that all they're about?"

I told him that theoretical analyses were often quite subtle, that some theorists showed impressive ingenuity and that, in many if not all cases, theoretical models were based on global interpretations of history. "Medieval, medieval and *more* medieval!" he volleyed out. "What'll you tell me next, that they all worship a pigeon?"

At that point Vita, who'd been lurking out in the hall, came in and clobbered him with a pillow.

Looked out the window this afternoon and saw Hal pausing in the courtyard, in running shorts, with his golden retriever and Doppler on leashes. I couldn't help calling Doppler's name, and he went wild, dragging man and dog all over the place.

When the Alexandrian library was founded about 300 B.C., various expedients were resorted to for the purpose of procuring books, and this appears to have stimulated the energies of the Athenian booksellers, who were termed *biblion kapeloi*. In Rome, towards the end of the republic, it became the fashion to have a library as part of the household furniture; and the booksellers, *librarii* (Cic. *D. Leg.* iii. 20) or *bibliopolae* (Martial iv. 71, xiii. 3), carried on a flourishing trade. Their shops (*taberna librarii*, Cicero, *Phil.* ii. 9) were chiefly in the Argiletum, and in the Vicus Sandalarius. On the door, or on the side posts, was a list of the books on sale; and Martial (i. 118), who mentions this also, says that a copy of his First Book of Epigrams might be purchased for five denarii. In the time of Augustus the great booksellers were the Sosii. According to Justinian (ii. I. 33), a law was passed securing to the scribes the property in the materials used; and in this may, perhaps, be traced the first germ of the modern law of copyright.

—ANONYMOUS, "Bookselling," *Encyclopædia Britannica,*
    11th edition

FOUR MEMORABLE PERFORMANCES

The LORD showed favour to Sarah, as he had promised, and made good what he had said about her. She conceived and bore a son to Abraham for his old age, at the time which God had appointed. The son whom Sarah bore to him, Abraham named Isaac [that is, *"he laughed"*]. When Isaac was eight days old Abraham circumcised him, as God had commanded. Abraham was a hundred years old when his son Isaac was born. Sarah said, "God has given me good reason to laugh, and everybody who hears this will laugh with me."

—New English Bible,
Genesis 21:1–6

1. A SHOCK TO THE MEDICAL WORLD

Overheard on June 7, 1990, in the canteen of the Veterans Administration Hospital in Batistoni, New York, where Gerald Underwood has been a patient for more than twenty years. The speakers are Waltraut Himmelfarb, a volunteer patient's companion, and Dr. Bernard O'Shea, physician in charge of Ward B.

O'SHEA: Thanks for waiting, Waltraut. I needed Ensign Underwood's file and this pad to take it all down on.

HIMMELFARB: Diss iss a vunderful sink, Doctor.

O'SHEA: You say it happened today.

HIMMELFARB: Diss very mornink, Doctor. I veeled heem oudt on de terrace, ass I alvays do venn de vetter iss gut. Every day, venn de vetter iss gut, I veel heem oudt, ver he faces de Hudson Wiffer andt de sun iss on him, andt myself I sit on de etch off a pik flowerpot, andt I read to him on de Piple.

O'SHEA: That's here in the file, Waltraut. Ensign Underwood's pulse rate improves when he's being read to.

HIMMELFARB: Diss happen many years now, Doctor. I haff read to heem *five years*. But today iss different. In five years vee go true de whole Piple *sree times,* andt today vee get pack to de stardt. Today I reed heem apoudt Gott, who made de whole vorlt, andt apoudt Adam andt Eefe, andt apoudt Noah, knock voot! who surfifed de flutt, andt apoudt old Apraham. Andt Apraham und Sarah, his lawful vife, day haff no kids, andt day gettink oldt, andt Apraham, you know, mess aroundt a liddle vid de floosies. But Gott said to Sarah, You vill haff a son, and Sarah laugh und say, Who me, an oldt lady? I *amp not apel* to haff a child. But Gott say, Just you vait, you see who laugh last—

O'SHEA: Waltraut—

HIMMELFARB: I know, I'mpe gettink der! I wememper every momendt of diss! Well I just get to de poindt ver Sarah hass her son Isaac, und she says she is goink to laugh, andt I look up, andt de ensign *iss lookink at me!*

O'SHEA: But doesn't he always look—

HIMMELFARB: No, not like dat, not wid de empty eyes. He looks at me vid *pik peautiful plue eyes,* all avake like a child's, andt he puts his handt on mine as I holdt de pook, andt—

O'SHEA: *He moved?*

HIMMELFARB: Den I stardt to cry, Doctor. I cry for joy, like I'mpe cryink now. Andt he squeezes my handt, andt he says—

O'SHEA: *He spoke?*

HIMMELFARB: He visper, "Waltraut, read dat pardt again." Andt he iss cryink too.

2. HARPER BRILLIANT AT AMAGUCCI'S

From across the room, they might have been playing bridge, but closer up, if you could have edged between the tightly packed tables at Amagucci's, you would have seen the wineglasses and prosciutto–fresh fig appetizers on the table, seen that the cards the four had stacked in from of them were scrawled with book titles. Harper, looking unprintably attractive in an off-white silk blouse and silver necklace, sat across from Sig Bazoom, her editorial director, a small, totally bald man with roundish features, dressed in a white linen suit with yellow shirt and purple bow tie. The company was completed by Zaz Caldecutt and Barona Rhine, two very fashionably attired young women who were, like Harper, editors for Wolper McNab. Two bottles of Orvieto Classico stood open on the table. The mood was cautiously festive.

Bazoom, who had listened in turn to reports from his three subordinates, took a sip of wine, straightened his tie, then brushed his pile of cards aside with the air of a man completing a task. "Thanks, ladies. That kind of rounds it out for spring '91. Twenty-one new titles, and we've got it all: murder, incest, wellness, espionage, child rearing, homespun humor, erotic gossip, come on, come on, help me—"

"Melon therapy," said Harper.

"Another, even better, baseball story," said Barona.

"Sing Along with Inner Child," said Zaz.

"All right, all right," continued Sig, growing more enthusiastic. "Melon therapy, another even better baseball story, little girls with depressed fathers, Sing Along with Inner Child, and Whales I Have Known. Is that everything? Could we ask for anything more?"

"It's a lively list, Sig," said Harper, and added meaningfully, "much livelier than this fall's."

Bazoom reddened from neck to scalp. "So what's with this fall? It's sick or something? It's got problems or something?" Sig was waving his hands in the air, trying to flap her.

Harper stayed calm, at least on the surface. "Sig, the *problem* is that it has no problems. It's simply *tame,* Sig. Sound minds and bodies, the great outdoors, seven novels about subtle family interactions, three about women's inner voices, two of authentic ethnic testimony. It's a respectable list, but *tame.*"

Sig's face fell. "Compared with Hammond and Fig?" he asked meekly.

Harper nodded. "H and F's fall list is very strong. Remember? They bid big on Lance Felladay and Zgooi Zomonga, and so they got the two hottest first novels of the year."

Sig shakily adjusted his tie. "So what do we do now, hide out in the Poconos?"

All eyes were on her now. Hair needed a brief shake. Now for the bombshell. "Not necessarily. We hit them with Adam Snell. His book's a knockout. He'll make Felladay look like Roger Rabbit."

Barona seemed impressed. "But how can you possibly get it on the fall list?"

"I've called Penrose Press. They'll give us everything for a song. All we do is change the imprint. We can get Ron to do a fast workup for the CAB in Denver next week, and if I phone today we can even get them to change the catalog."

Sig, whose face had been going through a symphony of contortions, now looked as though he had just found a crack in the world. "You mean you want to *change the list*?"

Harper was conciliatory. "Not change what's there, Sig, just add onto it."

"How big a run?" asked Zaz.

Harper made an upside-down smile. "Ten thousand, maybe, seventy-five hundred, nothing colossal. The size of the run isn't as important as the effect on our list. And we've very little to lose. *Sovrana Sostrata*'s a well-written book. It'll raise the list a notch and shake a gauntlet at Hammond and Fig, and then it's bye-bye, wait till spring."

Harper watched Sig's face move through two more shades of uncertainty. Zaz and Barona were spoken for, having been primed at the expense of a magnum of overpriced chardonnay at Caputi's the night before. Though not quite so dazzled by *Sovrana Sostrata* as she, they nonetheless saw it as a bold venture that might just catch fire.

Sig took a long pull on his wine and glanced timidly around the table. "So what's the consensus?"

Zaz and Barona made enthusiastic faces as Harper crouched to pounce. "The ayes have it, Sig. All we need is your promotional genius to sail it past Igor."

Sig now relaxed and brightened. "No problem there. He's been on my back about the fall list too."

But as Sig and Harper left Amagucci's after lunch, he let on that he did not see much in Snell's book. "Too old-fashioned, Harper. Too black-and-white. What's the use of writing like Hardy or Lawrence in 1990? But never mind, dearie. I respect your savvy. You haven't bombed yet, and here's hoping it works this time too."

Harper put on a kindly smile, desperately trying to conceal the joy that had welled up in her. Now she had work to do. She must keep trying to reach Snell. What was the man doing in a hospital? She must get a hold of Ron and write catalog copy and firm things up with Penrose Press and do in less than two days things that normally take weeks. And she must do it all in time to meet Harry at three o'clock Friday afternoon for a weekend on the Vineyard.

3. UNDERWOOD IMPROVES AT HARROLTON

One of Frank Underwood's many well-kept secrets, at least from the always curious and often envious ears of his colleagues at Washagon, was the Harrolton ranch. Ranch it had never been, at least in living memory, but Frank's dad had called it a ranch when, twenty-five years ago, he had picked up the little old house, with its 160 acres of rolling hills on the French River—ostensibly as an investment but really more in hopes of enjoying a second adolescence with his two teenage boys. Of course these hopes were doomed, first by the boys' incomprehensibly troublous attitudes toward each other, and then, tragically, by Gerald's injury and Frank's concomitant sullen retreat from the family hearth. Yet Frank and his parents remained politely in touch with each other, and as Mr. and Mrs. Underwood had not been west in years, Frank was the only one to visit and care for the property.

The ranch had a desolate beauty. Three miles of single-lane graded road down from the state road and then nearly half a mile of jeep trail (Frank garaged an old Blazer in Janeville) led up to the gray high-ceilinged Victorian that sat beneath two outsized Jeffrey pines, commanding a view of the river and semiwooded hills whose panorama did not yield another human dwelling. Couched on its shaded hilltop, in its almost magically year-worn Victorian grace, cruising time-wise through its summer ocean of cloudless, careless northern California days, the house palpably conveyed a kind of wisdom, a withdrawal from harried human affairs into an at once more primitive and reasonable world. How an overworked publisher like Harper, or a dedicated writer like Snell, would have loved it! Yet Underwood, immured as he was in his own private castle of anger, felt no such pleasure. The architecture, with its intimations of childhood ghost stories, vaguely frightened him, and he could not bear the long silences. He came there as a kind of caretaker twice a year, seldom staying for more than a few days.

But this summer brought new uses for house and land. Early in

June, days after learning of Snell's recovery, Underwood had shut up his Dulce home and driven, via Janeville (where he made several purchases) to the Harrolton ranch. There he spent a day in agitated preparation, marking, measuring and partly clearing a brushy area in the bone-dry valley to the south of the house. By evening he was so violently excited that only sleeping pills could buy him any rest. Next morning, when just past dawn he stepped out on the porch to survey the completed prospect, his equipment had changed from machete and shears to a rather battered-looking Remington .22-250 rifle, "varmint" model, fitted with a new 3X9-power scope.

Underwood looked down the hillside at a tribute to his own meticulousness, precision and determination: a landscape facsimile of the 180-yard shot which, fired some bright day in late summer or early fall from his chosen hiding place on Spine Hill in Dulce, would instantly exterminate Adam Snell. He held in his hands one of the most accurate long-range weapons available. Now his job was to calibrate the scope to the distance and perfect his own technique.

He donned a pair of earmuffs and steadied himself against a porch column. The valley began to resound with the sonic snaps of high-velocity ammunition.

A day of work and he was satisfied with his progress. The scope was adequately adjusted, and he was frequently hitting targets smaller than a human body at 180 yards. But frequently wasn't good enough, and stationary targets only approximated the challenge offered by a living being. He needed days, weeks more work. He must live with the gun until it became an extension of his own senses.

Yet the very next day saw a horrifying setback. A letter arrived from home. Gerald had moved, Gerald had spoken. His parents had driven to the hospital, and they had seen Gerald, and he had recognized them. His parents' exuberance and the potential reemergence of a newly articulate and sanctified Gerald threw Underwood into depression. He ate little, lay sleepless in bed, spent hours in the smothering heat of the faded living room listening to endless replays of country music on his CD player.

Days passed and the depression slowly lifted. The gross break in the psychotic armor had been recemented. Talking or silent, Gerald was a corpse to Frank, a closed case. The enemy, now somehow even more furiously hated, remained Snell. Target practice began again with a vengeance.

4. GAZZA ROASTED AT MAMMAL

Mammal Hall, which houses the administrative offices of the University of Washagon, is at once the oldest public building on campus and the only carryover from the now-defunct Washagon Academy of Veterinary Science, which it once contained in entirety. The building takes its name not from this historical connection but rather, more indirectly, from the remarkably lifelike animal sculptures decorating its otherwise neoclassical façade. The work of self-taught Washagon pioneer-cum-artist Hubert Tatnall, these granite heads portray the major mammals, both wild and domestic, of the Wishbone Valley in the middle of the nineteenth century. Arrayed above the Ionic columns of the portico, in heroic scale and as though thrust forth from the living rock, are the fox, the bear, the cougar, the cow, the pig, the deer, the elk, the beaver, the raccoon, the wolf and, in the center, Tatnall's acknowledged masterpiece, the horse.

It was right under this equine bust that Glanda Gazza, moving this Thursday afternoon with something less than a full head of steam, entered Mammal on her way to Thor Marshall's office, which was located on the upper floor directly to the rear. Gazza little relished the prospect of the meeting to come. She had been summoned by Thor to give a briefing, on the Snell case, no less, to that egregious populist and crank, Washagon chancellor of higher education Paul Edson. Nodding to Clorene, who grimaced knowingly, Gazza entered the broad-windowed sanctum sanctorum to find Marshall in an uncomfortable posture at his big desk, while a few feet to the left stood Edson, a sixtyish white-haired man of middle height and athletic build. Both men seemed frozen in the act of speech.

"Well, we'll get back to this, Paul," said Marshall awkwardly, as both turned to her.

"I believe we've already met, Professor Gazza," said Edson, shaking hands. They sat down. Across the desk from her, Marshall's broad face was dark against the bright windows, while Edson's face to the left, with its intense brown eyes, was focussed sharply in the afternoon light.

Edson pulled a thickish letter out of his breast pocket. "Professor Gazza, I have here a letter from one of your colleagues which avers in some detail that Professor Adam Snell is being discriminated against and, to some extent, persecuted, by members of your department, and with your knowledge and consent."

Gazza heard the inner trumpet and went into battle mode. "Who wrote—I mean, who could possibly say such a thing?"

Edson took the letter out of its envelope. "There's no reason to maintain confidentiality here. The writer's name is Quintus Adler, full professor, apparently a well-known Shakespearean." He whipped out a pair of tiny reading glasses. "Says here he made this allegation at a department meeting and so has no doubts that you're aware of his sentiments. Is that right?"

Small blunder necessitates tactical retreat. "Yes," parried Gazza, "I do remember now. But it was such a ridiculous accusation that I dismissed it out of hand."

Edson was persistent. "Wasn't it then seconded by Professor Edward Marlin?"

Gazza fought back. "In fact I think it was, but neither Adler nor Marlin knew what he was talking about. Both of them are mired up in a legalistic, hierarchical, thoroughly outdated way of looking at things. Our departmental review of Snell's work, if I may speak confidentially to you, was in the process of evolving a similar evaluation of him. We were deciding, in effect, that Snell's novel, which is his only major publication since promotion with tenure, did not measure up to departmental standards precisely for this reason. Adler and Marlin were only trying to defend the superannuated set of values they share with Snell."

Edson looked gently curious. "But aren't Adler and Marlin two of the most widely respected scholars on your campus?"

"That depends," answered Gazza, "on who's doing the respecting. They won attention doing traditional things. Now scholarship has simply passed them by."

Edson took off his glasses, pulled out a handkerchief and began to polish them with it, looking down at them as he spoke. "I have a suggestion for you, Professor Gazza, and also a question. My suggestion, first of all, is that you bend over backward being fair to Adam Snell. I don't know him or his book, but he's got rights like anyone else, and one of those rights is to publish anything that his fancy or conscience dictates. He's got tenure too, which means that, in recognition of what I assume to be substantial professional achievement, the university has granted him the freedom to publish his views without fearing for his job. We may not like what he writes or find it professionally respectable. On the basis of our opinions we may deny him promotion or salary increases. But that doesn't mean that we can revoke his tenure or apply unnaturally strict review standards to him and him alone. Is that fairly clear?"

Gazza struggled to restrain her fury. "Chancellor, are you trying to influence a departmental review?"

Edson looked over at Marshall, whose face remained darkly unreadable against the windows, then looked back at Gazza and smiled. "Let's say I'm trying to save this campus from legal embarrassment. Professor Snell's tenure here is guaranteed by your university constitution. Should this guarantee be violated in letter or in spirit, I could not in good conscience discourage him from defending himself in court." The chancellor then stretched like some house cat that had found an ideally comfortable place to lie down. "So much for my suggestion. Now for my question. You say that Snell's ideas and methods, and those of these two other professors, are outdated, and that yours aren't. What makes you so sure of that?"

"Where have you been for the last fifteen years?" Gazza boldly shot back at him. "Haven't you kept track of departmental demographics? Why, now we've got more theorists and theory-related scholars in our English department than any other kind."

Edson smiled again. "That goes without saying. But what are these scholars up to? How come a literary theorist has never won a teaching award on this campus? How come literary theory has no operative doctrine of education? How come, when physicists and chemists and sociologists and historians command big audiences on the lecture circuit, not a single literary theorist—correct me if I'm wrong—is ever asked to address a public audience?"

Gazza looked to Marshall for support, but his face remained dark and impassive. The rage welled up in her again, but she held it back. "You're wrong on two counts. First, public recognition has never, mark you, *never* been a dependable gauge of successful research. I can assure you that many literary theorists see their research as laying the groundwork for revolutionary social change. Second, you're passing judgment on us too soon. We're still in a period of transition. There's always confusion at the onset of a new order. And anyway, where does a chancellor of higher education get off trying to influence the direction of free research?"

The chancellor glanced at Marshall again, like some pitcher holding a runner at first, and then turned fully toward Gazza. "I'm responsible to the governor and the legislature for maintaining the quality of education on all our campuses, so whether teachers teach well or badly means a lot to me. More generally, my mission is to encourage a healthy relationship between learning in general and society at large. Large-scale academic movements like literary theory are bound to have an impact on this relationship." He turned slightly and motioned at the window. "Look out at society, Professor. We're facing environmental emergency and massive poverty and all sorts of crime. Our products are no longer attracting world attention, and to make things worse our corporations, mad for quarterly bottom-line profits, are cutting research-and-development budgets to the bone. If evolutionary success lies in adaptation and development, then we have apparently bought out of evolutionary success. To a large extent I see these selfish and panicky attitudes mirrored in individuals, even college students. How does literary theory speak to these problems? What values does it recommend to students and scholars?"

Gazza was too furious to speak.

"Let me answer for you, Professor. Literary theory, at least as Adler's letter describes it, not only has no antidote for these public disorders but would seem in its lack of values—its relativism and materialism—actually to encourage them. My guess is that its manifest lack of social relevance will make your field at best a passing vogue, at worst a tragic institutional blunder."

"Values, relevance, tragic," fumed Gazza. "What a taste you've got for art deco words!"

Marshall suddenly and hoarsely broke his silence. "I must agree with Paul that the words he uses remain meaningful, um, especially in terms of public policy. I'm so thoroughly convinced by what Paul's said that I'm going to write a memo to you and your colleagues suggesting that it might benefit all if you turned your attention to some of the issues he's raised."

Gazza fixed a death-dealing stare on him. *The faithless bastard! He's gone over. And only two weeks since the fat ass was lolling in my bed!* She turned the Gorgon beams on Edson. Why beat around the bush? "I assume then that you're not happy with the direction our department has been taking."

"Quite candidly, Professor, I'm appalled." Edson was folding up the Adler letter and putting it back in its envelope. "I've got to be back in Arcadia by five. Thor, if we could take a few minutes to discuss . . ."

They're kicking me out of the room! Gazza rose, glared balefully at each of her antagonists, turned with a lethal swing of her shoulder bag, burned her way through the outer office and headed across campus in a hormonal intoxication of rage. *The dirty masturbators! That self-righteous simplistic manipulating demagogue Edson! He's out to muzzle academic freedom! That cringing double-dealing mealy-mouthed snake Marshall! He sold me out to get the presidency!*

Arriving at the English-department office, she shouldered past two secretaries who wanted to speak to her, slammed her office door, savagely smashed her heavy bag against the books that lined her wall and, as books cascaded every which way to the floor, sat down and sprawled across her desk, sobbing heavily.

The fuckers have taken my job!

The spread of Christianity naturally created a great demand for copies of the Gospels and other sacred books, and later on for missals and other devotional volumes for church and private use. Benedict Biscop, the founder of the abbey at Wearmouth in England, brought home with him from France (671) a whole cargo of books, part of which he had "bought," but from whom is not mentioned. Passing by the intermediate ages we find that previous to the Reformation, the text writers or stationers (*stacyoneres*), who sold copies of the books then in use—the A B C, the Paternoster, Creed, Ave Maria and other MS. copies of prayers, in the neighbourhood of St Paul's, London,—were, in 1403, formed into a guild. Some of these "stacyoneres" had stalls or stations built against the very walls of the cathedral itself, in the same manner as they are still to be found in some of the older continental cities.

—Anonymous, "Bookselling," *Encyclopædia Britannica,* 11th edition

CHAPTER 5

THE FURNACE OF TRUTH

Sad is the man who seduces many women in search of variety,
for he will carry monotony to everything he touches. Far wiser
is he who finds in one woman many women, for in acknowledg-
ing her dignity he attains dignity himself. Wisest of all, though
dangerously near the furnace of truth, is he who finds in all
women one woman, and she infinite.

—SOVRANA SOSTRATA,
Gesta

Room 927 of Mother of God Hospital faces north, commanding
through its large window a view of the Wishbone River as it winds
patiently toward its faraway meeting with the Pacific. To the west as
you look down-valley are the green-bosomed Newcomb Hills; to the
east, rising more abruptly, are the foothills of the Lion Mountains.
Snell's bed faced east, and some mornings just after sunrise he was
able to catch the sun glinting against a distant white crag.

When Snell could get out of bed, he asked for a chair and table
by the window. Here, day after day, he would sit working at his
laptop computer, sipping hot chocolate or ice water and glancing up
now and then at the splendid view. His friends politely shunned his
work hours, visiting instead in the late afternoon or evening.

By early July Snell's continued presence at Mother of God had
become a topic of speculation among the staff. His fractures, neither
of them originally very severe, were knitting famously; his counts
were all normal; he had regained healthy muscle tone; and all the
neurological tests were good. Yet Maynard, citing the physical and
psychological ordeal that his patient had suffered and the occasional
headaches and dizzy spells he still experienced, recommended prolonged hospitalization. Was Maynard being overcautious, or was he
in cahoots with Pierce to incarcerate Snell for his own protection?
The police guard remained at the door.

In either case Snell would have been a willing prisoner. The prospect of being homicidally attacked by an unknown assailant of formidable strength and fanatic conviction held little attraction for him. With his leg still in a light cast, he enjoyed the luxury of service. And the writing conditions were excellent. Not just the peace, the quiet and the Wishbone view, not just the monastic simplicity and concentration of life within a single room, but the whole symbolism of mending and recovery appealed to him profoundly. "After all," he inquired in his journal, "isn't an artist's life honestly lived a kind of slow recuperation, a recovery of lost spirit, a knitting of broken time?"

Snell's own time had suffered a pleasant interruption on the morning of June 11, when Harper Nathan's unaccountably familiar bell-like voice, heightened a bit by her own excitement and piped his way on a new long-distance service that made her sound next door, informed him that *Sovrana Sostrata* was to be republished by Wolper McNab in the fall. Snell listened silently, breathlessly, with an onset of postconcussion dizziness followed by a mild case of shock. He excused himself prematurely, promising to call back soon. He leaned his head against the pillows and, closing his eyes, remembered the desolation in the Jungle.

So they've rescued us both now. And Sovrana's rescued for good.

His head swam. The thought of publication by a major press, of national distribution and publicity and possibly even reviews, had not occurred to him in years. And now, without his having lifted a finger, it was all but a *fait accompli,* in the hands of an angel-editor who called his work a "miracle" that might well "stun" the novel-reading world. Snell thought of Odysseus carried sleeping from the oared Phaiakian ship, placed sleeping on his beloved soil. Let Gazza try to fire him now!

Yet the news also carried danger. It could be a bugle call to Libricide, a blow that might excite him to action or even escalate his malice into rashness. Could it be kept secret? Secret at least until the fall, by which time Pierce might have a lead on Libricide? Alert now, Snell phoned Pierce's office and left a message.

The next evening brought more news of exciting but ambiguous character. Knocking at the door woke Snell from a light nap, and Quintus Adler, looking even more massive than usual and rather solemn, emerged into the room, awkwardly deposited a brown bag with a bottle of some sort in it on the bed, and took up a dramatic standing position by the window. "Glanda's resigned as head," he announced.

Snell blinked. "But she'd never—"

"Marshall forced her to, and apparently the chancellor forced Marshall. And the chancellor was acting on a letter from me. Edson's a fairly reasonable man, for an administrator."

"Quintus, how did you do it?"

Adler roared with delight. "Remember, my lad, our spiritual forebears, Marcus Tullius Cicero and Marcus Fabius Quintilianus. Cicero used rhetoric as a bludgeon against massed and violent odds, and remarked more than once that rhetoric was powerful only when empowered by the honesty of its wielder. Quintilian stipulated that the source of all eloquence was the heart. I'll tell you how I did it. *I meant it.*"

"But won't it get you into trouble?"

The big man beamed with excitement. "Possibly, but I doubt it. Marshall and Gazza will think I'm Edson's boy now. And your review case is going to be turned around and conducted fairly."

"Who's going to be head now? Hal again?"

"Don't you wish!" said Adler glumly. "Glanda's crew still has a big majority, and as long as they do they'll either pick one of their own or some neutral-looking character they can control. And they've got themselves a beauty."

Snell thought a moment. "You mean Web Hollins?"

Adler roared again. "Right on, man! Webster Hollins, eternal bibliographer, pasty-faced purveyor of platitudes, old Professor Steal-a-Feel, who finally bagged that archetypal grad-student coquette Salem Pogue, Mr. Committee, whose only regret is that he wasn't born one. Of course I'll nominate Hal, and you and Sarah and seven or eight junior faculty will vote for him. But Glanda, even Glanda in disgrace with fortune and men's eyes, walks around with twenty-five votes in her pocket. And that old pocket of hers, seamy and rat-infested as it is, also contains the lock, stock and barrel, so to speak, of Web Hollins."

"But isn't that too transparent? Wouldn't Edson notice?"

"Probably. But I think everyone will give Web the benefit of the doubt because he's a so-called moderate. Edson's meddled about as much as he safely can. If he wants to accomplish anything really solid, he'll have to dump Marshall and start repopulating the administration wholesale. And that's likely to be too tall an order even for him."

Snell thanked Adler for what, in the pallid arena of academe, had to be considered an act of uncommon valor. Adler pulled out a photocopy of the Gazza-felling missive and presented it to his colleague. "Read it for the style, Adam," he said in parting. "I think I managed one or two good paragraphs."

In the dreamily long summer days that followed, Snell turned to his new book, *On Wonderment*. On the surface his mode of operation was harmless enough, even rather staid: the laptop computer, the regular hours, the meticulous use of the journal and other secondary files. But Snell's subject matter, style and organization of material suggested lunacy in its purest form. The subject matter, first off, had no apparent rationale or coherence whatsoever. Snell wrote about nature, art, abstract ideas, personal experience, science, history, psychology, without the slightest effort to connect these fields at all. His style was patently inconsistent, including, sometimes within the course of a single working day, satire, tragedy, conversational anecdote, philosophical discourse, humor and belletristic essay. And as for development, there was none at all. Snell would simply pick up an idea, ride with it for what it was worth, let it go, and open up a new page. His only homage to system was the network of abbreviated subject codes that might someday allow him to draw related sections together out of the increasingly vast miscellany of discourse.

His friends responded to these exotic activities with various degrees of concern. Sarah, whose feelings toward Snell had grown undisguisedly affectionate, feared for his sanity. Adler referred to Snell's project as Briareus, the hundred-headed monster. Emmons feared some bitter and violent response from the theorists.

But there were more sanguine responses as well. Worried as he was, Emmons could not help comparing Snell with Renaissance humanists—Alberti, Machiavelli, Erasmus, Rabelais and others—who combined genuine learning with the ability to speak effectively to the general reader. Schmutzhauf and Edward Marlin (who now visited Snell occasionally) were even more positive. To Schmutzhauf, Snell's M.O. was reminiscent of a great tradition in modern science. "This is a perfectly valid way to work," he asserted. "You collect *everything,* no matter how incoherent it appears. You don't stop collecting until you've collected everything that's in your power to collect. And then you let it all *ferment* inside of you. Darwin worked this way."

Marlin put it differently. "Adam's having a dialogue with himself. He's exploring mental geography—not just his own but that of his culture as well. He's tempting pure chaos but opening himself up to real discovery. No one's ever found order in himself or society without first having a love affair with disorder, noting word by word the proceedings of Babel."

As Snell worked on through the summer, patiently, industriously, sometimes lost in musing, sometimes ravished by inspiration, a rationale of sorts began to emerge. In the course of months of amorphous expression, he had found himself returning repeatedly to a number of major experiences or images. Dozens of otherwise disconnected ideas had clustered around each of these constructs, and more important, each of them had come to symbolize a particular species of human emotion. In a flash one day Snell saw that by organizing his book around these constructs, one per chapter, he could unify nearly all of the material that he found compelling. Using a software database to search the whole manuscript for relevant title codes and aggregate them in new categories, he was able to reorganize four hundred pages of material in a single day.

Now what had been an ocean of inquiry snapped into focus as a potential book, and passages written days or weeks apart suddenly congealed together as parallels or antitheses. The entire fabric of the work melted out of chaos into form, a form, however, which retained for its vitality the chaotic energy that had spawned it. Snell felt that he had struck gold. In a way that few writers would find comfortable, he had bypassed the established rules of invention and discovered an authentic voice.

Snell's nine constructs (he called them his nine "places") were united by the single theme of wonder: the human capacity to feel that irreducible compound of joy and amazement, of strangeness and familiarity, in the presence of some suddenly apparent truth. An abandoned church in a forest near a shopping mall. The Michelangelo staircase in the Laurentian Library in Florence as Snell climbed it to read the first Latin translation of Plato. Plato's dialogue the *Timaeus*. A photograph of the Crab Nebula. A large standing dead tree off 101 north of Eureka. A computer program of the so-called Mandelbrot set. A painting of Mozart as a child. Da Vinci's portrait of Ginevra dei Benci. Louis Armstrong performing Fats Waller's "Ain't Misbehavin'." Each of these "places" became the mental location for a different form of wonder, for a special series of meditations, and the purposed role of all nine series, converging as they did on the hub of a central idea, was to render up, if discursively and rather shaggily, an honest and inclusive image of wonder and the phenomena that inspire it.

It was mid-July, and now Snell, strengthened in body and endowed at last with a consuming sense of artistic purpose, was writing with a passion over eight-hour daily stretches that left him exhausted in late afternoon. This intensity harked back to the days of composing *Sovrana Sostrata,* but two elements had changed profoundly. Sovrana, once the dominant voice in his art, was no longer his muse. He had buried her, as deep and finally as the sad farmers who hacked her unconsecrated grave into the rocky Chianti soil—or so he assumed. And concomitantly his writing now lacked Sovrana's fire. Gone were the taunting aggressiveness, the wanton exhibitionism, the oracular concision. In their place was a mellower vision, a discourse at once more leisurely and appreciative. In *Sovrana Sostrata* Snell had pulled down the temple walls. Now apparently he wished to construct a new temple of his own design.

I once asked him if *On Wonderment* implied any rejection of the tragic vision of *Sovrana Sostrata* or retreat from its bold positions. After a moment's pause he replied that to him truth had several "bodies," that some of these bodies were terrifying, some beautiful, some bizarre, some simple. To him each of these bodies carried an unmistakable stamp or signature of cosmic reality. Yet one body of truth could glaringly contradict aspects of one or more of the others. And the existence of all the other bodies made any one of them, however riveting it might be, incapable of holding the full picture.

Then *Sovrana Sostrata* and *On Wonderment* were just two different bodies of truth?

"As near as I could come."

With the new organizational rationale came a change of authorial attitude sweeping enough to alter the very shape of time. Before he conceived of his nine "places," Snell was expressing the past, foraging in his own mind for the spiritual institutions that gave him human identity and individual definition. Now the thrust instead was toward the future: toward a bound and printed book that would verbalize these institutions and give them lasting shape.

It was characteristic of Snell to speak to his friends of these unlikely inspirations and heroic designs in simple, almost homespun language, and with a green-eyed twinkle of humor.

Harper Nathan, now apprised of her new author's melodramatic adventures, telephoned regularly, sometimes to go over details of *Sovrana Sostrata*'s republication, sometimes to inquire after the new project. A second book-length manuscript, submitted soon after the first, would be of great use, she said, in establishing Snell as a good publishing risk. Harper showed lively interest in the burgeoning *On Wonderment,* even during the early days when Snell, as he artlessly admitted, had no words to describe it. She suggested paying a visit to Dulce in August, in order to "discuss matters in depth."

Pierce dropped in often over the summer to relate ongoing findings about the Likely Libricide Candidates and to advise Snell about the security measures that would have to be taken after his release from Mother of God. One July afternoon, when Snell had knocked off work a bit early to watch the Athletics play Kansas City, the lieutenant appeared with a copy of *Sovrana Sostrata* peeking out of his jacket pocket. Snell expressed surprise at being included in Pierce's casual reading.

"It's business," said the policeman cheerfully. "If I'm going to figure out who this book could make mad enough to kill, I'd better know what's in it."

"What's your guess?"

"Well, from a first reading, I reckon either a puritan or a born-again or a nihilist. The puritan would hate the sex in the book. The fundamentalist wouldn't be able to take the treatment of God, especially in that sermon of hers. And the nihilist would freak out at your sense of commitment."

Snell wondered whether these conclusions had helped Pierce narrow his Libricide list.

"Not yet. Born-agains are pretty easy to spot, and there are none of them on our list. Puritanism and nihilism can run underground, so to speak, and we haven't gotten enough on any of our candidates to pin either one on them. In fact we're sort of stalled. Which brings me to today's shocker. Adam, I've decided that we should start hooting and hollering about the republication of your novel, that we should announce it to your department head and the campus news bureau and anywhere else we can."

"You mean you want to lure him out."

The lieutenant gave him a serious doctorlike look. "I see it this way. If we keep the news secret, we let him write his own calendar. He could work up a classy game plan, full of fail-safes. This way it's us who are writing the calendar. We can make him attack when we're good and ready for it. And there's also the chance that this news plus your incredible survival plus the publisher's interest in your new book will flummox him—that he'll let you go and look for an easier mark."

Snell admitted a bit grimly that the idea had merit. "When do we break the news?"

"A week or two after you're released from here."

"And when will that be?"

"I'd say about three weeks. You know darn well you're strong enough to walk out of here right now. But we want you to build yourself up. Your fitness has never been more important to you than now. Dr. Maynard's going to tie you in with the sports-injury clinic next door. They can run you through a sort of full-spectrum exercise program for a couple of hours a day, and in three weeks we can have you looking and feeling like Captain Marvel."

Snell shrank visibly. "You mean I may have to defend myself."

Pierce became doctorlike again. "Yes, Adam. We can only do so much. How does that make you feel?"

"Scared," said Snell.

"I'd be scared myself," replied the policeman. "But I feel scared many times in my own job. I was scared when I fired my gun at the Homestead and scared the last time we had to overpower a drunk. Sometimes I wake up at night, scared to death of a society that allows extremes, rewards them, breeds, protects and nurses every conceivable kind of kookiness. But you can handle fear in two ways. You can go into the shock syndrome and feel faint and shut down your systems. Or you can go into fight-or-flight and either run away or defend yourself. You've got to cultivate that fight-or-flight response. And you need a strong body, if only to run away better with."

"Then running away wouldn't be cowardly?"

Pierce grew more intense. "You'd run from an angry hornet, wouldn't you? *I* sure would. Libricide's like an angry hornet. It doesn't make any sense defending yourself if it's safe to run away. But you've got to be ready to fight back if he doesn't give you a choice."

Snell turned to his exercise program with such zeal that he went to bed aching every night. The combination of writing and physical exertion made his time dramatic—the more so because his days of relative safety were now numbered. One evening he came back to his room, sweating and panting, from two hours of lifts and stretches, to find a large gift-wrapped package on his bed. The card, which bore a small reproduction of Turner's *A First-Rate Taking in Stores,* read

> *To Adam Snell—*
> *For silent running*
> *—From the Adam Snell Squadron*
> *July 20, 1990*

and in the carton was a new laser printer. Snell had refrained from using his old printer in the hospital because of its annoying loudness. Now he could print in silence, first in the hospital and later at home, where silence might come in handy too. The next day he installed the printer, filled up the paper tray and instructed the machine, with a few keystrokes, to print out the four hundred pages of the *On Wonderment* manuscript. It began to do so, at the rate of about one neatly printed page every ten seconds, and while it was printing the writer cleared the screen and began composing new material.

So Snell and his technological ally worked on together, the man for the first time thrilled by an awareness of his trade's paradoxically heroic implications, the machine laboring beside him in conspiratorial silence.

In Henry Anstey's *Munimenta Academica,* published under the direction of the master of the rolls, we catch a glimpse of the "sworn" university bookseller or stationer, John More of Oxford, who apparently first supplied pupils with their books, and then acted the part of a pawnbroker. Anstey says (p. 77), "The fact is that they [the students] mostly could not afford to buy books, and had they been able, would not have found the advantage so considerable as might be supposed, the instruction given being almost wholly oral. The chief source of supplying books was by purchase from the university sworn stationers, who had to a great extent a monopoly. Of such books there were plainly very large numbers constantly changing hands." Besides the sworn stationers there were many booksellers in Oxford who were not sworn; for one of the statutes, passed in the year 1373, expressly recites that, in consequence of their presence, "books of great value are sold and carried away from Oxford, the owners of them are cheated, and the sworn stationers are deprived of their lawful business." It was, therefore, enacted that no bookseller except two sworn stationers or their deputies, should sell any book being either his own property or that of another, exceeding half a mark in value, under a pain of imprisonment, or, if the offense was repeated, of abjuring his trade within the university.

—ANONYMOUS, "Bookselling," *Encyclopædia Britannica,* 11th edition

CHAPTER 6

———◄════►———

A DAY IN HELL

ADVANCED DIAGNOSTIC ERROR MESSAGE

CODE	DESCRIPTION
01x	Undetermined problem errors
02x	Power supply errors
1xx	SYSTEM BOARD ERRORS
101	Interrupt failure
102	Timer failure
103	Timer interrupt failure
104	Protect mode failure
105	Last 8042 command not accepted
106	Converting logic test
107	Hot NMI test
108	Timer bus test
109	Direct memory access test error
121	Unexpected hardware interrupts occurred

—From a computer manual

Millennia of spiritual torment and centuries of religious dispute might have been spared by the simple recognition of the female identity of God.

—SOVRANA SOSTRATA,
"Abominable" Sermon

W hile I was writing the first draft of this book, I asked several friends and colleagues to read the manuscript and give me their opinions. Seven stout hearts graciously agreed. Although responses varied widely (from "*Book* will be required reading on every American college campus" to "Kill this thing before it kills you"), all were united in one emotion: the desire to know more about Frank Underwood.

"What does he eat for breakfast?" one asked me.

"Does he have any sex?" another inquired.

"What does he read?" chimed in a third, and so on.

Lurking behind all these questions, I assume, was the curiosity, universal among all ages, nationalities and religions, about the private and intimate operations of evil—a craving so acute that many of us, I fear, would rather see the nakedness of an ugly soul than that of a beautiful body.

My own preferences are quite different. I take no particular relish in Underwood's private life. In fact, he rather frightens me. There's a certain vitality and dark resoluteness about him that unnerves me, to the extent that often as I write I cannot relieve myself of the feeling that at any moment he might appear through the office door to my left, bearing some blunt object and little good will. Other times I excessively identify with him. I think of him as uniquely my own, almost as a familiar spirit. I feel that revealing, nay publishing, his intimate experience would breach my own guilty privacy. Yet art must be served. I gave in to my friends' request and agreed to describe in some detail a day in the life of Frank Underwood, provided that I could be concise and businesslike in my descriptions, and that I could choose one of the more eventful episodes of his summer at the Harrolton ranch. I further agreed to answer any pertinent questions they might have along the way or after my narrative was complete.

Journal of Events, Harrolton Ranch, Monday, July 23, 1990

6:50 A.M. Underwood wakes to clock radio, lies for minutes on his back in bed, open-eyed. (Q: *Why?* A: He's reconstructing an obscurely dream-damaged world in some sort of tolerable image.)

6:57 A.M. Underwood, clad only in Jockey shorts, walks heavily into hall and bathroom, brushes teeth, defecates, washes hands.

7:09 A.M. In the living room, Underwood finds a country-music CD and inserts it into the portable player on his desk. To the loud accompaniment of twanging music and whining voices he spreads a soiled white comforter on the floor. He straps a twenty-pound weight to his left leg and performs sixty leg lifts, thirty of them isometrically prolonged, in four different positions. This repeated with right leg. Then a few stretches. Then the set of leg exercises is repeated in entirety. Then more stretching. It's hot already in the living room, and Underwood is sweating heavily. He folds comforter and replaces equipment. The CD player stays on at high volume.

7:59 A.M. Underwood showers, using deodorant soap and anti-dandruff shampoo. He shaves with a blade razor and slaps on some aftershave. He brushes his hair and reviews himself at length in the mirror. In his bedroom he dresses in jeans, a plaid mother-of-pearl-buttoned western shirt and well-worn black work boots, consulting a mirror again. (Q: *Why does Underwood spend so much time looking in the mirror?* A: You might say he's looking for the mark of Cain.)

8:30 A.M. Underwood breakfasts on cornflakes with milk and sugar and a fresh peach cut up and scattered into the bowl. He drinks two cups of percolated coffee, black. He washes dishes, puts things away and runs a damp rag over the counter and table.

8:51 A.M. Carefully removing his Remington varmint gun from its case, Underwood puts on his earmuffs, goes out to the porch, braces himself against his favorite column and very patiently and meticulously fires twenty-five shots downhill at his target. Back in his living room, to the nerve-deadening complaints of a digitally remastered lovelorn cowboy, he cleans the Remington and puts it away. It's 9:30 now and very hot.

9:30 A.M. Underwood turns off the CD player. He takes his Stetson from its hook in the living room, locks up his house, and walks down the porch steps to the orange Blazer. It starts up with a throaty old-muffler sound, and he turns on the A/C and a country-western radio station. Once the A/C is blowing cold he shuts his windows and very patiently guides the Blazer down the jeep trail to the state road, where he turns right and heads for French City.

10:10 A.M. After an uneventful trip at legal speeds, Underwood provisions himself at Safeway (hamburgers, hot dogs, milk, ice cream, white bread and major trade-name versions of beer, soda pop, candy bars, toilet paper, jam, peanut butter), and then parks at Wild Goose Sports and Feed, where he spends some minutes. He walks to the bus station, where he picks up three parcels. Sweating, he plods back to the Blazer, U-turns to the gas station across the street, pumps himself some fuel and drives home.

12:17 P.M. Arrived at the ranch, Underwood checks for signs of intruders' entry, surveys his property carefully from porch and rear window and carries in his acquisitions. The CD player with its familiar music goes on loud again. In the kitchen, he unpacks and stores the Safeway items. He walks to the living room, where he unwraps the parcels. Item number one is a rakishly styled pistol. It is a single-shot weapon with a fourteen-inch barrel, designed to fire high-velocity ammunition with an accuracy superior to that of most rifles. Item number two is a hard vinyl case for the gun. Underwood checks the pistol's action. He removes a new scope from its card-board box and installs it on the pistol. He fishes from a bag a kind of Velcro bracelet and puts it on his left forearm. (Q: *Did he buy the pistol in Dulce and ship it from there?* A: No. He bought it in Mon-taho, where he owns a ski condo, has established residency and can legally purchase firearms.)

1:08 P.M. His stride now somewhat slowed by the effects of heat and nervous tension, Underwood steps into the kitchen, washes his hands and douses his sweating face with water. He makes himself a large chocolate milk shake, complete with two raw eggs, in the blender and, still standing, drinks it hungrily straight from the blender pitcher. He sits for several minutes at the kitchen table, motionless, face cupped in hands. (Q: *What's he thinking about?* A: Nothing at all.)

1:35 P.M. He washes and replaces the blender pitcher, goes to the bathroom, urinates, washes his hands and returns to the living room. Without loading the pistol he walks out to the porch, braces himself against the porch column, sights a target with the unloaded gun and squeezes the trigger. The pistol has a more sensitive trigger than the varmint gun and seems somewhat harder, even for hands as strong and steady as Underwood's, to aim. (Q: *Why the new gun? What's wrong with the varmint gun? Why doesn't he fire the pistol at the targets?* A: He can't use the varmint gun to murder Snell because it's too bulky to carry up to Spine Hill in safety. The pistol, on the other hand, will fit in a knapsack. He has several reasons for not using the pistol on his home range, including a fear that somehow he might be seen and a desire to simulate the much wilder conditions on Spine Hill.)

1:53 P.M. In the kitchen he pours sun-brewed tea into a large ther-mos, adds lots of ice and sets out more tea to brew. He dons his Stetson, puts pistol, earmuffs, ammo and tea in the Blazer and shifts the transmission into low range. One hundred yards below the house an old jeep trail, barely perceptible in the grass, runs off steeply downhill to the left. He takes it at a crawl. In ten minutes he is on another hill, out of sight of the house, on a part of the property whose dusty soil shows no sign of human visitation. The heat is stifling. He sets up deadwood targets in the grass at the bottom of the hill and walking uphill paces off a distance of about a hundred yards. He braces himself against a nearby oak tree and commences firing, carefully saving every empty shell casing and occasionally pausing for gulps of tea. By 3:00 he has fired a hundred rounds. (Q: *Why does he save the shell casings?* A: He wants to cover his tracks. High-velocity bullets, once fired, are too distorted to identify, but shell casings often show marks characteristic of a single weapon.)

3:12 P.M. Back at the house, Underwood cleans and stores the pistol, showers and puts on fresh clothes similar to his earlier attire except for the tennis shoes he now wears instead of boots. Iced tea in hand he returns to the living room, where the contents of the third parcel lie waiting on the coffee table. These are a powerful laptop computer and a number of 3.5-inch disks. To a pandemonium of country music he clears some unopened family letters from the top of the oak desk at the west end of the room, places the computer on it, flips up the folding screen, pulls out the cord, plugs it in and turns it on. The screen instantly springs to life, going through a series of automated changes that culminate in a long list of titles. Underwood examines these titles carefully and, apparently satisfied with them, clears the screen and begins to write slowly. (Q: *Why hadn't Underwood brought his computer with him in the car?* A: I'm glad you asked me that. You see, Underwood's lengthy stay at Harrolton hadn't been planned very far in advance. Two days before departure from Dulce he faced the dilemma of how to continue his essential theoretical research while far away. Underwood, you see, felt most uncomfortable working without ready access to scores of recent books and articles by other literary theorists. The books, which he owned, had been duly boxed and loaded into the Porsche. The articles, which came from twenty-six different journals, were more of a poser. Underwood had a kind of inspiration. He instructed his departmental secretaries to use their new IBM scanner to save forty-three articles onto his computer's hard drive and to send him the computer when the job was done. Q: *Why didn't he just have the articles photocopied?* A: As what follows will show, that would have been a far more sensible idea. But Underwood wanted to use his computer's huge memory to simplify his own writing. With one-thousand-odd pages of current research in the computer, he could do word searches, finding out in minutes how many of his colleagues and competitors had made reference to specific ideas. He could also, via his word-processing system, borrow whole paragraphs for quotation at the expense of five or six keystrokes. And symbolically he would have what to his mind would have seemed the closest equivalent to Faustian power: portable, nearly instantaneous access to the aggregated genius of his profession.)

4:45 P.M. To the twang of the banjo and wheeze of the fiddle, Underwood works at the computer, occasionally pausing to sip tea or munch on a refrigerated Clark bar. His fingers fly as there rapidly unfolds on the screen the superstructure of a major project, the book that will unshakably solidify Underwood's reputation and further endear him to moguls like Floconne de Mais and Ewig Schabe. The sun is beginning to peek through the reddish gingham curtains of the northwest window, and the air is acid hot. He pauses to drink and begins writing again. In the heat the computer gives off a strange mild smell, vaguely reminiscent of the model-train transformers he and Gerald played with as kids. He remembers the little engine racing around their living room in the winter twilight, puffing real steam, its tiny light throwing a dim yellow patch on the tracks before it. *No more of that.* Searching for a concept, Underwood runs through a variety of screens and fetches up a recent article by Sandy Eule. Suddenly he pauses and looks up as though inspired. Why not put all forty-three articles into one huge file that he can call into memory? That would immensely simplify all his searches. Sweating profusely now, he summons up the file menu and begins the job. He titles the mammoth new file WHOLTHNG.BOO. His agile fingers manage complete file maneuvers in seconds. Twenty minutes later the monster file is in memory and ready to be saved onto the hard drive. As the CD player thunders with girlish delight, Underwood presses the SAVE key, and the machine replies

Document to be saved: C:\WHOLTHNG.BOO

Tonight ain't nothing gonna slow me down,
Wanna hear a band with a country sound

Underwood signals the affirmative by hitting ENTER, and in turn receives the new signal,

Saving C:\WHOLTHNG.BOO

Gonna dance every dance till all the boys go home.

But seconds pass, and nothing happens. The message remains on-screen, but the screen is frozen, and the hard drive, which ought to be flashing green, is dark as death. Underwood's face freezes in sweaty panic. His fingers try a succession of keys, ENTER, SAVE, EXIT, CANCEL and then, as a last resort, ESCAPE. A minute passes with no change, except Underwood's slow frustrated realization that he has hit a glitch and that his only available option, one that will clear the memory of his entire WHOLTHNG.BOO file and the word-processing system itself, is the red button RESET on the right side of the machine. Pressing RESET will void the machine's memory of his new WHOLTHNG.BOO file, but after resetting he can boot up and start work again. Fortunately he has saved his book project, his precious project, in relatively complete form on the hard drive. The CD trembles with a plaintive song of lost love. He hits the button. The screen goes blank. He waits for the automatic boot-up, but instead the screen goes through a few abortive attempts at expression and ends up with

121 Unexpected hardware interrupts occurred
705 Unintelligible logic

I wanted to die
When you said we were through

followed by a burping noise and

1273 Irreconcilable parameters
1790 Fixed disk 0 error

I've forgotten somehow
That I cared so before

followed by a loud *beep,* a very nasty electrical smell and a series of words and rapidly escalating numbers that finally resolve themselves into

666 Intolerable disk damage
127 files destroyed
0 files intact

At last I am free,
I don't hurt anymore.

Shaking from head to toe, Underwood presses RESET again. More electrical smell. The backlight on the screen flickers and dies. Fingers of black fume begin to rise from the cooling vents. Now moving with the slow furious clumsiness of a movie monster Underwood grabs the machine and rises, simultaneously overturning his chair and ripping the cord from the wall socket. Computer in right hand, he lumbers through the screen door, and as the door zaps the wall to its left, he hurls the computer off the porch and into the brown grass of the hillside. He walks woodenly into the house, reemerging with the varmint gun. *Crack!* Struck by a round of high-velocity ammo, the laptop jumps airward. *Crack!* Underwood catches it with another round in midair, projecting it twenty feet downrange. *Crack!* A third round misses as the laptop falls to rest nearly upright, a now-dusty corner still visible above the grass. Underwood fires again, aiming just under the visible corner (*Crack!*), and the land-scape erupts into a momentary circus of glass slivers, keys, wires, plugs, boards, cards, ICs, expansion slots, switches, drives and panels. Underwood slowly lowers the gun. He stands rigid in the outrageous heat, crying. He walks into the house, where the CD is still blaring. He aims the gun hip-high at the CD player, which responds with one final *"I don't care anymore."* He does not fire. He lowers the gun again and sits down on the green velvet couch across the room from his desk. His face stony and white, he cleans the gun and puts it back in the closet. He goes to the bedroom and lies down on his back on the bed, to remain, stiff, motionless and open-eyed, until long after dark. The music plays on.

Any more questions? Hey don't all ask at once!

Q: *Why didn't he shoot the computer with the pistol?*

A: The varmint gun was a repeater. Please pay more attention.

Q: *Does Underwood get any sex?*

A: I can't answer that at present. By the way, have you got a dirty mind or something?

Q: *If I didn't, I might not have followed this story up till now. But come on, you've obviously been teasing us about Underwood's sex life, holding something back. Why, for example, if he's so good-looking and upwardly mobile, didn't Gazza try to seduce him?*

A: Good question. In fact, the idea occurred several times to Gazza, but each time it was quashed by an unspecific, instinctive impulse of restraint. For more on this subject, if there is any more, you'll have to wait a while.

Q: *When you answered my earlier question, you called Underwood's world "dream-damaged." What did Underwood dream about?*

A: Underwood's obsessively recurring nightmare is of being bested and shamed in a one-on-one confrontation with another man. In adolescence, this dream enemy always either was or resembled his brother Gerald. After Gerald's injury, Frank stopped dreaming so directly about his brother and "cast" his dream, so to speak, with vaguely fraternal types under different guises. Most recently the opponent, who in the dream not only is of fearsome strength but also seems to carry with him the wrath of God, is Adam Snell.

Q: *Why the big milk shake with the egg?*

A: A bodybuilding fad. People with the right metabolism and lots of exercise can turn that stuff into muscle. Note also that today Underwood only exercises his lower body. Many bodybuilders are convinced that muscles grow better on a day-on, day-off schedule, so Underwood has been alternating upper- and lower-body exercises.

Q: *For a well-heeled academic with theoretical pretensions, Underwood has curiously flat tastes in food and drink. You speak of white bread, hot dogs, candy bars, etc. Isn't this an anomaly?*

A: Is it or isn't it? Anyone else have an idea?

Q: *Could it be that he's fixated in adolescence?*

A: So far as I can see, that's it. It's well known clinically that many neurotics and psychotics have behavioral traits characteristic of youthful periods in their life. These are seen as telltales of serious and unresolved problems affecting the patient during that earlier time. Underwood's upset with Gerald, you may remember, reached crisis proportions during his early adolescence, a time when boys go for white bread, sweets, hot dogs and other similar treats. This theory also would explain Underwood's taste in casual attire and music.

Q: *You say "So far as I can see" and "This theory also would explain" as though you weren't sure you're right. Come off it! You're the author, aren't you? How about taking responsibility for what you've done and telling us for sure?*

A: I wish I could. But you see I'm at a crazily excited period in composition when I'm writing reams a day, and the characters are calling their own shots, and the book is at least temporarily out of control. It's no longer a dead text I'm handling, but rather a self-sustaining ecosystem, an autonomous life form that drinks up my energy each day and leaves me exhausted. I can't take full responsibility, in the normal sense of that word, or fully explain down to the last detail why things are happening as they are.

Q: *Was Underwood thinking at all about Snell that Monday?*

A: Good question. As he lay on the bed after his computer disaster, he thought about Snell quite a lot. He blamed things on Snell, you know. He vowed to take it all out on Snell. But earlier? Emphatically not. Underwood has a thoroughgoing way of fixing on the details of life and exxing out everything else: associations, implications, inner messages, what have you. That's how he has managed to put Gerald or Snell, or anything else that has threatened his balance, out of his mind.

Q: *Underwood, then, has a plugged-up mind? I mean, a mind where various sectors are completely walled off from one another?*

A: More or less. This phenomenon occurs in lots of violent personalities. The violent part is, so to speak, in a separate file, out of normal consciousness. And when the personality switches into violent mode, the other files are similarly immobilized.

Q: *What's happening to brother Gerald?*

A: I almost wish you hadn't asked. Gerald Underwood's story is in a sense much more interesting than his brother's, and certainly more entertaining. Can you believe that the man has gained twenty-five pounds in a month? [*Gasps of astonishment.*] Can you believe he's walking? [*Louder gasps, some applause.*] Dr. O'Shea says it's the weirdest case he's ever seen, and he's writing the whole thing up for the *Saratoga Journal of Medicine*. Gerald's been transferred to a sports-therapy center in Ohio, where he's in a training program that's not all that different from Snell's. Compos mentis in every other way, Gerald has insisted with childish stubbornness that Waltraut Himmelfarb accompany him with her Bible, and Mrs. Himmelfarb, a long-widowed concentration-camp survivor with a fascinating story of her own, if the truth be told, has—

Q: *That's enough about Waltraut for now. But while we're on the subject: We've asked a number of pertinent questions, and your replies have been helpful enough. Since you clearly knew that all this information was relevant, even exciting, why didn't you include it in the text in the first place?*

A: That is all part of my innovative stylistic strategy. You've all heard of "intertextuality," the idea (done to death by interpreters like Gazza and Underwood) of a text subtly commenting on other texts or on itself. Well, I've invented a new concept that I call *extratextuality,* consisting of things readers won't ever know unless they ask the author personally. In fact, I may even put blank pages in the text, so that readers can write questions on them and send them to me.

Q: *Very interesting. Can we get on with the story now?*

A: With pleasure. What would you like to hear?

Q: *You mean we've got a choice? How about one of those sections where we hear a bit of everything?*

A: Your wish is my command.

Q: *But wait. One more question: Why does Underwood's computer break down?*

A: Oh, it's kind of a combination, you know, of a very hot room, a gimpy fan and a card slightly askew in its slot and—

Q: *Come on, cut the technicalities. Aren't you implying that no vessel of discourse, not even an apathetic computer, can tolerate the volume of pure bullshit that Underwood had put into his?*

A: I'll tell you later.

Q: *Why not now?*

A: I'm using a computer myself.

"The trade in bookselling seems," says Hallam, "to have been established at Paris and Bologna in the 12th century; the lawyers and universities called it into life. It is very improbable that it existed in what we properly call the dark ages. Peter of Blois mentions a book which he had bought of a public dealer (*a quodam publico mangone librorum*); but we do not find many distinct accounts of them until the next age. These dealers were denominated *stationarii,* perhaps from the open stalls at which they carried on their business, though *statio* is a general word for a show in low Latin. They appear, by the old statutes of the university of Paris, and by those of Bologna, to have sold books upon commission, and are sometimes, though not uniformly, distinguished from the *librarii,* a word which, having originally been confined to the copyists of books, was afterwards applied to those who traded in them. They sold parchment and other materials of writing, which have retained the name of stationery, and they naturally exercised the kindred occupations of binding and decorating. They probably employed transcribers; we find at least that there was a profession of copyists in the universities and in large cities."

—ANONYMOUS, "Bookselling," *Encyclopædia Britannica,*
11th edition

CHAPTER 7

NINE BAGATELLES

Time and grilled cheese wait for no man.
—Sovrana Sostrata,
table talk

The shortages will be distributed among the poor.
—Soviet witticism

1. A MEMO

University of Washagon
English Department
Dulce, WS 100989

July 24, 1990
TO: Professorial Faculty
FROM: Webster Hollins, Acting Head

I know that you will join me in congratulating Adam Snell on the republication of his novel *Sovrana Sostrata* by Wolper McNab. I am most pleased to note as well that Wolper McNab is negotiating for the rights to Adam's new book of creative nonfiction, *On Wonderment.*

You will also be happy to learn of Adam's pending release from Mother of God Hospital.

2. A PASSAGE FROM *HEGEMONY*

"Literalizing the Decentering," an article by Sanford Eule and Glanda Gazza in *Hegemony: A Theoretical Quarterly,* published by the University of Washagon English Department, Vol. 4, No. 2 (July 1990), 1–96, pp. 73*ff.*

. . . Heidegger, De Man, Saussure, Eule, Derrida, Schabe, Habermas, Siskin, Kristeva, Thwackum, Lacan, De Mais, Underwood, Mishunk,

Govnjuk, Baismacou, Barthes). This is not to say that Theory qua Theory is of a specific cast or category, or that it can be quantified or limited or defined or institutionalized as per ideology (Govnjuk). It *is* to say, however, that Theory in all its known or probably knowable forms, and no matter how much its followers may disagree about details, partakes of a certain *esprit,* or you might say *Stimmung,* that seems to distinguish it from other forms of inquiry and by the same token to demarcate its enthusiasts characterologically and politically from adherents of other methodologies (Fetzel, Pfitzer, Schlucker, Poucabolas). Therefore, it seems safe to say that when we speak of "decentering" we intend silently after that participle "in a specific direction," and when we use the word "subversive" we add mentally "in special ways of our own." This insight relieves what would otherwise have been a bothersome syndrome: the "frontier mentality" assuming that the decentering and subversion of essentialism and structuralism, like some Pandora, opens up a "free" range of inquiry and expression, and presuming to introduce, onto the same field of action that *we* have cleared, forms and positions unfriendly to our spirit (Frangalha, Dreck). Given our present role as stewards of authority in so many literature departments across the continent, we may feel justified in using—in fact obliged to use—that authority to direct inquiry along healthy and historically necessitated channels and away from such eddies, marshes and beaver dams as might impede it.

Simply put, *exclusionists should be excluded* (Fetzel, Pfitzer). And good riddance!

3. OVERHEARD BY OUR OPERATIVES

LOCATION: WEBSTER HOLLINS RESIDENCE, 325 MALTBY WAY, DULCE
CHARACTERS: WEBSTER HOLLINS, ACTING HEAD OF THE UNIVERSITY OF
WASHAGON ENGLISH DEPARTMENT, AND HIS COMPANION, SALEM
POGUE
DATE: July 24, 1990
TIME: 23:45–23:57.

SALEM POGUE [*from bed*]: Have you brushed your teeth?

WEBSTER HOLLINS [*from bathroom*]: OK. [*Sound of tap water and brushing.*]

SALEM: Coming to bed now? Where are you going?

WEBSTER: To the kitchen. Want anything?

SALEM: What are you having?

WEBSTER: I think—a carrot.

SALEM: No thanks. [*A pause. Kitchen light goes on briefly, then is extinguished.*]

WEBSTER [*getting into bed*]: *Chomp chomp.*

SALEM: Webster.

WEBSTER: Shalem. *Chomp.*

SALEM: Couldn't we, um, do our Jay and Daisy thing tonight?

WEBSTER: I'm feeling kind of—off. Maybe this weekend we can get a bottle of wine and—*chomp.*

SALEM: Can we afford it?

WEBSTER: Don't you remember? Fat times are coming.

SALEM: Of course! How wonderful! You're department head!

WEBSTER: Well, we *will* make more money, but I'm not sure how wonderful it's all going to be. Glanda's fit to be tied, and I think I'll never be able to keep her out of my office. There's gossip on campus that we're being unfair to Sarah Wilkins, and then of course the Snell fiasco. People outside the discipline can't seem to understand why we took Adam amiss.

SALEM: And after he wrote such a *shocking* book!

WEBSTER: I *know*. How can such a stereotyped—

SALEM: Salacious, reactionary, ideological—

WEBSTER: Insinuating, opportunistic, sexist—

SALEM: *Rapist* book get published by a major press?

WEBSTER: Maybe that's just it. Adam has a kind of vulgar ca-chet, like some sort of literary beer ad. He'll probably make the best-seller list and cash in for a million.

SALEM: It's funny. He always seemed like such a nice, gentle sort of man. Say, um, sure you're not up for a little, say, Jane Eyre and Rochester?

WEBSTER: Sorry, Salem. *Chomp.* Sure shows how appearances can deceive. Adam probably's not as learned as he makes out to be either.

SALEM: I know! That new book of his—

WEBSTER: What's it called? *On Wonderment?* What a farce! Why there's no *scholarship* on wonderment. It's a nonsubject, a catchall that a fortune-hunting charlatan can ramble on for three hundred pages about. *Chomp chomp.*

SALEM: Another carrot? Oh, well. Webby—*Webby!*

WEBSTER: Mmm.

SALEM: Can't we try the new one?

WEBSTER: Mmm?

SALEM: Leda and the swan!

WEBSTER [*swallowing, then with authority*]: Salem, I've been meaning to talk to you.

SALEM: About sex?

WEBSTER: I guess that's what you'd have to call it. Salem, aren't you keeping up on your reading? Why, this stuff about females desiring males and all their need for regular sex with males has been shown to be a fallacy!

SALEM: A fallacy? What do you mean?

WEBSTER: Why—I guess—it's a kind of *phallocentric* fallacy: You know, something that's been imposed or, um, foisted on women by centuries of acculturation to male dominance. And that's a fact.

[*A Pause.*]

SALEM: Webby?

WEBSTER: Yeah.

SALEM: Well, if it's a *fallacy,* then what've I got between my legs? And what's it for, anyway? Have I got a fallacy between my legs?

[*Snoring.*]

SALEM: Webby!

WEBSTER: Hm?

SALEM: Sorry I got mad. Tell me what to read, and I promise to read it. By the way, *I*'ve been reading the most wonderful book. It's by a man from India named Dr. Poona. It says that animals are really wiser than people.

WEBSTER [*sleepily*]: How so?

SALEM: Something about their not being able to talk.

[*Silence, then snoring.*]

4. HARPER BEAGLES

Guenevere and Sigmund Bazoom
Request the Pleasure of Your Company
at
A BEAGLING
Sunday, July 22
Brunch 10:30 A.M., Hunt 12 noon
Hare Farm
Wahamsett, L.I.
R.S.V.P. (516) 555-2095
(Dress Ruggedly)

Smile, Face. I'm greeted at the front door of half-timbered Hare House by the wildly enthusiastic Gwen Bazoom. *Speak, Mouth;* and Mouth obliges with "Gwen! I'm so sorry I'm late! I forgot about that roadwork on the Queensboro Bridge."

Large, solidly built, green-linen tunic crackling with electrostatic energy, voice uncommonly high, hostess Gwen squeals, "Not to worry! Not to worry! Everybody's late! *We're* even late! Come on in—we're gorging ourselves." Gwen throws out an arm and tugs me through the back of the entrance hall and toward the buffet on the terrace off the dining room. *Remember, Face, you're enjoying this. You're having a good time, Face.*

Onto the big slated terrace, pleasantly shaded by trellised Concord grapevines, and into Beau Monde à la Bazoom. Sig himself, as though extrasensorily alert to my arrival, breaks out of a pack of larger men, he resplendent in purple tennis shirt and orange shorts, bugle hanging from neck, arms outstretched. "Angel! My life is complete!"

Alerted by this modest greeting, eighteen men or so turn around and gaze and stare and gawk at me. OK, so you think I'm attractive. Can't you louts find a better way of showing it? *Smile, Face; speak, Mouth.* "Thanks for inviting me, Sig."

He offers champagne in a huge cut-glass goblet, and I can tell you, champagne has looked worse. I take a gulp and almost choke, but it's beginning to help already. Belly pipes up: Waddabout some food? *Pipe down, Belly, we're not alone.* Sig's back again, hands me a mammoth Wedgwood plate ("Enjoy!"), and the big table's crammed with ham, pastrami, roast beef, turkey, whitefish, lox, pickled herring, Genoa salami, caviar, salmon mousse, pickled eggs, mounded potato salad, melon salad, green salad, pasta primavera salad, fat dill pickles and giardiniera, with a whole end devoted to Gorgonzola, Brie, Roquefort, Stilton, Emmentaler, Edam, Provolone and ricotta, and another to baguettes, croissants, matzos, pumpernickel, sourdough, bagels and three kinds of rye. Steady now. Resting goblet on table I take some rye from Bread City, some ricotta (*Excuse me Sammy*), some ham and potato salad, and now I can lean back on this post and feed the inner woman.

That tastes good—just another sip and I'm stable enough to observe this bunch of bold hunters. How funny they all look in shorts! Every one of them a big name in the biz. Fat Francis Mastino, godfather of best-sellers, tipsy already in his red-suspendered lederhosen. Watch out, Francy—you might trip and flatten a beagle. Harriet Dunstable, who gave us Lew Buggam's blockbusting trilogy *Grunt*, *Growl* and *Snort*, looking hung over in a Mets cap and tennis dress. Curly-headed Jamison McTeague, boy wonder of Garris and Soup, makes eyes at that aging New Age vamp Giselle Parana. And around them a little galaxy of moguls, each dressed after his or her own private idea of the aristocratic Long Island beagler, none looking exactly ready for *Country Life* prime time. What a farce! Why the hell am I here?

Harper, you're here because you'll do anything short of prostitu-

tion to get Sig to make Adam Snell an offer for On Wonderment. *Otherwise you wouldn't—*

Sig makes a joyful noise on his beagle bugle and a distant chorus of yelps (Gwen must've been stationed at the kennel door) gains volume with alarming speed and all of a sudden we're awash in maybe twenty beagles, barking, foraging, peeing on potted plants, rolling over and rubbing their backs on the floor, trying to climb up people's legs. Some favored creature comes bounding in with a rolled-up newspaper that looks like the *Racing Times* in its mouth and presents it to Sig, and a minute later we all break up when Sig looks down to find Fat Francis on all fours with a book in *his* mouth and takes it from Francy and sees that it's a copy of Francy's firm's *Spanish Trumpeter,* which edged out our *Noble Gas* on the best-seller list last year. Sig lets go a cry of pain and tosses the book backward into the dining room, where beagles rush in after it, and I've suddenly got my eyes closed thinking of them all, those formidable hucksters, four-legging it around the terrace with books in their mouths and peeing on the peonies. But Sig's blowing his horn again. "*A la chasse!*" he shouts, and bounds off up a woody trail at the back of the terrace with the army of dogs at his heels. Gwen is suddenly among us shrieking "Follow him!" and before I know it we're all shouldering one another heedlessly along the path, and I get knocked into a raspberry bush by that little textbook snipe Baxter Biddle, who says something like "Back to you later" and vanishes down the trail. But I'm up again and bounding through the woodland to reach, after a minute or so, the glade where everybody's surrounding the intrepid Sig, who, fallen with a sprained ankle, lies literally covered by his own dogs, who make ecstatic opera noises in some confused opinion of having won the game.

We carry Sig back home to an ice bag and everybody gets a drink. Biddle is at me now, doing his "I'm very curious about who you *really* are" number as he shamelessly noshes on caviar and matzos, but I'm sipping wine and wondering why that rascal Harry has broken dates two weekends in a row.

Date a divorced man who has wistful eyes and suddenly goes invisible and maybe you're talking ex-wife.

5. FROM SNELL'S JOURNAL

July 23, 1990. Monday. 11:16 A.M.

Dry as a bone today, brain-dead. Stupid today, and stir-crazy, getting tired of this room and boiled-out food and Beautiful View. They let me out for two hours yesterday near sunset. Marlin and I walked by the river. Wonderful evening, great to be free. Prof. Marlin trying to figure out Machiavelli. Prof. Snell stealing sneaky looks at women in shorts. And occasional sneaky looks behind me. One of Pierce's boys shadowing.

Came back, had a snort of Blessed Quintus' bourbon, and then a call from Harper recounting at hilarious length her adventures *beagling* on Long Island at the home of her boss, Sig Bazoom. Bazoom cuts ludicrous figure as country gentleman, kennels twenty mischievous beagles, for no other reason than impressing fellow publishers with gaudy and inhumane attacks on rabbits. This time it backfired and he's on crutches with a sprained ankle.

Prompted by beagling and who knows what other East Coast-isms, Harper's going to take her vacation out here next month. I, that is if I survive, can count on meeting the midwife of my dreams in four weeks. I can feel in my bones that she's a Sovrana type, even down to that musical voice. Am I ready to meet this abundant spirit? But Harper seems nicer than Sovrana. She's down to earth and doesn't seem to play games.

Sarah just called to ask of all things if I had enough vitamins. I in a way—especially in my recent helpless state—must have called up one of *her* ancient dreams, because she's showing signs of violent affection. I wish I could feel that way about her. Something the matter with me? Not enough vitamins? And I'm a heel not to manage more sympathy for Sarah. Marshall's denied her tenure appeal.

Vita Turk appears with today's *Bugle*. Rival groups, we learn, have "reached accord" on the future of the Pisham Homestead. They're going to defoliate the mucca-grass and all the rest of the undergrowth, tear down the fences and a few trees and open the place up as part of campus. House to be allowed to dilapidate a bit more, then to be pulled down or rebuilt as a frontier museum.

2 P.M. and still no ideas about how to treat this section. Sometimes you just have to give up for the day, and sometimes when you give up, you have ideas.

A call from the newly elevated Web Hollins. He says he's "elated" by my success. Given his track record, I find that hard to believe. Hollins the classic example of genus *Academicus*. When I met him fifteen years ago he was rosy-cheeked, with big shifty too-opened eyes, like an outsized chipmunk, as though on constant alert, should any emergency decision crop up, for some hole to jump into or authority to consult. Now the face is shapeless and blotchy but the alert apparently is still posted. I've seen him, before votes at department meetings, reading Glanda's face for yea or nay.

Web's first move on hitting Dulce was to join every academic committee he could. His motives? Let me conjecture. First to garner every available crumb of power. Second to become action central for confidential information, which, of course, is also potential power. Third to impress everybody as being hardworking and responsible. This strategy got him tenure and promotion. After all, tenure and promotion decisions are made by committees.

Web and Glanda are probably laying odds on whether I live through October.

Betting on a murder? How uncollegial! If they saw my house in a week they'd have to up the odds. Pierce's safety measures include discreetly barred windows, a security alarm system, heavy curtains. Also I'm to get a gun and enough schooling with it to make accidental self-slaughter an unlikely prospect.

But Libricide is strong and smart. If he ever decides my life is worth his, I'm a goner. Imagine dying without any idea who this sedate lunatic is! The thought gives me chills. Pierce says it's got to be Ashenham or that kooky philosopher Wenderson, or it's the Devil himself. They've got everything they can on these two guys and could only get more if they announced their suspicion or made an arrest. And doing that, says Pierce, is out of the question because of the amount of evidence necessary to get a conviction. For us to catch Libricide, he's got to oblige us by coming out of the closet.

Ashenham's a thoroughgoing prig, vain, empty-headed, swaggering, divorced by two battered wives. Used to wrestle on TV; took up literary theory as an alternative to hamming it up in the ring. Seldom greets me, often glares at me. He fills the bill on paper, but I can't imagine him mustering the intensity to commit violence over a work of literature.

Wenderson's on medication for some disorder and has persecution fantasies hairy enough to get mentioned in his faculty file. One graduation day he climbed a cherry tree, academic regalia and all, and threw fruit down at his students. This sort would be likely to do almost anything. But then he and I barely know each other, and he's been very civil the few times we've met.

Bizarre scene just now with Schmutzhauf and Vita. Vita's brought mail and stops for a moment to enjoy the view. Door pops open, Schmutzhauf appears holding tissue-shrouded thing that looks like a bouquet, hands it to Vita who, muttering distrustfully, removes tissue and discovers it's a single yellow rose about a foot in diameter. She holds it, staring at it, and suddenly goes all white, threatening to faint on me, then regains color, hisses, *"God didn't make this freak!,"* throws flower on bed and scuttles off.

His bid for reconciliation with Vita having failed, Schmutzhauf sits down at the foot of the bed. I describe to him my misgivings about Pierce's Wenderson/Ashenham hypothesis. Schmutzhauf, in excellent form today after having outdone God, replies, "You know, Adam, Pierce may be a great cop. But the trouble with being a great cop, or being excellent at any profession—especially if you're senior—is that you tend to let the results of your case experience harden into a theoretical grid that you can then apply to anything new that pops up. It's a kind of mental automation that simplifies life, speeds up analyses. But it's blind to the exceptional case."

Thirty minutes now until physical therapy, and I'm actually eager for another day of groans. My therapist Kevin says my progress is stellar and that if I don't watch out I'll be in the Veterans' Games next year. He even gave me a recipe for muscle-making milk shakes. And Maynard says I can jog again as soon as I'm released, provided (adds Pierce) I do it during the day and don't build up a fixed itinerary. Libricide might lay a mine or something.

Now I know why I'm so wooden-headed today: I'm fascinated by that creep. He's out there somewhere, maybe near me, in living color, breathing through every second of time that I occupy. He has a home, a history, a museumful of human detail. Yet I can't even *imagine* him. I, such hot stuff to dream up Sovrana as my opposite. But Libricide's another opposite, a blind-side opposite or infernal antipode, who just like Sovrana may have much in common with me. Or in fact, I suppose, identify with me profoundly—but negatively.

Nine chapters of *Wonderment* and nothing on evil? I suppose that's OK. We wonder at good things, are appalled by evil. What's wondering got in common with being appalled? That strange combination, that surprise duet of disbelief and acknowledgment. You can't believe that any human being would open up with an assault gun in a trolley, but look over there—right there!—there's somebody doing it. You've suddenly got to believe it, but can you acknowledge it as *human*? Yet you can't come near to self-knowledge unless you acknowledge extreme evil, imagine it in yourself.

That's it. Libricide's invisible to me in *two* ways: one, because he's physically hidden, and two, because I can't imagine him. And I can't imagine him because I'm your normal American intellectual-in-the-street, a moral coward, a harmless ignoramus, a tweed-jacketed sitting duck.

Try a new one on Pierce tomorrow. Take out a blank notebook and a pen. Tell him: "Let's be creative. Let's model ourselves a Libricide."

6. A PRESS RELEASE

From the University of Washagon News Bureau, August 8, 1990

Professor Simon Misthotos, head of the Department of Biology and Agricultural Science, has confirmed reports that Professor Warren Schmutzhauf of his department will receive this year's Krupp Prize for his isolation of the ultra–rapid growth enzyme muccasin during experiments with the hybrid mucca-grass. This $400,000 award will bring to a total of $1,372,915 ("and counting," as Prof. Misthotos put it) the prize money that Prof. Schmutzhauf has received since the publication of his discovery in June. His other honors include the Howitzer Prize, the Luger Prize, the Humanitarian Service Award from the International Food Corporation, the Nonsectarian Spiritual Frenzy Award and the *Playboy* Self-Improvement Prize.

It was further announced that Texas billionaire Benedict Snark has donated $20 million, in part to support Prof. Schmutzhauf's future muccasin research and in part to advance progress in other University programs of Prof. Schmutzhauf's choice. To house these projects, Prof. Schmutzhauf has purchased the Warren Gamaliel Harding Elementary School building adjacent to campus and leased it to the University for the rent of $1.00 per year. The eastern half of the building, he announced, will be devoted to muccasin research. Plans for the western half are pending.

Professor Misthotos further stated that a substantial portion of the Snark grant would be used by Prof. Schmutzhauf to fund additional positions in the Department of Environmental Economics.

On other fronts: Mildred Adamson, widow of late Professor of Philosophy Jonathan Adamson, wishes to thank an anonymous donor for payment of $714.50 in medical expenses incurred by Adamson during his last efforts to complete his lifetime project, a reinterpretation of Plato's *Laws*.

7. ON GRAY VELLUM, UNDATED

Henry Stuart
District Court Judge

Dear Harper,
    It is wretched of me to write rather than tell you this in person, but

I am afraid that the sound of your voice, not to mention the sight of you, would in an instant undo weeks of distressful deciding. What I have had so much trouble deciding, as well as what I have decided, you've probably already guessed from my dreadfully indefinite behavior of late. I have been seeing Sue again and I think we are going to patch things up. In any case I'm going to do my damnedest to make the relationship more loving and communicative than it was before. How can I manage this? What makes things different? I've known *you* now, Harper, and loved you, and always will. But in knowing and loving, giving and listening, I was reminded more and more irresistibly of what I had failed to do in the past, of a thousand missed opportunities and gifts refused. I was driven into a past that I had largely ruined and conceivably could repair. Forgive me for trying, my dear, even if this poor explanation makes you feel like an object of use. Or better, don't forgive me, and find yourself a man, if there is one, worthy of your beauty and spirit.

Yours,
Harry

Over her Saturday-morning coffee, holding the letter in her right hand and the square gray envelope in her left, reading it over now once again, admiring the strong graceful handwriting (must have been an old fountain pen), Harper sat motionless at the kitchen table in her York Avenue apartment. A steamy breeze, freighted originally with East River barnacles and flotsam and more recently with papaya juice, boiled hot dogs and Rudolf the Master Dry Cleaner, licked the torn envelope flap, caressed the white skin of her upper chest, comfortably bare between the lapels of the loosely tied bathrobe. Harper laid letter and envelope down on a pile of already-opened mail and sipped the now-cold coffee. Unfamiliar with the handwriting (Harry always phoned) and seeing no return address, she had saved it for reading last of all, thinking it an invitation, perhaps even a note from some long-lost friend or secret admirer. Then she saw the letterhead and knew, before she read a line, the purport of the elegant script. Terrible words, faint reasons, insulting humility. But can a rejection ever be merciful? Can the cutting hand heal the wound it makes? She thought momentarily of her own work, of the thousand equally false-sounding and uncomfortable ways she had tried to rephrase the simple message that she was returning, unaccepted, an author's book.

But hadn't they at least other publishers to submit to, new avenues to try?

Well, so did she.

Propping her right elbow on the letters, she rested her brow on her hand. Her robe had slipped open now, leaving her breasts bare. No matter, she thought. No one could see. Her cheeks went wet with tears. No one could see, or touch, or kiss. Harry had honored her, and made love to her with courtly gentleness and the patience of middle age. Harry's fine eyes, loving and still as she spoke to him of this or that, would whisper that he understood the enigma that she lacked the language to express, her twinned desires to be cherished and to be free. Now, with a gesture as irrevocable as it was polite, he had emptied her world.

She had seen it coming, but not believed it.

Where could she turn? Where else but to her work? Her eyes dry now, she rose, refastened her robe and made fresh coffee. There was much to do. A stack of new manuscripts lay on her night table, crowned by Westerley Firkin's unreadable cookbook epic, *Meals for Males*. Better do the worst first. Dragging the Firkin from the pile and bringing it into the kitchen, Harper smacked it down squarely on Harry's letter, got pencils and Post-its, and sat down to read. She glanced up at the calendar. Firkin might take her, flat out, three days, and there were four more scripts after that. Working nonstop, she might be able to trim down her schedule, fly to Washagon a day or two early and come at last face-to-face with the mysterious Adam Snell.

8. GERALD UNDERWOOD TO HIS PARENTS, AUGUST 11, 1990

Dearest Mom and Dad,

Sorry that my temporary move to the Midwest has made our meetings less frequent, though as you will see below, I've got a plan to change all that next summer. I can't tell you how good it was to see you every weekend for that first month, how very sustaining it was to see and hear your joy at each slow improvement I made. I hope that, after having given you so much grief in the past, I'll never disappoint you again.

For my own life—the new life I have happened into—I am too grateful to find words of thanks. I jog five miles a day and fool around with the piano (just exercises, mind you) in the evening. And every afternoon—that is, when her arthritis isn't acting up—Waltraut and I go walking in the Keenan Game Preserve. We marvel together at the birds, their immense variety of species, their complex patterns of behavior, their remarkable, inexhaustible *involvement* in everything they do. How seldom we see, in our Western urban world, a human being coming anywhere near those tiny animals in concern or engagement with life! I've been reading extensively about the state of the world, especially about the ways in which our nation, whose name was once synonymous with vitality, seems everywhere to be losing pace and conviction.

This brings me to my only piece of news. I've been accepted in the new Ph.D. program in environmental economics at the University of Washagon. My plan is to study the ways in which environmentalism, which is to me the new American frontier, can be an incentive for economic recovery and growth. There are similar programs in Florida and California, but I'm choosing Washagon in order to be near Franky. He may not have answered any of our letters, but I'm convinced that seeing me more or less in one piece again will bring him out. If so, what about a big reunion at the ranch in June?

One final note. You ask whether I remember anything of my many comatose years. Indeed I do, but what I remembered was so deep in my heart, so to speak, that for weeks after awakening I was not *aware* of remembering it. It was, quite simply, the feeling that I was living *in* the Bible, that the Bible was like my homeland, stretching vastly in space and time, that Jacob and Daniel and Matthew were my brothers, that they all spoke with German accents, and that I moved like a slow caravan through their history and had no existence outside of it. Only one thing more: A woman was in that land—who, I don't know—definitely not a Bible woman, definitely no German accent, but a woman who came to me in the desert now and then and looked at me with compassion and spoke to me.

Your loving son,
Gerald

9. A TOCCATA FOR SILHOUETTE

Toward the southeastern corner of Underwood's country land, an old roadbed runs down toward the river between grassy hills. Rumor has it that it was once employed for bringing gold ore down from the mines, but a number of less romantic uses, some of them relatively recent, could have accounted for the leveled trail with its occasional skewed rails and bleached ties. Underwood comes there now, in early August, rewriting the landscape with his own ardent purpose and putting the little valley to a use which, in general tone if not specific detail, might remind it of a wilder past. Dark against the sky in the morning he stands, on the giant brow of hill, his body still as a dead trunk, his head crazily tilted, his hands cupping as though in reverence the stock of the target pistol pointed downward at the roadbed, his one opened eye glued to the scope.

His quarry is the ground squirrel, rodent of the squirrel family, genus *Citellus*. Ground squirrels love the roadbed and inhabit it in force, because of the winter stream that runs beside it, because the oak and bay trees growing there make convenient locations for their burrows, and because of the delectable acorns, berries and insects that naturally abound there. In quest of such booty and generally having nothing more to fear than the occasional strike of a hawk, a squirrel will forsake the safety of burrow or grass, leap up on a section of track and stand upright, rapidly glancing to and fro. Underwood catches them one by one in his scope, knowing that he has about thirty seconds at best to steady himself and fire. As the morning wanes and the track gets hotter, the aiming time shortens.

Today, for the first time, Underwood doesn't miss a shot. Some little animals disappear into the grass on impact; others explode into fragments; others do brief, oblivious imitations of birds in flight. Morning in the valley is boxed neatly into deafening reports followed by slow recoveries of calm. Vultures make huge dilatory circles in the sky; ravens watch cannily, hidden in shadow, from the branches of hillside firs.

It's frightening to behold the man's concentration, more frightening if, closer up, you see that he is days unshaven, that his shirt is drenched in sweat and that, as he lowers the scope, removes an empty shell from the breech and carefully chooses a fresh round from a cartridge holder on his left wrist, his face is that of one in nightmare. The pain is before him now, formidable enough to drive him from his impeccable hygiene of the past. But his shooting technique has been perfected. He is as though part of the strange little gun he holds. Still as a Zen master he addresses his distant target, and conveys its projectile on bevel-flat trajectory with the dread sureness of a vindictive god.

At 1 P.M., dehydrated and dog tired, Underwood picks up his cartridge bag, turns and walks down the other side of the hill to the Blazer. Half blinded by sweat, he takes the steep and narrow trail at a snail's pace. In the trash-littered ranch kitchen he turns on the radio, gulps iced tea, showers and dresses in fresh jeans and shirt. Returning to the kitchen, he begins stuffing two weeks' worth of cans, bottles and uneaten food into a black garbage bag. When the stuffed and smelly bag has been stowed in the truck, he buses dishes and silverware to the sink, cleans the table and countertops, sweeps and mops the floor and washes, dries and cupboards the dishes and silverware. He gets and twists open a long-necked bottle of beer, drinks deeply from it and saunters into the living room, which is in a similar state of chaos. Patiently he reduces the room to its old order, vacuuming in the end the faded Indian rug.

Underwood lies down supine on the velvet couch. He falls asleep immediately, and does not wake until the shadows are long and a cool breeze from the north gently lifts the red curtains. He groans, stretches, rises, gets another beer and sits down at his desk. On the newly cleared surface, two kinds of correspondence are arranged in separate piles. To the left are the still-unopened family letters, many from his father or mother, but some in a new and gradually stronger hand of frightening and familiar beauty, all bearing, as he divines, the inevitable olive branch, the invitation to rebuild the loving family, the intimations of tearful joy. He cannot open these letters, yet cannot throw them out. To the right, unmistakable in their drab format, a pile of recent departmental memos, relating among many items of lesser note the heroic tidings of fray between Gazza and Edson and the concomitant unexpected rise to power of Webster Hollins. Yet atop these and dwarfing them in importance is a three-week-old memo from Hollins whose contents even now provoke in their beholder a look of uncomprehending outrage: the publishing success of Adam Snell. Underwood resists the impulse to snatch the paper and tear at its offending words. He turns instead, as though for consolation, to a squarish carton that has been shoved against the wall to the left of the desk. He reaches for it, drags it toward him and swivels to face it. His right hand removes from it a sealed plastic bag of jellylike substance, his left an instrument resembling a walkie-talkie. These he examines briefly and, replacing them in the carton, extracts a lengthy instruction sheet, laced with boldface warnings and cautions. Turning, he spreads it on the desk before him.

.

PART THREE

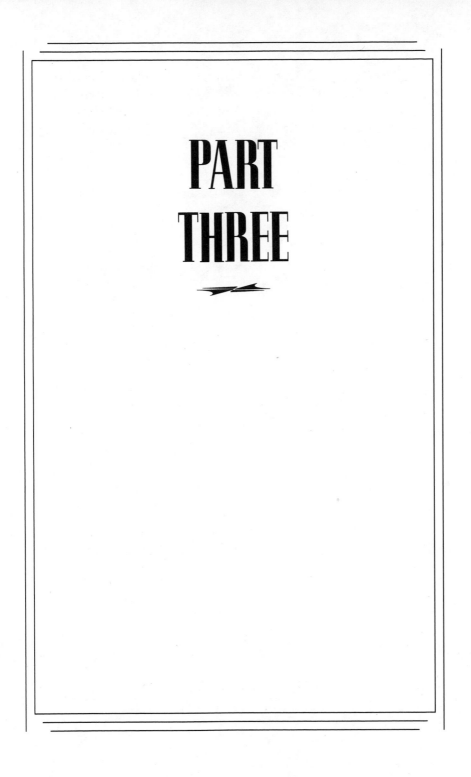

The modern system of bookselling dates from soon after the introduction of printing. The earliest printers were also editors and booksellers; but being unable to sell every copy of the works they printed, they had agents at most of the seats of learning. Antony Koburger, who introduced the arts of printing into Nuremberg in 1470, although a printer, was more of a bookseller; for, besides his own sixteen shops, we are informed by his biographers that he had agents for the sale of his books in every city of Christendom. Wynkyn de Worde, who succeeded to Caxton's press in Westminster, had a shop in Fleet Street.

—ANONYMOUS, "Bookselling," *Encyclopædia Britannica,* 11th edition

CHAPTER 1

THE COLLEGE-RULED NOTEBOOK

The Gate of Hell is the doorway to freedom.

—Sovrana Sostrata,
"Abominable" Sermon

Walk southward one block past Emmons' Fir Boulevard on the Slope, and you'll come to Park Avenue, a paved track even narrower and more twisting than Fir and roughly paralleling its course up Spine Hill. To 716 Park Avenue, a 1920s-era two-story white frame house on the downhill side of the road, Adam Snell was returned by Andrew Pierce in an unmarked tan Ford sedan on the morning of Wednesday, August 15. Another unmarked Ford was already parked by the house, and Snell, renewing contact with his abode after almost two months, watched with some reassurance as the bomb squad completed their routine search of his home and car. Less reassuring, however, were Pierce's parting words: "Take care, Adam. I'll stay in touch. And we'll make sure this road is patrolled." Snell mumbled something distractedly, looking down at his various bags and packages and suddenly remembering his first day of college, when his parents had left him desolately alone in the dorm and started off on their long drive home. The inevitable break had come. He was out in the cold.

He turned on the stereo in the living room and set to work to the strains of Corelli. He closed the curtains of the downstairs rooms, unpacked groceries and clothes and brought his borrowed laptop computer and his printer upstairs. Here he closed all the curtains except those facing westward across the valley and placed the computer in his bedroom on a small table by one of the west windows. As he was checking his files, the radio downstairs announced that it was noon, and not long after that a loud bark and frenzied scratching at the front door signaled his imminent reunion with Doppler. Snell jumped up and raced downstairs, forgetting for the first time that he had ever been injured. When he opened the front door the dog pulled

GAZZA: You might have better luck phoning Snell directly. I'll give you his home number. And thank you so much for the invitation to New Haven. We've indeed underestimated Adam if you, the world's leading literary theorist, and such eminent theorists as Professors L'Olla, Nugae and Thwackum—

DE MAIS: I tell you, literary teory *sucks*. I *discover,* don't you know, dat *literature,* I mean everydeeng dat's written down, from Shakespeare to ferry tickets, is just wee baby leetle part of a huge COSMOS OF DISCOURSE, a great corpus of HUMANIMAL SEMIOTICS! Dis *cosmos,* look you, eencludes *all meaning eentended or apprehended,* dat means *science, art, politics,* you name eet, *technology, plants, animals, sex.* Dat's right, *sex*! God, woman, *theenk of the fieldwork*! *Theenk of doing eet on a grant!*

HOBOKEN STRANGER

Daytimes he sleeps, tinny radio still blaring, in a little flophouse just off the docks. Five nights a week he security-guards at a big electronics warehouse on the north side of town. Other nights, you'll glimpse him, in jeans and jean jacket, heavily bearded now, sucking brown-bagged whiskey by the river, or provisioning at the meager shop downstairs from his room, or suddenly turning, with hulking purposeful stride, off a well-lit street and down an alley. He doesn't exercise now, and the flesh is heavier on him. He has no profession now, no expertise, and his handsome blue eyes, furtively downward-turned, have lost their arrogant keenness, their hunter's glint. He has no global agenda, no vaulting ambition now, only a dark intent, too warped for rationalization, too shadowed and oblique even for words, dumbly stalking him from day to day.

He has known the hardness that seemed his due, the gross solitude of freight yards in twilight, the sooty rat-trodden floors of endlessly swaying freight cars, the beds of wet grass by stinking estuaries, the urine-scented mud under bridge approaches. He has felt the cold knife blade against his neck and watched with dispassionate attention as his own hands ripped the knife from the man and forced it to the hilt three times into the writhing belly. He has plodded dumbly in the shouting sun beneath the billboards of truck routes, as his own sweat raised hell in his grime-stiffened shirt.

Now he sits by the river, just before work in the sunset of late summer, while a gaily painted tug tows a garbage scow, its heaped cargo the focus of a whirlwind of accusing gulls, downriver toward the Battery. The sun glints back at him brazenly off the Chrysler Building's roof and the tapelike vertical window facings of the Empire State Building. Of this enormous scene his withdrawn staring eyes make nothing but wholesale injustice and manifest chaos. The shell of his identity is gone, the neologistic aphorisms banked on their pat reductive system all fed to ovens of shame and fury, the laconic hauteur of the academic aristocrat laid low by floods of horror.

An alley cat ventures near him for food but recoils in the wind of a wild blow. Underwood rises slowly, grabs his lunch box and lumbers hunch-shouldered off the pier and to the right.

COLLECTIBLES II:
A BUNDLE OF LETTERS

PAUL EDSON TO WARREN SCHMUTZHAUF

September 17, 1990

Confidential

Dear Professor Schmutzhauf:

> Iam redit et virgo, redeunt Saturnia regna,
> iam nova progenies caelo demittitur alto.

Allow me to express my admiration, first for the brilliant work leading up to your discovery of muccasin, second for your equally inspired plan for disposing of Benedict Snark's generous gift to the University. Let me treat the two parts of your plan in the order in which you presented them:

Your decision to set aside $1.5 million for a Mucca Professorship in Humane Letters will strengthen the University in a most deserving and needy area. I heartily commend your stipulation in the draft charter that this professorship, the richest and most honorific on the University of Washagon campus, be awarded to Adam Snell. I was recently able to get my hands on a copy of his book and find it a minor masterpiece, bespeaking intellectual insight and integrity of a high order.

Your generous support of the new Department of Environmental Economics will certainly make it the strongest department of its kind in the nation. Professor Gleuck is already on the prowl for outstanding candidates for the five new positions you have opened up.

Part Three of your plan, which calls for splitting the Department of English into "theoretical" and "essentialist" groups, locating the theoretical group in Mucca Hall as a separate Department of Literary Theory and restaffing the original Department of English with a requisite number of real literature professors, will greatly enhance the effectiveness of the humanities faculty and doubtless will be seen as attractive by all concerned. The benefits of this realignment are double. First, the Department of English will be restored to strength as a body considering literature itself, and not the theoretical manipulation of literature, the paramount element in an English degree. Second, literary theory's capacity, in and of itself, to edify and empower students will be tested in a fair arena.

Let me know if I can be of any further help in the implementation of your proposals. As you know, Thor Marshall was flattened by a skateboarder last month and is not likely to be back with us for some time. In his place I am today appointing Alex MacCrae Acting President.

> With best regards,
> Paul Edson
> Chancellor

GLANDA GAZZA TO VARIOUS COLLEAGUES

September 19, 1990
FROM: Glanda Gazza, Head, Department of Literary Theory
TO: Emerson Baismacou, Ardilla Biber, Robin Cuervo, Sandy Eule, Webster Hollins, Rainer Maulwurf, Evelyn Scamel, Orville Mishunk, Alois Stoat, E. F. Taupe, [etc.]

I trust that all of you will join me in accepting Warren Schmutzhauf's kind offer (now made official by Alex MacCrae) to house our new Department of Literary Theory in the western wing of Mucca Hall. I have visited these new offices and found them roomy and well equipped, complete with a large lounge/conference room to accommodate our doubtless frequent meetings and colloquia. I expressed concern to Warren about the curious smells that seem to be wafting over from his labs in the eastern wing, and he assured me that they were all organic and would be gone as soon as he passed on to a more advanced stage of research. For the moment, however, room fresheners are advised, and surgical masks may be necessary for the more sensitive.

Let me congratulate all of you on a great and, to me at least, unexpected victory for our group in particular and our movement in general. This term we will inaugurate the first independent Department of Literary Theory in the United States. Many campuses, I am certain, will follow our example.

I am delighted, finally, to inform you that Web Hollins has accepted President MacCrae's invitation to join us at Mucca Hall and accordingly has resigned the headship of the Department of English. Though not a theorist himself, he is at work on a massive bibliography of theory that will greatly simplify research in our field.

ALEXANDER MacCRAE TO SARAH WILKINS

September 19, 1990
FROM: Alexander MacCrae, Acting President
TO: Sarah Wilkins, Assistant Professor of English

It gives me great pleasure to inform you that your appeal for a reversal of the negative decision on your promotion and tenure case has been granted, and that as of September 15 of this year you have been promoted to Associate Professor with indefinite tenure. Details of these cases are normally confidential, but since our negative decision and prolonged deliberations may have given you cause for undeserved anxiety, let me inform you that your promotion is based on lengthy referrals from your publisher, leading environmental groups and nationally ranking professors in your field—referrals which my predecessor for some reason did not see fit to obtain.

I should note in closing that the complex and controversial nature of your case was responsible for an innovation which is likely to influence the way we handle promotions here at Washagon. While I was trying to evaluate the variety of conflicting opinions about your published and unpublished work, it occurred to me that my decision might be considerably enhanced if I actually read some of it. This I proceeded to do, and with great pleasure. I am currently drafting a memo to my associate deans, and to the chairs of all standing promotion committees, recommending that they initiate the practice (exotic as this may sound) of reading at least a few pages of candidates' publications.

Let me congratulate you on your fine work and encourage you to continue it at Washagon.

ANDREW PIERCE TO ADAM SNELL

[From Andrew Pierce, lieutenant, Dulce police department, to Adam Snell. On the back of a postcard (*reverse:* Lorenzetti's painting *Buon Govèrno*) from Siena, Italy, September 20, 1990:]

Dear Adam,

Buon giorno and *ciao!* Thanks for telling me about this town. I've never seen such a fabulous City Hall. Also I greatly favor the two-hour lunches and the afternoon naps that follow. The cops here tell me that the crime rate during that period is real low.

Last week we rented a Fiat and visited villages very much like the one in which your Sovrana bit the dust. Beautiful countryside; handsome, hardworking people. The women around those parts look *much* too nice to have stoned a philosopher to death, though I must admit that her riding around naked on horseback might have been sort of a provocation.

See you in October,
Andy

In the first English Copyright Act (1709), which specially relates to booksellers, it is enacted that, if any person shall think the published price of a book unreasonably high, he may thereupon make complaint to the archbishop of Canterbury, and to certain other persons named, who shall thereupon examine into his complaint, and if well founded reduce the price; and any bookseller charging more than the price so fixed shall be fined £5 for every copy sold. Apparently this enactment remained a dead letter.

—Anonymous, "Bookselling," *Encyclopædia Britannica,* 11th edition

CHAPTER 4

RETURN

They went quietly down into the roaring streets, inseparable and blessed; and as they passed along in sunshine and in shade, the noisy and the eager, and the arrogant and the froward and the vain, fretted, and chafed, and made their usual uproar.

—CHARLES DICKENS,
Little Dorrit

The world's fate hinges on the difference between truth and lie.

—SOVRANA SOSTRATA,
Gesta

S nell's neighbor in the crowded first-class cabin of the 757 was a puffy-faced gravelly voiced New York options trader named Pete, who wore a mauve Ralph Lauren tennis shirt, a dauntingly posh camel's hair blazer, knife-creased blue trousers and snakeskin loafers. He'd been in Washagon, he said, to visit his racehorses. He grimaced a lot, in a Bogart sort of way, especially while stealing snide glances at Snell's ironed khakis and geriatric cordovans. "What brings you to New York?" he finally asked, clearly meaning "What the hell are you doing in first class?"

Himself somewhat uneasy in the showy champagne-and-leather ambience (Sig Bazoom had said, "Nothing but the best for our Adam—that is, if you don't mind me calling you Adam"), Snell explained that he was actually going to a launch party for a new book.

Pete was incredulous. "You mean they give parties for books? Next you'll tell me they baptize 'em."

Just out of Denver there occurred an unsettling event. Banking eastward after a westward takeoff the big plane suddenly aborted its muscular climb and began drifting anemically southward about a thousand feet above the hills. Something was the matter. Snell glanced at Pete, still sipping his champagne, still intent on *Tennis Today*. Someone turned on the P.A. and left it on, staticky, chaotic. Then the captain, who sounded on the verge of swallowing his own tongue, said, "We're going back," turned off the P.A. and went into a steep bank.

Snell looked at Pete again. Pete *knew* now, face of fear, knuckles white on the wineglass stem, bulging eyes fixed on the seat ahead of him, *Tennis Today* slipping from his lap. Snell turned to his other neighbor, across the aisle, a florid man whose fingers had frozen on the keys of his laptop. "Think it's an engine?"

"Maybe a bomb," said the man. This was enough for Pete. Now he had his wallet out, fumbling for a credit card and before you knew it he was past Snell and punching keys on the in-plane telephone at the bulkhead. One hand on the headpiece, one hand distractedly pushing away the stewardess who was trying to get him back to his seat, he barked a few orders into the phone and returned.

"Call your family?" Snell asked.

"My secretary," Pete croaked.

"About your will?"

"Will, shmill," said Pete. "I told her to shred paper."

Engines throttled back, the plane floated groundward on a shallow glide path. More static from the P.A., and then the voice of the chief stewardess announcing with thinly disguised pique that she was as much in the dark about what was going on as anyone else. Snell looked past Pete through the window at the brown October hills and suddenly wondered what the blazes he was doing on the plane. Had he fought off Underwood to be barbecued, along with side orders of nachos, peanuts and options trader, in flaming first-class wreckage? Were launch parties spiritual communions of such magnitude as to warrant the risk of incineration? He groaned. But then, he was a writer, and this was part of a writer's job.

And he would have three days with Harper. Who wouldn't risk crashing for that?

Snell could see a fire truck waiting at the near end of the runway as they landed. Taxiing to the gate, the captain came over the pipe again, this time apologizing for earlier silences, explaining that the problem had been an "overheated" pressurization system and announcing a one-hour delay for repairs.

The second takeoff from Denver, far more satisfactory than its predecessor, found Pete in a drunken stupor in Snell's seat (a favor begged by Pete so as to be nearer "the amenities") and Snell enjoying the view from the window. When the plane leveled off he asked for bourbon and sipped it, thirty-five thousand feet over the Nebraska plains, in an ecstasy of relief. The emergency seemed to have purged him of more than mere fear: of anxieties lingering from summer, of tensions from his new professional responsibilities, of nervousness about New York. His body felt strong again, and he now yearned in the most uncomplicated way to see Harper and embrace her and present telling arguments for her relocation to Dulce.

There was also news to share. Underwood had been traced, via the testimony of battered and terrorized transients, to the greater New York area. He'd been connected with a homicide in Toledo and described as a psychopath in full bloom, a sullen violent darkness-loving man, liable to accesses of catatonic depression and fits of bestial rage. The FBI was on the case now, the man's prints were in circulation, and the lightest bookable offense, even a drunk-and-disorderly, was likely to spark an identification and land him in prison for life.

The Dulce campus, meanwhile, was hopping with activity. Ralph Adorno, the ailing president, had made an unexpected recovery and taken up the reins of power again; while Thor Marshall had announced his intention to step down and return to research in business statistics after his release from Mother of God. The grounds division was beautifying select areas of the Pisham Homestead, and the office of security had posted, with little hope of their being obeyed, a number of prohibitions against skateboarding on campus. The English department, now under the benign leadership of Hal Emmons, was at work reviewing job applications by the thousands.

Yet for productive activity nothing matched Mucca Hall. The east wing bubbled, popped, rumbled and hissed as Schmutzhauf's people tested mucca-grass applications from gasification to chewing gum. The west wing resounded with the whine of computer printers and the chirping of excited voices. A sudden and unexpected dearth of students had left the theorists with great spans of time on their hands, and they weren't losing a moment. Some had started enormous research projects. Inspired perhaps by Web's bibliography, Glanda Gazza had embarked on a seven-volume *History of Literary Theory,* which would cover the subject from the early nineteenth century (which for her was the literary equivalent of the Big Bang) right up to the present. Alois Stoat, the Foucauldian, had broken ground on an equally ambitious *History of Wounds* (whose first sentence, posted on his office door to the great approval of his colleagues, ran, "A wound is an intrusion into the posited Self"); while the irrepressible Emerson Baismacou was conducting a nonstop seminar on his recently published *Oracle, Orifice* and his soon-to-appear *The Text as Undergarment.* Supported by a massive government grant, E. F. Taupe was eloquently advancing the thesis that all known forms of heterosexual activity were processible rape; while Sandy Eule was rough-drafting a polemic which asserted that books were not written by people, or, if they were, they were not books.

Others, driven on by news of Floconne de Mais's newly announced study of humanimal semiotics, had occupied the Committee Room where, almost from dawn to dusk, braced with copious infusions of coffee and interrupted by scarcely a student, they debated intractably subtle distinctions in unintelligibly recondite terminology.

In spite of Warren Schmutzhauf's repeated protestations that he had eliminated all odors from the west wing, some theorists still complained of a mild sulfuric smell.

Gazza, who had emerged from the Edson debacle with scarcely a feather ruffled, seemed more robust and aspiring than ever. Attired in an endless variety of fashions, she lorded it over the department from an office full of potted plants and professional memorabilia, while three secretaries labored hour on hour to convey her correspondence, reports, announcements, commendations, memos and directives. Confident, outgoing, even jovial, she sponsored gala Saturday-night socials in the roomy lounge, exotic soirees characterized by unfamiliar modes of dress, minimalist music, Demerara rum, simultaneous speeches and, as the evening wore on, lantern-lit ululations.

Only one of her new ambitions had been thwarted. The illustrious Butzi Siskin, informed from afar of the Snell scandal, had diverted her course from Dulce to East Grapefruit University in Missibama, where she now sat as dean.

The sometime theoretical young lion Frank Underwood was all but forgotten by his ex-cohorts. Alone among the theorists, Rainer Maulwurf revered Frank's memory and remained in awe of his tragic intensity. Immured in his office, Maulwurf labored clandestinely among piles of theoretical texts and journals. His high voice was occasionally audible out in the hall, enthusiastically whining snatches of his own discourse. It was rumored that his scholarly project was to prove, with pitiless logic and watertight methodology, the ideological limitations of Adam Snell's *Sovrana Sostrata*—a task made even more heroic at present by Maulwurf's inability to find a copy anywhere.

But all that would change now. The book had been through production and was, as Harper put it, "at the warehouse." Snell had seen a copy of it himself, weirdly *déjà vu,* identical in almost every detail to the original Penrose Press edition. As the plane's tires screamed on contact with the New York tarmac, Snell wondered whether Underwood, Maulwurf and company were unlucky anomalies, or whether prides of rampant theorists, nihilists and fundamentalists, some perhaps of the psychopathic persuasion, would congregate in force against him. He wondered whether next year's Adam Snell Colloquium in New Haven, recently mooted to him in quasireligious tones by Floconne de Mais on the phone (he politely declined to attend), had been merely the front for some terrorist abduction. Maybe he shouldn't be so eager to see *On Wonderment* sail into print. But that couldn't be known till later. For now he concentrated on restoring to consciousness the still-sodden Pete (who asked if it all had been a dream) and then working his way through the warrens of La Guardia.

Snell waited in line forty minutes for the twenty-minute taxi ride to the Algonquin. After a nostalgic glance at the literary bar, he ensconced himself in his room, phoned Harper to announce his arrival, showered and, eclipsing the lights of Forty-fourth Street with a sweep of the curtains, settled himself in bed.

He would have little sleep that night. No sooner did head touch pillow than he remembered what the near-crash and its aftermath had made him forget: that, if police reports could be trusted, he was now within a few miles of Frank Underwood.

Next morning just past ten he turned right on Fifth Avenue and strode downtown through light, warm rain. The rain must have been the first of autumn, for seeking out the tiny unpaved plots of midtown, the sidewalk flowerpots, the trees behind the New York Public Library, it had evoked fresh odors of vanished flowers and made the wet air remember days of summer. His own memories of the city were mainly decades older than that, memories of a college boy's expeditions and experiments, of pretentious concierges and preposterous coming-out parties, of heroic lofts and vest-pocket *pieds-à-*

terre, of three-dollar eggplant parmigiano at Delmonico's and beery summer afternoons at the café of the Central Park Zoo, of sudden mad gyrations between holy and profane, of haughty overdressed girls from Vassar or Smith or Radcliffe suddenly naked and playful in townhouse bedrooms. The rain couldn't bring back *those* smells, of ginger-ale highballs and shampooed hair and My Sin perfume, nor the feeling of new reality, transfiguring revelation, that they had given him.

He passed Thirty-fourth Street and the Empire State Building and continued south. Now the morning smells of coffee and bacon and English muffins and frosted pastry wafted in from the numbered streets, as though to win him over from his course. But Harper had said not to eat breakfast, and he had a few blocks to go.

The receptionist at Wolper McNab's twentieth-floor office smiled wanly, as though sizing up Snell's tweed jacket and khakis immediately as those of some first-book author or pesky submitter, and keyed in Harper's extension. In seconds Harper was there, radiant, smiling as she came round the corner, and without a word she took him by the arm and led him back that way past a few open doors to her office at the end of the hall. They hugged warmly. "Sure you haven't eaten?"

"Not since the plane."

She made space for him on a little blue couch by a coffee table bearing abundant lox, bagels and cream cheese. "I'll be right back," she said, and in her absence he admired the south-facing view which comprehended, in the muted colors of the wet day, an extraordinary complexity of urban architecture culminating in the Woolworth Building. He looked around. Harper's rather large office reminded him of his own dining room: no decorations to speak of, three sides lined floor-to-ceiling with books. But Harper's were samplings of Wolper McNab harvests, sometimes in quantities of two or three per title.

Harper returned beaming, placed a bottle of chilled Asti Spumante on the table, pulled up a swivel chair and sat down facing him. "We will call this a brunch," she announced. "We can go out for coffee later. May I serve you?"

Snell consumed two succulent bagels and was much refreshed by the sparkling wine, which seemed to bring its own memories of summer and youth. The mild morning intoxication brought home more fully his delight at seeing Harper again, and he relaxed into this feeling as she related to him her own remembered impressions of Dulce. She hiccupped, and both broke out laughing.

"This'll get you fired," said Snell.

"No way," she said, hiccupping and laughing some more. "Sig's in Nashville, haranguing the sales reps. I'm boss while he's away." There was a pause as they looked at each other sweetly. It occurred to Snell that he'd not yet told Harper about his close escape on the plane out of Denver. As he did this her eyes got very serious, her presence more intense. "You poor man," she said, coming over to sit beside him and putting her hand on his arm.

He put his other hand on hers and, as he avouches, has never let go of it since.

At ten-fifteen the next morning Snell and Harper were at her York Avenue apartment, doubtless discussing some philological nicety or other, when the phone started ringing and wouldn't quit.

"I won't answer," said Harper as it rang and rang. "Bosses don't have to answer phones. And besides, I'm not home."

"Somebody very much wants you to be," said Snell, handing her the receiver.

Harper accepted it with a frown. "Hello? Kit! How—what? Are you hurt?" Her eyes got bigger as she listened to some lengthy narration. "Is he dead? . . . Yes I can. I'll bring Mr. Snell himself."

She hung up, turned to Snell and held him at arm's length. "There's been an explosion at our warehouse in Hoboken. A man's been killed. The police think it's Underwood."

Guiding the Mercedes deftly down Forty-second Street toward the Lincoln Tunnel, she told Snell more about the call. The Kit in question was Kit Henslow, the warehouse chief, a Londoner who'd abandoned England because he " 'ited warm beer," known throughout the firm for his good humor and love of his work. As usual he'd been up with the birds this morning, opened the warehouse and clocked in at eight-fifteen. Immediately he'd smelled smoke and traced it to the main storage area. The lights in the big room had blown, so he went in with a flashlight.

"By himself?" queried Snell.

"You haven't met Kit," answered Harper. The storage area was cavernous and enormous, like half a football field, but Kit hadn't had far to look. Aisle Two was in absolute chaos. All the books stacked on the left wall near the entrance had come down and were now heaped in a pile about six feet high, some still in their cases and some loose on the floor. Pages, spines and a million bits of packing material were everywhere. The heavy acrid smell ("Stinkin' like 'Ides, it was") suggested explosives.

Kit called the police, who told him to vacate the building at once and who soon arrived en masse, together with fire trucks and an ambulance. He had waited outside, drinking coffee with his staff and the firemen, while the bomb squad cleaned up the mess. It was twenty minutes before they found the man, lying at the very bottom beside a twisted aluminum ladder. The rescue people were called in, but he was quite dead and had apparently been so ("All stiff 'e was, like a mouse in a trap") for several hours. The man carried no ID, but he was obviously the bomber. The wireless detonator was still in his jacket pocket.

"What made them suspect it was Underwood?" Snell asked as they left the tunnel and turned off for Hoboken.

"A file photo of him had just been posted at the station. They recognized the face. They're checking fingerprints now, but we can make a positive identification."

"What do you keep in Aisle Two?"

"Aisles One and Two are staging areas. Kit stores new deliveries from the printer there until they can be put where they belong."

"And my book?"

"*Sovrana Sostrata* definitely would have been on Aisle One or Two."

They parked near a massive gray building of awkwardly neo-classical design, around the front of which a miscellaneous crowd of about fifty were clustered. One of them, a huge bald mustached man in overalls, came running to the car.

"It's 'im! Miss 'Arper, it's 'im! The prints match!" Harper hastily introduced Snell. "Come quick, Mr. Snell. Thiy've lide him out in front. Don't you go a-lookin' now, Miss 'Arper. This ine't a pretty sight."

But Harper insisted on seeing the body. Henslow imperiously made way for them through the crowd, and Snell found himself looking down at a strangely small-looking white-shrouded form on a stretcher that had been set down on the sidewalk. "Are you Professor Snell?" asked a hawklike man in a gray hat from across the stretcher. "I'm Captain Maier. We've been waiting for you. Uncover him, Leo."

The shroud was drawn past the shoulders, and Snell faced his sworn enemy for the last time. Underwood wore a jean jacket over a plaid western shirt. The head was turned rigidly to one side. The skull was bloodily dented in, but the features remained intact. The eyes were half shut showing only white, the lips, as though about to speak or snarl, pulled slightly back from the teeth. "That's Underwood," said Snell, catching his breath. He had expected a tragic, pitiful sight. Instead the face now disappearing beneath the shroud bespoke, as though undyingly, malicious intensity, terrible purpose.

Two paramedics picked up the stretcher and slid it into the ambulance. The ambulance doors slammed, the crowd began to disperse, the police thanked Snell and retired. Henslow, who'd been off telling his staff they could leave for the day, rejoined Snell and Harper in front of the warehouse.

"Must've set 'is charge and touched it off 'appenstantially on the way down the ladder," remarked Kit, lighting up a cigar. Snell suddenly remembered *Sovrana Sostrata*. Had Underwood succeeded a second time in destroying his magnum opus? He looked at Harper, who with the same question on her mind posed it first.

Henslow had words of comfort. "No, Miss 'Arper. *Sovrana Sostrata*'s minely sife. 'Is bomb shredded one kise of 'er, but the explosive punch, so to say, got shunted up to other kises on top. These were certain of our mijor classics kises, Tolstoy and Shikespeare and Dickens and the like. It's a kise of *Little Dorrit* what done 'im. Stove 'is 'ed in right proper, she did."

"I've got to call Gerald," Snell said to Harper.

"Do it from my apartment. Thanks, Kit. Let us know what's damaged as soon as you can."

"Wite just one moment, Miss 'Arper." Kit was already bustling back into the warehouse. In a minute he reappeared with two boxes of books, one slightly scorched but intact, the other, which he carried easily with thumb and forefinger, ragged and mutilated. " 'Ere's a fresh kise for your complimentaries, Miss 'Arper. And this 'ere one's a souvenir for you, Professor."

Snell accepted the devastated box, rummaged into the wreckage it contained and withdrew a single copy of his book. It felt pathetically light in his hand. The black-lettered white cover, with its strangely prescient profile of his heroine, was more or less intact, but the book's shape had been distorted by the force of the explosion, and the text was variously burned, gouged and frayed into confetti.

"I'll treasure this one, Kit," he said, slipping the book into his jacket pocket. "It's been revised by the world's leading authority."

POSTSCRIPTS

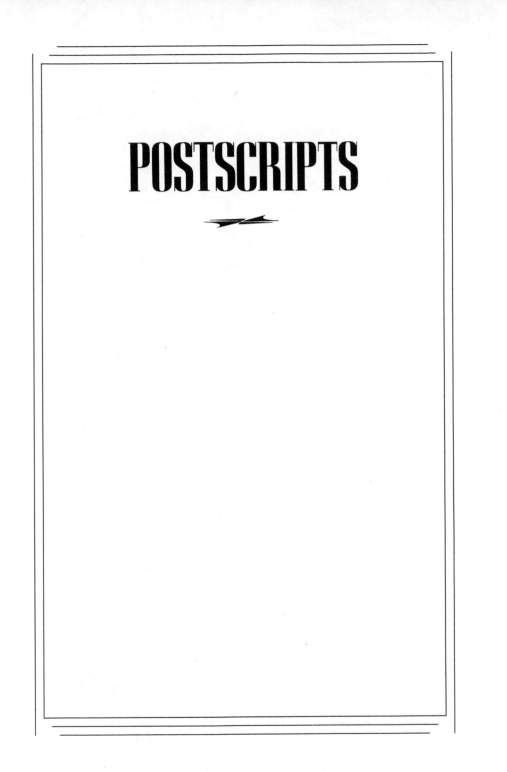

POSTSCRIPT 1

by Adam Snell

I take up pen with great reluctance. For months I have delayed, hoping that a massive confusion, born of malice and compounded by poor communications, would either subside of itself or be put to rest by accurate media coverage. But now I have no choice. The imminent global paperback reissue of Robert Grudin's *Book,* with simultaneous translations into twenty-three foreign languages, precludes any more modesty or hesitation. The world has got to know the facts, and unhappily I am at the moment the individual most capable of recounting them.

I must begin with the unpleasant task of exposing a slander. In a letter to *The New York Times Book Review* dated June 17, 1995, Glanda Gazza, then of East Grapefruit University but previously at the University of Washagon, created a national furor by claiming that I, not Robert Grudin, was the real author of *Book.* Grudin, she brazenly declared, was himself a fiction, a figurehead trumped up in a project that she termed "the megalomaniacal self-aggrandizement of Adam Snell." Corollary to this project, she continued, was the propagation of libelous material against her, her colleagues in the now-defunct Department of Literary Theory at Washagon, and the theoretical establishment at large. (For readers who wish to be reminded what literary theory was, an informative if choppy account is given in Grudin's book. See especially the Handlist of Terms on pp. 62–63.)

Using this letter as a sort of clarion call, Gazza commenced against me the much-publicized legal action, which, after five years of hearings and appeals, has finally been concluded in her total disfavor.

Why a hoax so preposterous as hers inspired any indulgence at all from the courts or excitement from the press, there are three credible reasons. First, the huge popularity of *Book,* which stood number one on *The New York Times* best-seller list for so many months that the editors retired its number, served as a beacon to the curious. Second, these "curious," who comprise, I regret to say, a substantial percentage of the reading public, have traditionally characterized themselves as preferring distasteful fictions to innocuous realities. Third, the talented author of *Book*, who might otherwise, with bold and decisive strokes, have put these fictions to rest once and for all, was not present to do so. On April 12, 1992, Captain Andrew Pierce of the Dulce police department had telephoned me with the tragic news that Robert Grudin had disappeared.

I regret that in a mere half-page the reader will know as much about my friend's disappearance, or his possible whereabouts, as I have learned in several years. But first it will be necessary to supply some background:

In early December 1990 Robert Grudin, a Chicago writer with whose work I had some acquaintance, telephoned me urging that I tell the story of my recent adventures in a book. I unconditionally declined, citing first of all the exigent demands of my current work (*On Wonderment,* which I then planned to publish during my own lifetime, having grown to over nine hundred pages in manuscript with no end in sight) and secondly the fact, now made clear to me for the thousandth time, that no document of naked truth, be it of the most harmless nature, will ever be warmly received by society. When Mr. Grudin asked me why then I continued writing myself, I responded that if he looked at *On Wonderment* in its present form, he would see truth so attenuated by anecdote, modified by humor and protected by poetic metaphor as to appear, to the untrained reader, no different from the diurnal essayistic gossamer of this or any other age. Apparently convinced by this reasoning, or at least by my conviction in embracing it, Mr. Grudin then made the proposal that initiated the literary enterprise now known as *Book*. He himself would write my story, he said, not as a venture into truth but rather as an exotic diversion and cautionary tonic for the inventive, if I would agree to provide technical assistance and stylistic oversight.

I replied to him that, because this proposal personally affected others besides myself, I would have to call him back. During the next week I conferred with my wife, who gave conditional assent, and Ensign Underwood, who generously endorsed the project on the grounds that his brother's tragic story, if told in authentic detail, might be of some use to society. Chancellor Edson, the newly promoted Captain Pierce, Doctors Maynard and O'Shea, Professors Adler, Emmons, Marlin, Schmutzhauf and Wilkins, and Dr. Gallard all approved the project and warmly pledged assistance; others were not consulted. Grudin we knew to have apt descriptive and reportorial skills, as well as a lively imagination. On December 13 I phoned him back, agreeing to the project on the following conditions:

- that my relationship with Harper Snell be treated with delicacy;
- that Grudin's contact with me, whether by telephone or in person, be limited to the later afternoon hours (my writing day ends regularly at 3 P.M.); and
- that I would retain full authority regarding quality control, including the right to veto and even destroy a manuscript that did not meet my standards of decorum and authenticity.

These Grudin accepted in writing.

That he might conduct the many hours of local interviewing and research necessary for his purposed undertaking, Mr. Grudin became recipient of the first Schmutzhauf-Snark Fellowship for Extradisciplinary Studies. In the winter of 1991 he came to Dulce with his wife Anastasia, her brother Giovanni, seven Grudin children, two sets of in-laws, a number of other unidentified relatives, a family psychologist and five species of pet, rented a vacant fraternity house and commenced research. The project did not go smoothly. Colleagues in the now-defunct Department of Literary Theory speedily caught wind of it, subjecting Mr. Grudin to harassment so vehement that only (we must assume) the formidable population of his household prevented their daring physical assault. Difficulties internal to the project were even more threatening. Grudin's frenetic pace of research and composition began to wear him down. He complained of visions, bouts of delirium and persecution fantasies; his work slowed. The project touched nadir in January 1992, when Grudin, suffering from depression, exhaustion and an apparent overdose of health-food remedies, was briefly hospitalized at Mother of God.

My journal for January 14, 1992, records a visit to the hospital, during which he complained of recurring dreams in which Sovrana Sostrata appeared as a living human being and Frank Underwood as a resurrected demon.

Clearly something had to be done. I conferred with Warren Schmutzhauf, that unplumbable well of ideas, and we visited Grudin at Mother of God on the twenty-first with the proposal that, together with Adler, Gallard, and a few other associates, we would form a kind of *Book* support group, to meet, weather permitting, for a communal jog every Wednesday afternoon, followed by a beer-and-pretzels session at Dingo's. During these sessions he could share his ideas with us, solicit technical advice and generally cathart his anxieties. This plan he readily accepted. Within days he was hard at work again. A pleasant memento of our communal sessions is Part Two, Chapter Six, of this volume, in which some of our questions and comments, somewhat fictionalized and excluding (at my request) my own, are recorded.

Yet one eccentricity, apparently some side effect of his deliria, characterized Grudin's behavior thenceforward. A syndrome of behavioral aberrations suggested that he was overidentifying with his own composition. He would catch himself calling his wife Sovrana. He developed a passion for milk shakes. He purchased a Remington XP-100 pistol and regularly practiced at a range in Mud Canyon. Conversational slips like "I'm going into the book today" and "Sorry, I didn't hear the phone ring—I must've been in the book" suggested that he conceived of the memoir less as a physical artifact than a mental place, a kind of house or vessel with its own inner space and time, that could wholly include him, accommodate, envelop his being. Authorial foibles, like his idea of having readers write in with questions and his absurd request (denied by Wolper McNab) that his publishers expand the book to include updated calendars and blank pages for names and addresses, hint that he actually wished his readers to join him in this spaceless environment. Though there were no blatantly neurotic symptoms, it was clear that Grudin had, temporarily at least, become obsessed with his work, and that he had appropriated my real-life experiences, together with those of Harper, the brothers Underwood and others, as things psychically his own.

I must confess having felt some jealousy at this, even a sense of disinheritance, as though someone, admittedly with the best of intentions and my full consent, had deprived me of my immediate past. I particularly regret what he may have considered my rather curt behavior toward him on the very last day I saw him, April 10. It was over sherry in his study, a spacious, amply windowed chamber comprising the whole top floor of his rented fraternity house. After a week of frenzied revising, he had completed a final version of *Book*, and the typescript now sat, thick, neat and white, on his broad, sunlit writing table. He couldn't, I remember, keep his eyes off it. Small brown eyes, given in the normal course of life to frequent recessions of trance and sparkles of inner merriment, they now flickered nervously between me and the book on the table, as though afraid the thing would grow wings and flap itself out through the window. After a few faint efforts at conversation, he tossed off his sherry and made it clear that I was to leave. "Sorry, Adam, I'm unfit for human company today. The book's going off express tomorrow, and I've simply got to get into it one more time."

That unpleasant idiom again. I spoke on impulse. "That's easy enough, Bob. Your problem's going to be getting *out* of it."

He didn't answer but looked directly at me, his eyes unfocussed as though by some inner confusion.

That was nine years ago, almost to the day.

Unlike my own, my friend's disappearance was complete. There were no writer's journals to consult, no suspects to research or interview. The Gazza faction, so obstreperous at first, had lapsed into silence, and Captain Pierce had no reason to suspect that any of them would dare to compass an offense so recently, and with such disastrous results, attempted by one of their colleagues. Captain Pierce simply threw up his hands. No violence, no signs of malice, he said. It's got to be voluntary.

But if voluntary, why? And where? The possibility grows that we will never find out. The Grudin family bore up as best they could, with Hamilcar and Drusilla (the two oldest children) growing into the void to assume parental roles. Anastasia grieved silently and devoted herself to the children, long inwardly sure, she once told me, that her husband was not dead but would reappear, fresh as new, some morning at breakfast. Recently, after the passing of the eighth year, she (to our great joy) accepted a marriage proposal from Quintus Adler.

. Several of the Grudin pets conceived an observance of their own. For days after Grudin's disappearance, three cats, two dogs and a gibbon ape were noticed sniffing curiously through every room of the big house. After a week this activity subsided, and the animals took to passing every night in a common heap under the bookshelf that bears their master's final literary production. The custom is maintained to this day by those of them that survive.

I remain unconvinced that my friend is dead. The reader will forgive me for taking advantage of this huge international printing to solicit clues as to his whereabouts. Anyone who has seen him or heard

of him, anyone noting in some colleague or acquaintance manifesta-
tions symbolic of some hidden personal history, should write to me,

> Adam Snell
> Department of English
> University of Washagon
> Dulce, WS 100989

if possible sending a photograph or sketch of the individual.

Now I take my leave of you. If you learn nothing else from my
story, please learn that the way is never easy for an individual who
abandons the trodden path on an expedition of discovery, but that
the rewards are often worth the trouble, and even the perils faced can
be sources of enlightenment. If you ever read *Sovrana Sostrata,* do so
with mercy toward a writer who became helpless subject to the
dictates of his heart. You will hear from me again on the publication
of *On Wonderment* which, as my will stipulates, will appear no
sooner than six months after my medically verified death. When that
event occurs is in the hands of Providence, which has treated me up
to now with bounty far beyond my merit, and in which I place my full
trust for the future.

POSTSCRIPT 2

(Unsigned)

> Most true it is that I have look'd on truth
> Askance and strangely; but, by all above,
> These blenches[21] gave my heart another youth,
> And worse assays prov'd thee my best of love.

Beneath me, beneath me, down sun-bleached crests and granite palisades, the Gulf of Corinth stretches fathomless, an azure kingdom of thought. *Turn, and look.* See the province of wind, where the water-skin wrinkles and blurs as wavelets flaunt and pucker. See the province of calm, a world's-eye deep as its Maker's love. *Come closer; nay, closer still. Kneel down before me. Each of you touch the hem of my robe.* From where I sit, I could unriddle for you earth's

---

[21]Blenches: "turnings-aside, swervings away [from constancy]" (*Riverside Shakespeare*). The quote is from Sonnet 110, lines 5–8. Hello once more, dear reader. You may have thought that I was dead, indigestible verbal meat in the offal of the slobbering hound Tusker (who died at once upon eating me, poisoned by a dram of truth, and has since been condemned to chase Frank Underwood through Hades), but though I no longer inhabit the world of flesh and shredders, I am more truly alive than I have ever been. I have gone to a place where tongues are true and hearts light, where the moonlight sparkles in fountains and the sun smiles through tears, where hearty speech and rich learning abound in inexhaustible profusion, where texts cry out for us and editors cannot delete us. No vicious curs here, but Argos, faithful companion of the young Odysseus; Bendicò, beloved cohort to Prince Fabrizio of Salina; and single-thoughted Doppler, all resting dreamily in beds of asphodel, all rising in joy to frisk in columned courtyards, sip honeydew and sit attendance by the feasting table. My twenty friends are here, young as youth, steeped in honor and ever eager for new service to inquiry. And most wondrous of all, Sovrana is here, more beautiful than words could make her. She frequents our convocations, sits at our tables, speaks—nay, sings her speech to us. To her I have bound myself in everlasting service. I run errands for her, happily do menial chores, seek out, to indulge her rich fancy, philological odds and ends of all sorts. My labor is its own reward, but if reward in overplus can be imagined, reward to transfigure and justify and exalt my whole existence, it will be from a momentary touch of her hand.

dread oracles and the ghostly dialectic of stars. Without turning I could unlock the brazen house of Death and etch its secrets in your ears. Without moving a finger I could open the Book of Life and read you the Lessons of Joy.

I could show you where life and death meet like two hands clasped behind the back of Time.

Each of you speak my name.

You are true acolytes, blind to obstacle yet inwardly acute, alert to no errors save your own, enduring hunger and mockery for the solitary delight of mere perception. I have seen your cramped offices and stooping garrets, tasted with you the cheap wine and coarse bread, listened as you strained before drowsy classes to teach the act of thought. *I accept your worship; I grant you favor.* And I shall visit you, sometimes in your dreams, or when dreams linger like watery reflections in your wakened eyes; sometimes at work, when your mind, twisted and taut as an Ithacan bowstring, relaxes into revelation; sometimes in meditation, when the masks of science fall and give way to a simple reverence; sometimes at play, when power and office, effort and pretense, dissolve into the music of laughter. And even when I am absent my blessing will nest in your souls: a glint of promise, a pure intention.

Leave me now. Turn, descend the long trail.

What, one disobeys? Know you, sir, the power of my wrath? Have you—stay, I recognize you now. You're bad boy Snell, intricate Snell, stubborn rascal who tried to write me into time. Come back here, kiddo! Don't smile and simper. I know your ways. Praise me to the moon; then, when I'm not looking, marry the first broad you meet! Ahem. Yet you did well enough, I must admit. And as a writer you have built fair.

But don't presume too much on your good fortune, no matter how well deserved, or grow proud in the bosom of prosperity. Your plan to delay the publication of *On Wonderment* is both arrogant and timid. Truth doesn't sit waiting in anterooms. It disdains politeness. It walks straight to the throne. They'll hoot at you, of course, and carp about details. But no one will attempt to destroy you this time. Mammon has smiled on you now, and Mammon's followers, try as they may, cannot withhold a certain respect.

You have learned well. Your schooling is almost complete; but the mind, ever shy, balks at turning the final page. You have worshiped the bud of truth and never seen the flower. Come close to me,

Snell. Look into my eyes, touch my face with your hand. Undo my robe now, there, by that silver fastening. How easily it falls! Look at me, Snell. Raise your head, open your eyes and hear my words of love:

You loved me as a woman and wrote of me in a book. Yet the woman died and the book was published and I sit here unchanged. You pined for my intimacy and sought my love. Yet they were there for you before you wished them and will endure after your death.

Open your eyes, behold me truly now.

I am your book, Adam. I am open to you. Come to me.

A B O U T   T H E   T Y P E

This book was set in Sabon, a typeface designed by the well-known German typographer Jan Tschichold (1902–74). Sabon's design is based upon the original letter forms of Claude Garamond, and was created specifically to be used for three sources: foundry type for hand composition, Linotype, and Monotype. Tschichold named his typeface for the famous Frankfurt typefounder Jacques Sabon, who died in 1580.